Daryl paused,  protective of her he felt.

Was that the element of his character that Kara had sensed? The key factor that had drawn her back to him with her outrageous request? She knew the truth—that he cared about her enough that he would move mountains to see she was safe.

"Isn't there anything I can say to change your mind? Daryl, I don't want to be alone in this. I want you. I feel safe with you, if that counts for anything."

He leaned in and pressed his forehead against hers. He stroked a hand down the back of her head, then cradled the nape of her neck. "It counts for a lot. And while I'm still not convinced I'm the best man for the job, I'm not going to walk away and leave you exposed until I'm certain you're no longer at risk."

"Does that mean you'll take the job? That you'll protect me?"

"Of course I'll protect you...until we find a better option."

Dear Reader,

Welcome back to Cameron Glen! I've had so much fun revisiting the Cameron family and giving the younger generation a chance at their own happily-ever-afters. Up this month, Daryl, the adopted son of Neil and Grace Cameron.

When Daryl meets an Irish lass on an overseas flight who is wreathed in mystery and clearly frightened by... something, his instinct is to protect her. What follows is beyond his wildest imaginings, but once committed, he is all in.

For Kara O'Quinn, doing the right thing has come with a cost, and now she must hide from a powerful man who wants to destroy her. But fate brings a handsome and kind stranger into her life at just the right moment, and she knows her life will never be the same... assuming she lives that long!

Happy reading,

Beth

HER CAMERON BODYGUARD

BETH CORNELISON

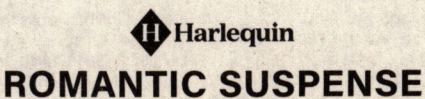

ROMANTIC SUSPENSE

If you purchased this book without a cover you should be aware that this book is stolen property. It was reported as "unsold and destroyed" to the publisher, and neither the author nor the publisher has received any payment for this "stripped book."

Harlequin
ROMANTIC SUSPENSE

Recycling programs for this product may not exist in your area.

ISBN-13: 978-1-335-47190-1

Her Cameron Bodyguard

Copyright © 2026 by Beth Cornelison

All rights reserved. No part of this book may be used or reproduced in any manner whatsoever without written permission.

Without limiting the exclusive rights of any author, contributor or the publisher of this publication, any unauthorized use of this publication to train generative artificial intelligence (AI) technologies is expressly prohibited. Harlequin also exercises their rights under Article 4(3) of the Digital Single Market Directive 2019/790 and expressly reserves this publication from the text and data mining exception.

This is a work of fiction. Names, characters, places and incidents are either the product of the author's imagination or are used fictitiously. Any resemblance to actual persons, living or dead, businesses, companies, events or locales is entirely coincidental.

For questions and comments about the quality of this book, please contact us at CustomerService@Harlequin.com.

TM and ® are trademarks of Harlequin Enterprises ULC.

Harlequin Enterprises ULC
22 Adelaide St. West, 41st Floor
Toronto, Ontario M5H 4E3, Canada
www.Harlequin.com

HarperCollins Publishers
Macken House, 39/40 Mayor Street Upper,
Dublin 1, D01 C9W8, Ireland
www.HarperCollins.com

Printed in Lithuania

Beth Cornelison began working in public relations before pursuing her love of writing romance. She has won numerous honors for her work, including a nomination for the RWA RITA® Award for *The Christmas Stranger*. She enjoys featuring her cats (or friends' pets) in her stories and always has another book in the pipeline! She currently lives in Louisiana with her husband, one son and three spoiled cats. Contact her via her website, bethcornelison.com.

Books by Beth Cornelison

Harlequin Romantic Suspense

Cameron Glen

Mountain Retreat Murder
Kidnapping in Cameron Glen
Cameron Mountain Rescue
Protecting His Cameron Baby
Cameron Mountain Refuge
Her Cameron Defender
Her Cameron Bodyguard

The Coltons of New York

Colton's Undercover Seduction

The Coltons of Owl Creek

Targeted with a Colton

The Coltons of Alaska

Colton's Second Chance

Visit the Author Profile page
at Harlequin.com for more titles.

Chapter 1

So far, no one had noticed her. Or, at least, no one had accosted her, glared at her or asked for a selfie with her. That was progress.

Kara O'Quinn kept her eyes down and her jacket's voluminous hood up as she made her way through Amsterdam's Schiphol Airport. Her disguise, such as it was, was working, and, with a little luck, she could get to the United States, make it through customs and keep a low profile at the rented house on the beach until things calmed down.

Please, oh, please, let things settle!

Her flight wasn't scheduled to board for another twenty minutes, and she didn't want to mill about in the crowd clustering near the gate. Biting the inside of her cheek, she decided to duck into the loo. She could hide in a stall until the last minute then head straight onto the airplane.

Really, Kara? Has it come to hiding in the loo?

She vacillated, not wanting to think her life had come to such drastic measures, but as she scanned the other passengers, one older man with a paunchy stomach did a double take and narrowed a dark look on her.

Bloody hell! The toilet it is, then. Schlepping her carry-on and backpack, she wended her way through the bustling airport to the closest women's restroom, stewing over how tired she was of the venom, the hate directed at her. The lies told about her. The smear campaign against her designed to protect the person who truly was guilty of wrongdoing. A person she'd trusted. A person she might have even loved, if he'd given them a chance. If only she'd kept her mouth shut…

Enough. Weren't the tabloids and the public vilifying her enough without berating herself for her choices? She took a deep breath, trying to calm the roil in her gut. She just had to avoid being recognized and her escape from London leaked to the press for a few more hours. One transcontinental flight, one more short hop to the North Carolina coast and one Uber ride to her rental house, and she'd be in the clear for at least a while. Americans really didn't know her the way Brits did. Her movies weren't popular in the States, and most Americans weren't avid followers of Premier League football—er, soccer—the way citizens of the UK were. Ted Lasso may have piqued Americans' interest, but she doubted any were rabid fans like the ones who worshipped Ian and the Knights, as they did at home.

Home. She wasn't even sure where home was now. Not with Ian. Not London, all things considered. Maybe not even the United Kingdom. She'd been driven from her adopted home by people willing to sacrifice her on the altar of greed. Did she move back to Ireland to live with her parents? Not now. Not yet. She couldn't bring her troubles, the harassment to her family.

She sighed. Eventually, someone in Kitty Hawk would recognize her. Word would get out. The paparazzi would show up, stake out her rental house and make her life hell again. But for now, North Carolina would be her safe haven.

Kara squeezed her eyes shut and fought back the tears. She was determined not to waste any more tears on Ian or his betrayal.

Head high. No regrets. Move forward, Imogen had texted this morning, and Kara treasured her personal assistant's morale boost. Imogen's last text had read, I'm here night or day if you need me. Remember, everything is arranged in my name.

Everything except her airline ticket, that was. Kara prayed the flight attendants and gate agents weren't fans of British cinema or tabloid readers. If one of them recognized her name…

She heard the last call for boarding her flight announced, and she hurried to her gate, flashed her boarding pass to the gate agent and towed her rolling bag down the Jetway. The flight attendant at the door to the airplane asked for her boarding pass and, keeping her gaze down, Kara held it up for the woman to read. Hearing a small gasp, Kara lifted a quick glance to meet the attendant's eyes. She saw recognition there and gave her head a subtle shake, her expression silently pleading the woman wouldn't expose her identity.

With a warm smile, the woman nodded and said, "Welcome aboard."

With a wave of her hand, she directed Kara to the coach class cabin. Imogen had apologized for the economy seat but had told her the first-class section was full when she made the reservation yesterday. Kara had dismissed her concern. She had bigger problems than where she sat on the overseas flight. She made her way to the correct row and found the window seat next to her was occupied by a Black man, whose broad shoulders and long legs filled his seat and spilled slightly into hers. He glanced up when she stopped in the aisle and looked around for a space in the overhead bin for her carry-on.

"Let me help you with that," her seatmate said, flashing her a devastatingly handsome smile.

"Oh, I can—" Kara started but cut herself off as he squeezed out of the row, because it was clear, as short as she was and as full as the storage bins were, she, in fact, could not.

Her seatmate reached for the handle of her small rolling suitcase, and his warm hand brushed hers as she passed the bag to him. He slid some other bags to one end of the bin, making room for hers, and hoisted her suitcase with ease. As her seatmate started to return to his seat, she caught the glare of the same man who'd been eyeing her at the boarding gate. A ripple moved down her spine. She surely did not want that man staring at her all the way across the Atlantic Ocean.

She caught her seatmate's arm as he started folding himself back in the narrow space. "Wait, I—would you like the aisle seat? I mean…you have long legs, and I was thinking…"

The Black man blinked and tugged his mouth in a crooked smile that made his dark eyes twinkle with mischief. "If you're willing, I'd be real grateful."

He wiggled back into the aisle, and as she squeezed past him into the seat, she brushed against his sturdy frame. Clearly every bit of his large body was muscle, sinew and bone, because she surely didn't feel anything soft on him. She tucked her backpack under the seat in front of her and hastened to fasten her seat belt, since the cabin attendant was already making announcements about preparing to leave the gate.

Her seatmate stuck his wide hand out, smiling again with a flash of white teeth. "I'm Daryl."

She stared at his hand for a beat before taking it and tipping up a quick grin. "Nice to meet you."

Oh, bollocks. Is he going to be a talker? Is he going to interrogate her about what the media was reporting about her life, her mistakes, her relationship with Ian? Would he be snapping secretive selfies with her while she slept? Maybe he'd get the message if she kept the hood of her jacket up and shielding her face?

As she busied herself with looking occupied, he said, "Sorry, didn't catch your name."

She paused, cast a quick, irritated side glance at him. Was that his idea of a joke? Or... She tugged the edge of her hood back a bit to study his face more fully. His expression was guileless, pleasant and...so handsome.

His eyes were a warm, rich shade of brown, his chiseled cheeks and squared chin worthy of a Harrods model. With a tumble of her pulse, she realized he honestly didn't recognize her. A pressure in her chest eased a little. If he truly didn't know who she was or the tumult her life had been in recent weeks, she wasn't going to tell him. She was running to the US to escape her recent infamy, after all, not feed it.

And so, she fumbled for a name and heard herself saying, "Imogen."

"Pleased to meet ya, Imogen," he said, a distinctly American accent—was it Southern?—thick in his reply.

He turned then and settled back in his seat. He pulled

headphones from his bag and slid them on, giving her peace.

Or relative peace, anyway, because now that they were in the air and she wasn't focused so keenly on avoiding detection by fans or the media, her thoughts shifted to the metal death tube that was hurtling her over a vast ocean.

Her fear of flying, or possibly her many layers of clothing, caused a thin layer of perspiration to dampen her face. Just the same, she waited until the flight was well underway and the other passengers seemed settled into movies or books or naps before she lowered her hood and started peeling out of her anorak.

As she tugged and grappled with the jacket, another set of hands was suddenly helping her remove the layers, and she flinched instinctively. Too many times in recent months, paparazzi or upset members of the public had grabbed at her or pushed her or otherwise hostilely invaded her personal space. She snapped a startled look to her seatmate, who quickly raised both palms to face her and flashed a charming grin. "Sorry, just looked like you were stuck."

She released the breath she'd sucked in and tried again to free her arms. "I think you're right."

"May I?" he said, gesturing to the jacket sleeve.

"Thank you." She watched his expression for any flicker of recognition, now that her anorak was off and her hood removed. She wore no makeup and had her thick auburn hair loose, so that it could swing forward and hide her face. But in that moment, hot as she was, she'd tucked her hair behind her ear. Her seatmate—Daryl—had a clear view of her face.

But...nothing. Either he truly didn't recognize her or

he was scrupulously polite about not drawing attention to her. Either way, her tension uncoiled another notch. When she gazed out the window, where the white clouds and bright sun testified to the quip her grandmother used to quote that above the rain, it was always a sunny day, she could even relax a wee bit. Her eyelids grew heavy, and soon she was easing into the first real sleep she'd had in weeks.

Only to be jolted awake some time later when the plane encountered turbulence. Kara gasped as the airplane dropped sharply, then shook violently. Half asleep as she still was, she couldn't contain the whimper of fear that slipped from her throat. She gripped her armrest tightly and squeezed her eyes shut, trying not to think about a crash landing or the plane coming apart midair.

"Not a happy flier, I take it?" The silky baritone voice cut into her wild imaginings.

She angled a look at Daryl and frowned. "More like a terrified, reluctant flier."

"Would it help if I explained that turbulence is just pockets of air, and that it's quite common and nothing to fear?"

The plane jolted and dipped again, and she wheezed, "No." She gritted her teeth, swallowing another whimper as the plane vibrated and shuddered again. When this rumble passed, she gave Daryl a quick, wry grin. "That's the thing about irrational phobias, they don't care about reason or scientific explanations. They just…are."

"Right. Got it. Like my fear of spiders. No reason to be afraid of the creepy little things, but I still hate, *hate* going in my parents' tool shed, because invariably there's one in there somewhere." He screwed up his face and gave a shiver of disgust, adding in a dark contemptuous voice, "Lurking. Taunting me with their beady eyes and sticky cobwebs." He gave his head a quick shake. "Blech!"

She couldn't help it. She laughed, imagining big, strapping Daryl freaking out over a spider in a tool shed. Covering her mouth, she muttered, "I'm sorry. I don't mean to make light of your arachnophobia. I only… You don't seem… I mean—"

The airplane lurched again, and she gasped, pressing her head back against her seat and bracing her arms. When the flight smoothed out again, she rubbed her damp hands on her yoga pants and blew a breath through pursed lips. If she weren't already so twisted in knots from the turmoil of her life over the last three months, she might be able to handle the turbulence with more decorum, but the juddering airplane felt like an allegory of her life. Everything shaken and completely out of her control.

Another violent dip and shudder renewed the frantic scramble of her heartbeat, and she groped for the armrest, only to find Daryl's hand already there.

When he started to move his arm, the fuselage gave another lurch, and she grabbed his hand as she emitted a frightened squeak. Clinging to him, she muttered, "I hate this. But I hate myself more for acting like a git over it."

Where she'd been clutching his fingers before, now Daryl turned his hand so he could fully fold her hand in his. His expression turned pensive, and when she tried to tug her hand free, he squeezed gently, saying, "Tell me about yourself, Imogen. What do you do for a living?"

She blinked. So he truly didn't know who she was. She considered answering truthfully, but why spoil the unassuming rapport she had with him? She opted for a slight alteration on the truth. "I work with children's charities, using playacting to help children who've survived trauma to express their feelings in a safe environment."

That was true. She had volunteered in that capacity earlier this year, until the organization asked her not to come anymore because of the disturbance the paparazzi was causing the children.

Daryl lifted his eyebrows and nodded. "That's great. A noble endeavor. Do you have any children of your own?"

She opened her mouth to answer as the airplane shook again, and another jolt of terror chased through her. She clutched his hand and held his gaze as she shook her head. "N-not married. No children. You?"

"Ditto. Not married. No children."

"And your profession?" she asked.

"I recently finished my commitment to the US Army, and now I'm in the reserves. I worked in IT in Germany after leaving West Point, and now I do basically the same, but as a civilian back in the States." He grinned. "Which is to say I'm a computer geek."

"A geek?" She gave him a measuring look. "You're quite fit to be calling yourself a geek."

He wrinkled his brow in thought and used his free hand to stroke his chin. "Geek is a state of mind. A love of computers and science and math."

"Nothing wrong with that," she said, lifting a corner of her mouth. She'd certainly had her fill of athletes and their ilk lately. A change of course would be welcome. Not that she was sizing Daryl up for a relationship. He was a stranger on a plane to whom she'd bid farewell in a few hours.

He smiled back, saying, "I'm glad you think so. My

family teases me about it sometimes. I've been a geek since way back. They like to say I had my nose in computer games as soon as I could hold a remote." He laughed, and the sound was rich and sweet like warm sticky toffee pudding. "Shocked them all when I tried out for and made the high school football team."

Her stomach dropped. Football.

She must have frowned, because he tipped his head. "What? You don't like football? Oh, wait. I hear a British accent. American football. Not soccer."

She ignored the sports reference and hoped to change the topic with, "More of an Irish accent actually. I moved to England when I was eighteen." She shot him a teasing expression. "And you're the one with the accent, Yank."

"What?" He feigned offense. "Everyone knows Americans don't have accents. We speak the true English language."

She sputtered a chuckle. "Uh. Hello? The language has England right there in its name."

He nodded. "Touché."

"Oh, French now?"

"Trust me, you do not want to hear my French. Talk about an American accent!" He rolled his eyes. "I can manage enough decent German to get by in Frankfurt, but Parisians look at me like I'm insulting their mother."

The airplane shuddered again, and Kara realized what Daryl had been doing—distracting her. She'd actually laughed, and for the past few minutes, she hadn't thought about the mess she left in London or the metal death tube soaring over the ocean and scrambling them like eggs.

"Thank you," she said quietly, giving him a grateful smile.

He squeezed her hand, and she returned one in kind.

She was reluctant to release his grip, absurdly feeling as if their linked hands were a connection to safety for her. Or that Daryl gave her the strength she needed to carry out her crazy plan to go underground on the American coast until the tempest with Ian blew over. To his credit, he didn't rush her to release him. Just sat with her fingers wrapped snugly in his on the shared armrest.

Surprising herself, she said, "Tell me more about Daryl. Who is this family that teases you about your geekdom?"

One eyebrow sketched up. "You really want to know or are you just being polite?"

An hour ago, she'd preferred silence and anonymity. A few minutes ago, her answer would have been politeness. But she found now, gazing into his kind brown eyes, she truly wanted to know more about this American ex-soldier, geek and thoughtful soul. "I really do."

Chapter 2

"All right," Daryl said. "Feel free to stop me when you've heard enough. I can get carried away talking about Cameron Glen and the Cameron family."

"Cameron Glen?" she echoed, canting her head in query.

"That's where I grew up. It's my family's property in the Smoky Mountains of North Carolina. A little slice of paradise, really."

She turned to face him more fully and leaned her head against the seat as she listened to him regale her about fishing at the property's ponds as a boy, helping clean the rustic rental cabins, the seasonal beauty of the lush landscape, playing tag in the rows of Christmas trees on the surrounding hillsides and watching the constant parade of wildlife. He waxed warmly about Valley Haven, the friendly small town just miles from Cameron Glen and, most important, his large, loving family.

"My parents had five kids. I'm the youngest. There's Emma—she's the oldest. Then Cait, Isla and Brody. So, yeah. Big family. I was the 'bonus kid' who came along fifteen years after Brody."

Kara gaped at him. "Fifteen years! What a surprise for your parents!"

He shook his head. "Not a surprise really. My birth mother was a close friend of Mom's, and when my real mom got cancer and knew she was dying, she asked Mom to adopt me. Grace and Neil, my adoptive parents, say it was a no-brainer for them. They were happy to add me to their ranks."

"How old were you when your birth mother died?" she asked, leaning closer to him.

"A baby. Two, I think. I have pictures of her, but I don't remember her."

Kara pulled a sad expression, and he held up his free hand, dismissing her condolence. "It's okay. I love her for giving me life and making sure I was taken in by the Camerons, but I was too young to feel any pain in her loss. The Camerons have been nothing but good to me, and I don't have any regrets."

"Is that where you're headed now? To see your family?" she guessed. The plane was headed to Atlanta after all, and he said Cameron Glen was not far away, in the Smoky Mountains.

"Yes. I'll drop in and see them first, but I have business in Durham at Duke University at the end of the week. I'm doing a couple lectures."

"Geek and professor. That is impressive."

"Not professor. Just a guest lecturer," he said, smiling modestly. "And you? Where are you headed, Imogen?"

Her pulse stumbled hearing her assistant's name and reminding her of the lie she'd told him, the chaos she was escaping and the truth she needed kept quiet. "A sabbatical."

"Oh. Where about?"

She was suddenly very conscious of the other passengers seated around them, who could yet recognize her or overhear this conversation and leak the information to the press. She fumbled for a response. "Well, I'm, uh, playing that by ear."

That was half true. This whole trip, this mad dash to leave London and hide out had been last minute, planned by Imogen in a rush. She was largely trusting Imogen to have everything sorted by the time she reached the next step of her journey.

Daryl scrunched his face in puzzlement, but didn't press for more information. "Spontaneity has never been my forte, but more power to ya."

"There you go with the French again," she teased, wagging a finger.

He pressed his mouth in a moue of thought. "No, I'm pretty sure *ya* is straight up American Southern."

She bumped him playfully with her shoulder, chuckling, something she'd thought she'd forgotten how to do.

Over the cabin's intercom, the flight attendant announced that they were past the turbulence now and cabin service and lunch would be served soon.

Reluctantly, Kara released Daryl's hand. "Well, if the turbulence is behind us, then I don't need…" She exhaled and sent him a look of gratitude. "I appreciate the distraction."

"Any time."

Exhaustion sank into her in the aftermath of the adrenaline spike, the lost sleep in recent days and a pleasant sense of well-being that Daryl evoked. She felt…safe. As if she could let her guard down for a few minutes and he'd protect her.

Why she should believe that she didn't question. Only

he'd looked out for her when the shaking, swooping airplane had upset her, so maybe she could get a little rest and…

A jaw-cracking yawn rose from nowhere, and Daryl cut a side glance to her. "If you want to catch a nap, I'll wake you when lunch comes."

Her eyes closed, and she could feel sleep stealing rapidly upon her. "No. If I'm asleep, don't wake me until we reach Atlanta. I need a nap more than I need food."

She wiggled and turned, trying to get comfortable in the narrow seat with barely enough legroom to move her knees.

Daryl reached up by her temple and showed her how to flex the headrest for a tiny prop to lean against. "Sleep tight."

Turning to the screen on the seat back in front of him, he began scrolling through the video offerings then slid his headphones back over his ears.

With his attention fixed on the film he'd selected, a thriller with car chases and a Hollywood leading man storming across the screen, Kara studied Daryl closer.

His thick fringe of eyelashes highlighted the friendly warmth of his eyes. His square jaw, as if needing to counter the eyelashes, had a masculine, square cut, and he had the sort of symmetrical facial features that casting directors loved. His light brown skin had a lustrous, healthy glow she envied, and his lips looked buttery soft. Sensual. Kissable. Unlike hers, which were chapped and which she'd anxiously bitten so often recently, they'd bled. Her esthetician would be shocked at how Kara had let herself go since she left Ian. She'd just not had the energy or desire to bother with more than basic skin care.

Her attention lingered on his mouth as she grew sleepier. Yes. Kissable. She'd bet Daryl was a brilliant kisser. Not that she'd ever know, but it was a pleasant thought to take with her as she drifted off to sleep.

Imogen was sound asleep when the flight attendant finally rolled her cart down the aisle with the tiny microwaved meals that passed as airplane food. When the attendant leaned in, clearly about to rouse Imogen, Daryl waved her off. "She asked not to be woken up. But if you'd bring her a pillow and blanket, I think those would make her more comfortable."

For the last several minutes, Imogen had been scrunched sideways, her head at an odd angle that had to be giving her a crick in her neck. A different flight attendant delivered the blanket and pillow a few minutes later, and Daryl carefully covered Imogen and tucked the pillow under her cheek when she stirred.

Shifting his attention to his meal, he attempted to cut his chicken with the provided plastic utensils without much luck. When he fumbled open the plastic bag his roll came in, his fingers slipped, and he accidentally poked Imogen in the ribs with his elbow.

Daryl cringed and held his breath as she grunted, shifted and fell back asleep—with her head on his shoulder. He muffled a laugh. Sure, he could ease her back, lean her head the other direction, but honestly, he enjoyed the sweet aroma of her hair, a light floral scent. He could tell from the dark smudges under her amazing green eyes that she needed every bit of sleep she could get on this flight. Even before the turbulence sent her into a tailspin, he could tell something had been bothering her from the moment she rushed on board at the last minute. Something beyond typical stress over making her connection.

He angled his head to study her lightly freckled cheeks and ivory complexion. Her pale pink lips were chapped and had clearly seen some abuse from her teeth, lending credence to his suspicion she was anxious over something in her life. She wore no makeup that he could tell, but her skin had a healthy glow and her long auburn hair shone with a burnished luster. Daryl sighed, a nudge of protectiveness making his chest tighten. She looked…vulnerable. Lost. And having so many women in his family who he cared deeply for, he couldn't help but wonder—and worry—about Imogen's story.

Imogen slept hard for the next six hours, even through another patch of turbulence due to a storm as they approached the airport. Only when the plane touched down with a jarring bump in Atlanta did she wake with a confused and groggy expression. She glanced at the blanket on her, then sent an embarrassed look to him when she clearly realized she'd been leaning on his shoulder.

He grinned at her, hoping to dispel some of her mortification. "It's fine. You obviously needed the sleep, and I wasn't going to risk waking you."

She yawned and raked her hair back from her face, then, after looking around the cabin, she pulled her hair forward again so that it formed a curtain around her cheeks. After wadding up the blanket and stuffing it on the floor, she struggled to put her jacket back on. He reached over to help, and she muttered, "Thank you." Her lilting accent charmed him all over again.

He really was a sucker for an accent. Who was he kidding? A lot of things about her appealed to him, not the least of which being how attractive she was.

When she settled back in her seat, hood up, he couldn't help but tease her just a bit. Leaning closer, her said softly, "By the way, you snore."

She snapped a wide-eyed look to him. "Did I?" She covered her face with a hand and moaned. "Sorry."

He held up his thumb and pointer finger an inch apart. "Only a little. I was more worried about you drooling."

Her jaw dropped and pink stained her cheeks. "Tell me I didn't!"

Daryl bumped her shoulder with his. "You didn't. Fortunately."

She pinched the bridge of her nose and shook her head as she chuckled.

When the captain announced that passengers could use their phones again, Imogen pulled out hers and checked her texts.

Daryl began gathering his belongings and putting them back in his backpack. He switched off airplane mode on his own phone then checked the airline app for any information about his connecting flight to Asheville, only to find it had been canceled. "Well, damn."

"Folks, I have good news and bad news," the captain said over the intercom. "While we were one of the last planes allowed to land, this storm has settled in and, due to lightning, all outgoing flights have been grounded indefinitely for safety. Please check with a gate agent if you had a connecting flight for further information."

A general groan rose from the other passengers.

"Grounded?" Imogen repeated, her shoulders sagging.

Daryl already had his weather app open looking at the

radar picture. "Ouch. It's a big one. Could be hours before this mess clears." He showed her the screen with the large, slow-moving storm illustrated in bright reds and yellows. "My best advice? Hurry and book a rental car, if you don't mind driving in rain."

"But… I don't drive."

"Like…at all?"

She shook her head. "Because I—" She clamped her mouth shut, stifling whatever explanation she'd started.

"In that case, you should book a hotel room. Quick. You, me and about ten thousand other people will be spending the night tonight either at a hotel or in the airport. I know which one I prefer."

Kara's gut swooped, realizing the truth of what Daryl was saying. She pulled out her phone and started texting Imogen again, updating her on the situation and begging her to arrange both a hotel room and a car to pick her up. Spending the night in the Atlanta airport would mean hours of trying to avoid being recognized and the inevitable questions about *why* she was in Atlanta instead of London.

The other passengers started deplaning, and she kept her head down, avoiding eye contact with anyone—especially the surly guy who'd glared at her when they'd boarded. When Daryl stood, he reached in the overhead bin and got her carry-on down for her, putting it in the seat he'd vacated.

She sent him an appreciative glance. "Thank you. For everything."

Kara hoped he read in her smile all that *everything* included. His understanding and distraction during the turbulence. His kindness. His shoulder for her nap. The many ways he'd eased her anxiety in the past few hours, when she'd thought she was about to crumble under the strain of Ian's betrayal and all the fallout.

In response, Daryl gave her a flirtatious wink and a small wave as he followed the line of passengers down the aisle. "Take care, Imogen."

A pang of regret pierced her as she watched his broad back disappear down the aisle and off the airplane. Once the other passengers had largely gone, she finally slid out of her seat and dragged her bag off the plane. Tugging her hood forward, she trundled up the Jetway and into the concourse, dodging a group of travelers standing around a lighted board that blinked red as more and more flights were canceled.

Her phone vibrated, and she checked the incoming message from Imogen. "Driver arranged. Meet at taxicab exit. No rooms near airport. Reserved suite at downtown Marriott. Good luck."

She exhaled her relief knowing she had a room and a car—*bless you, Imogen*. Now to find a bite to eat, since she's slept through the meal on the flight, and what Americans discretely called a restroom before she headed to customs.

An hour later, she finally cleared customs and made her way to the doors by baggage claim where Imogen had said she'd meet her driver. She searched the busy lobby for a man standing with a sign that read Imogen Jones, since Imogen had set up all of her travel arrangements in her own name to provide an extra layer of anonymity for Kara, but Kara saw no man with such a sign.

"So far so good?" a voice said close to her ear, and her

pulse leaping, she whirled to find Daryl standing next to her, grinning in his boyishly charming way.

She clapped a hand over her racing heart. "Blimey, Daryl. Don't sneak up on people that way!"

He chuckled unrepentantly. "Did ya get a room and ride lined up okay?"

She nodded. "Yes, in a hotel downtown. You?"

"Downtown? Oof. That's a hike."

"A hike?"

"Downtown is a long way, relatively speaking, with high traffic, like most cities. I got a room outside the perimeter anyway. Haven't checked the app to know how far it is, but I grabbed what I could." His phone pinged, and he checked the screen, frowning. "Well, that's my Uber." He lifted a hand. "Bye again. Nice to meet you."

"Cheers," she called as he walked away. Then under her breath added, "Very nice to meet you."

Daryl cast one last glance over his shoulder to the spot where Imogen stood, looking lost—head down, pulled into herself—and he cringed internally at her body language. Why was she trying to make herself small when she had so much to offer? Someone had done that to her, he could well imagine. Someone had hurt her. But what could he do other than wish her the best and pray she found happiness and strength down the road?

Puffing out a breath, Daryl carried his backpack to the busy driveway where taxis, hotel vans and Uber drivers were lined up, hustling passengers into vehicles. Traffic in adjacent lanes backed up and impatient drivers honked. He spotted a bearded guy leaning against the hood of his black sedan, his bare arms folded over his protruding belly, and strolled toward him.

"Hey, I called for an Uber, but my app is acting up right now. Are you here for Daryl by any chance?"

"Naw," the guy said, giving Daryl a snarling up and down look. "I ain't no Uber driver. I'm pickin' up my brother."

Daryl started to tell the rude guy that he was at the wrong door, that this area was for public transportation only, but at the edge of his vision, he noticed a small SUV whip into a recently vacated spot at the curb. The Uber decal was prominent on the door and front windshield, so Daryl hustled to the passenger side window. "You picking up Daryl? Going to the Meadow Lark Motel?"

"Yep. Need help with a bag?" the driver, a young guy with a Clemson T-shirt, called from the driver's seat.

"No bag. Just my backpack," Daryl said, climbing in the back and tossing his pack on the other seat.

The driver held out a hand, introducing himself as Ted, motioning to a box of free snacks and asking about Daryl's flight. Daryl exchanged pleasantries, commenting on the bad weather. As he fastened his seat belt, he ducked his head to look out at the busy sidewalk…and spotted Imogen coming out the terminal door. She raised her head to cast a glance around the chaos of cars and stopped to push back the hood that impeded her view. He saw her lock eyes with Mr. Rude from two spaces ahead of them, and he wanted to shout out the window, *Don't bother with him. Wrong guy. Bad attitude.*

To Daryl's surprise, Mr. Rude pushed away from his vehicle, his head high and a smarmy, ingratiating smile lighting his face as he approached Imogen. Daryl watched the exchange between Imogen and Mr. Rude, while Ted grumbled about none of the other drivers allowing him to pull into traffic. She spoke to him for a moment, looking wary and confused. But he pried her bag handle from her, and she followed him to his black sedan, biting her bottom lip and frowning. He opened the car door for her, and when she hesitated, he gave her a push and slammed the car door. Mr. Rude all but threw her bag in the trunk of the sedan then rushed to the driver's seat.

A prickle of unease chased down Daryl's spine. Hadn't the rude guy said he wasn't a rideshare? Why then would Imogen think he was? Unless Mr. Rude lied…to Daryl or to Imogen. He thought about the wary confusion on her face when the man approached her, the way the guy pried the suitcase handle from her hand and the uncertainty on her face as he hustled her to the back seat.

Daryl frowned, the uneasy prickling swelling to a full-body assault.

Ted waved thanks to another driver as he pulled into the next lane.

Keeping his gaze on the black sedan, Daryl gritted his teeth. "Ted, I—"

As he spoke, Rude Dude poked the front fender of his black sedan into traffic, not so much *finding* space to pull over as *making* it, taking it and everyone else be damned.

Ted scoffed and waved a hand at his windshield. "Would you look at this guy? What an ass!"

Rude Dude darted out in front of Ted, and Daryl leaned toward the front seat as far as his seat belt allowed. "Change of plans, Ted. My friend just got in that car, and I have a bad feeling about it. There's an extra fifty dollars in your tip, if you follow that black sedan. I need to make sure Imogen is all right."

Chapter 3

Ted glanced back over his shoulder. "You want me to follow that black car?"

"You game?"

"Hell to the yeah! Let's do this!" Ted's polite-driver demeanor disappeared as he transformed into a NAS-CAR wannabe. Daryl was thrown back in his seat as Ted punched the gas and wove through cars in order to keep Rude Dude in sight.

"Teddo, my man, there'll be no tip if you crash into innocents or create a hazard in the process."

"It's cool, man. I got this."

Rain poured down, and lightning flashed in the clouds as Ted maneuvered through the airport traffic, keeping the black sedan in front of him. Another wave of concern washed through Daryl when the sedan merged onto Interstate 75 headed south. "Correct me if I'm wrong, but isn't downtown Atlanta north of here?"

Ted met Daryl's gaze in the rearview mirror. "Yeah. But you said you wanted me to follow the black car."

"Yeah, I do. Especially since the guy just went the wrong way on 75 to get my friend to her hotel."

Ted frowned. "You think the guy is up to something sinister?"

"I just know something about the situation stinks to me." Daryl rubbed his chin, wondering if he was sticking his nose where it didn't belong. Imogen wasn't his responsibility. She might even take offense at his following her. But from the moment she'd rushed on board the flight in Amsterdam, he'd gotten a vibe from her that something was amiss. Even without the turbulence rattling her, she'd looked…scared. And nothing in the ensuing hours had done anything to change that impression.

He knew if Imogen were one of his sisters or nieces, he'd want someone to intervene if they sensed a threat. He'd grown up watching all of the Cameron men and the husbands that came into the family act nobly, be protective, even face danger for the sake of their family. He'd carried that lesson with him to West Point and had a sense of duty and courage and honor drilled in even further. He set his jaw, acknowledging that he simply didn't have it in him to turn his back on Imogen while he had even an inkling she was in danger.

The black sedan passed several exits, any one of which could have been used to turn around had Mr. Rude simply gone the wrong direction by accident. Instead, he moved into the far left lane and accelerated, as if he realized Ted was following him. Ted pursued, skillfully weaving between cars as he kept pace with Mr. Rude.

They traveled for several minutes, getting farther and farther from the city. Daryl wished he had a way to call Imogen, check in with her, warn her the black sedan was taking her the wrong direction. *As if she hasn't guessed.*

When Rude Dude sped up, Ted grumbled, "Man, the guy is nuts. In this rain, to go that fast…?"

Everything in Daryl wanted to shout, *To hell with the*

risk! Stay with him! but did he dare encourage Ted to contribute to the danger Rude Dude was posing to the public?

"We don't need to make a bad situation worse. I hate for him to get away, but I can't ask you to risk an accident on a hunch that—"

"Hold the phone," Ted cut in. "He's makin' a move."

Daryl craned his neck, searching for the sedan in the flow of traffic. The dark car was barely visible through the veil of rain, but he watched the rear lights change lanes then cut in front of another car to take an exit. Leaning forward, Daryl aimed a finger at the exit. "Follow—"

He was thrown back in his seat when Ted cut the wheel to take the exit, as well. At the foot of the ramp, Rude Dude blew through the stop sign. He turned onto a dark two-lane country road heading into rural Georgia. Ted pumped the brakes once, checking for oncoming cars, then pursued. The twin beams of Ted's headlights created a narrow tunnel of illumination in the dreary night. Daryl balled his fists on his lap, wishing he could make Ted's small SUV go faster, wishing he could reach through the night and pull Imogen from her kidnapper, praying they didn't hydroplane or crash before they caught up to the black sedan. And when they did overtake Rude Dude? What then? He gritted his molars. *One thing at a time*.

"Ted, are you familiar with the PIT maneuver?"

"I am." Ted exhaled loudly. "It's pretty dangerous, is it not?"

"It is. I can't ask you to do it. But if you think you can, and do it safely—" Now Daryl sighed. "I think my friend is in real danger. I need to get her away from this guy. I know this puts you in a bad position, and you can say no."

"Hell, no. I'm in. If she were my girlfriend, my sister, you'd do the same for me. Right?"

"Hooah!" Daryl shouted from deep in his chest.

Ted barked a laugh and returned, "Hooah!"

Kara was pressed against the back seat, her body taut with fear. She braced her arms and legs as her driver took one curve after another far too fast for the conditions. Out her window, the night was dark and soaked, the landscape empty. They were nowhere near the city anymore, and knowing that sent a fresh shiver down her spine.

Full of dread and regret, Kara replayed the frightening turn of events, wishing she'd done so many things differently, rewinding the "if onlys," and castigating herself for choosing not making a scene or drawing attention over her own safety. Why hadn't she listened to her instincts?

But Imogen had texted that she'd arranged a car for her, and this man with the grizzled beard had known her name. Her *real* name. Caught off guard, she'd admitted who she was before analyzing the situation sufficiently. While she'd equivocated, trying to decide if this truly was the driver Imogen had arranged on short notice, the bulky man had hustled her into his car and had locked the door with a fob.

She'd scrambled to find the door handle as he raced around the back end, but it had a child safety feature engaged that disabled the latch. She'd been trapped as the man raced away, recklessly snaking through the other cars and speeding down the rain-soaked motorway. For a brief time, she'd clung to the hope that he was, in fact, her driver, and while his driving was atrocious, he'd soon let her out at the downtown hotel. But the lights of the city were behind them as he sped down the motorway, and she grew increasingly scared.

"Where are we going? Who are you?" She'd already asked the question a couple of times and been ignored. This time, however, he gave her a quick glance over his shoulder. "You can call me Floyd, and we're just going somewhere we can talk. Have a little fun maybe. I bet them hoity-toity newspapers you got in England would pay a whole lot of money for pictures of you hiding out here in Georgia, Ms. O'Quinn. Especially if you was nekid." He laughed until he coughed, and a chill seeped to her bone. Dear God. What did he have in mind?

"Let me out. Right now!" She tried to infuse the demand with authority, but her voice cracked.

He angled his head toward her. "Naw. Don't think so." Then in the dim light from his dashboard, she saw him scrunch his face as he glanced in his mirror. "What the hell?" Pressing his mouth tight, he said, "Hang on, darlin'. I think this guy is following us, and I'm gonna try to shake him loose."

Gasping, she gripped the edge of the worn seat as Floyd accelerated. She could feel the tires slip on the wet road, and she sent up a silent prayer she wouldn't die tonight in a car crash so far from home.

Floyd laughed again as if the high-speed race was the greatest fun. Fury spiked in her that he would so blithely put her life in danger this way. That he could presume to snatch her from the curb and scheme to sell pictures of her or...*worse*. Her stomach sank. She refused to sit here and do nothing to save herself, but...what could she do? The back seat door was locked. Her phone was tucked in the front pocket of her travel bag which the man had taken from her. They were hurtling down a country road, while Floyd tried to evade…

The car that was following them. Was it the police? Could she signal the other driver that she needed help? It was so dark. How would they see her?

She glanced around her, searching for tools, ideas, inspiration. Her shirt under her jumper was white. Could she use it as a flag? Tugging to loosen her seat belt, she twisted and pulled her arms inside her jumper and shirt, wiggling and pushing until they both came off over her head.

Floyd cut a look over his shoulder. "What are you doin' back there? What—" At that moment the back end of the car fishtailed, and Floyd battled the steering wheel to keep them on the road.

Turning on the seat, Kara first tried waving her shirt toward the back window. She quickly decided she needed a bolder move, dubious whether her efforts were visible to the other driver. The window. If she couldn't roll it down she would break it. She had to flag the other car. A voice inside her said the car behind them was her only chance of rescue.

Something white, some kind of rag or flag, emerged from the back passenger side window of the sedan. Daryl's pulse jolted. Clearly Imogen wanted to signal some message to them. Though she waved the cloth, it became instantly drenched and hung limply. But Daryl had seen enough. He had to get her out of that car, if only so he could speak to her, confirm her wishes.

His chest squeezed at the notion of seeing her again, looking into her green eyes, maybe touching her hand or drawing her into a hug. Less than an hour had passed since they had last spoken near baggage claim, but a skitter of wistful yearning filled him, a desire for her he couldn't explain.

When, after taking a curve *way* too fast, the black sedan fishtailed for a second time and nearly went in a ditch, Daryl knew they couldn't wait any longer. Time had come to act.

"Ted, we gotta end this, one way or another, before someone gets hurt."

His driver's hands tightened on the steering wheel. "Back off or cut him off?"

Daryl clapped his driver on the shoulder. "I know what I want, what I'd do, but it's your car, your decision."

Ted's jaw firmed, and his eyes narrowed. "And I know what I'd want if she were my loved one. Hold on tight, friend. Here we go!"

Daryl grasped the door handle as Ted accelerated on a straightaway. Ted had his job, but Daryl had his own. He needed a plan of action if—no, when—Ted stopped the sedan. How would he get Imogen from the car? How would he deal with Mr. Rude?

He snatched his backpack from the floor and rummaged through it, gathering supplies.

Ted moved his small SUV into the oncoming lane, edging closer until his front bumper was next to the rear quarter panel of the sedan. Before Ted could try to gently nudge the sedan, Rude Dude swerved into Ted. Metal crunched, shuddered and scraped with a screech. Daryl lost his grip on his backpack, which spilled on the seat.

Ted fought the steering wheel, keeping the SUV on the road.

Daryl's blood pumped harder, adrenaline buzzing through him. Anticipation was a physical thing, clawing at him. Spying the objects he'd been looking for, Daryl seized the tools and returned his attention to the chase.

Once Ted had his car under control again, he tried once more, inching nearer the black sedan...only to have to fall back and pull behind Mr. Rude again when headlights speared the night—a car headed toward them. Rude Dude gained some distance as Ted waited for the next straight stretch of road, another opportunity to make a move. Struggling to rein in his disappointment, Daryl balled his hands. "You got this, man. Do it!"

A red blinking traffic light flashed ahead of them, but the black sedan hadn't even touched his brakes. Ted shot forward again, moved alongside the other vehicle, and as before, Rude Dude reacted. This time, when the black car swerved into Ted's SUV, the sedan spun out and skidded from the road.

Ted nimbly avoided crashing into them, and when the black sedan came to a rest, facing the opposite direction, Ted jerked to a stop at an angle blocking Rude Dude from reentering the road.

Daryl unfastened his seat belt and shouldered open the back door before the SUV had fully stopped. He charged through the downpour to the driver's door and yanked on the handle. When it wouldn't open, he employed the items he'd taken from his backpack—nail clippers and a decorative wooden clog he'd bought his mother in the Amsterdam airport. Locking the nail clippers so that he had a metal tip, he drew back his arm and smashed the metal clippers into the driver's window. The impact cause a starburst crack, which was all he needed. Now he smacked the heavy shoe against the damaged safety glass, and it shattered.

In the back seat, Imogen gave a startled scream.

As Rude Dude recoiled from the splintering glass, Daryl reached through the broken window and grabbed the man's collar. He hauled Rude Dude closer and slammed a fist into the kidnapper's nose.

Rude Dude's hands flew up to cradle his face, curses flying. Ignoring the threats of his opponent, Daryl reached inside and hit the button to unlock all the doors. Then leaning past the whimpering man, he turned off the ignition. He removed the key and hurled the whole jangling set down the dark highway. Rude Dude wouldn't be driving off anytime soon.

As Ted appeared beside him, Daryl said, "Don't let him get out until I get her away." Without waiting for a reply, he opened the back door and leaned in.

Imogen gasped and scuttled away from him. Understandable. Everything about this situation had to be terrifying for her. Keeping his voice calm and soothing, Daryl asked, "Are you okay, Imogen?"

Her sharp inhale had a different tone this time. Surprise rather than fear. "Daryl?"

"Yeah." He swiped at the rain that streamed down his face and stung his eyes. "I saw you get in this jerk's car and figured out pretty quick he wasn't taking you downtown."

"Uh…no." Her voice wobbled.

He leaned farther into the back seat, dripping rain on the ripped vinyl. "Are you all right?"

"I—I, um…" She only stared at him for a moment before saying, "You came after me…to…save me from him?"

She seemed to be in shock. Also understandable, given the harrowing night. Given Rude Dude and Ted were tussling a bit and exchanging loud, blistering insults.

Daryl held his hand out to her. "Come on. Let's get you out of here. I'll have Ted drive you to your hotel."

She gave the downpour a considering look, then put her cold, trembling hand in his. As he helped her climb out of the black sedan, he held his jacket over her, trying in vain to shield her from the worst of the rain. With his arm around her, he hurried her to Ted's small SUV.

She hesitated before climbing in, lifting a wide-eyed look to him. "Wait! My suitcase…"

"Oh, right." Daryl replayed the moments at the airport when Rude Dude had thrown her bag in the trunk. "Wait here."

Returning to the black sedan, he called to Ted. "Hey, pop the trunk, will ya?"

Ted complied, and as he returned with Imogen's bag, Daryl called, "We've got her. Let's go." After loading Imogen's luggage in the back of Ted's vehicle, Daryl slid onto the back seat next to her. He was sodden and chilled, but relieved to have Imogen safe. He peered through the water-speckled window to watch Rude Dude stand beside his car for a moment, raging and waving a fist. Then the bearded man turned to begin searching the pavement for the keys Daryl had tossed away.

Ted settled on the driver's seat and slicked rain from his face and hair. "How long do you think it'll take the cops to get here? Before that SOB finds his keys and takes off?"

Imogen stiffened. "Cops? You mean the police?"

Ted glanced back at them. "Yeah. I mean, hell, he kidnapped you. Don't you want to file charges? I know I need an accident report to file with my insurance to get my car fixed."

Daryl surveyed Imogen's stricken expression, a building suspicion in his gut. "You have a problem with calling the police?"

"It's just… I'd rather we…not. Please. I can't have anyone know where I am. This would end up in the press and—" She met Ted's curious frown with a pleading gaze. "I will pay to have your car repaired. I'm so grateful for your help, but I only… Can we just…get away from here?" She angled her head to monitor Rude Dude's activity, worry deeply etched in her fragile features.

Daryl studied her, noting her phrasing. She was worried about the press picking up the story?

Ted twisted his mouth, clearly skeptical but thinking it over. "I suppose we are lucky he hasn't pulled a gun out of his glove compartment and shot us yet," he said darkly. "And despite our noble mission, I did break a few traffic laws myself in order to catch that guy." Ted buckled his seat belt and started his engine again. "You promise you'll help me fix my car?"

"I promise. Every pence." She furrowed her brow. "Or penny, rather."

Ted turned the steering wheel and pulled back onto the road, heading back the direction they'd come. "Pence, huh? Where are you from?"

"Erm," she said and hesitated as if weighing her answer. "Great Britain."

In the dark car, Daryl focused on Imogen as they drove away. Her bluntly nonspecific answer intrigued him. Again, her body language shouted at him—arms wrapped around herself, expression troubled, body trembling. Of course, much of that could be from the damp, cold weather. Except…she'd been in a similar state when she boarded their flight. Imogen was running scared, trying to escape something bad, and she didn't want to be found.

He had no reason in the world to feel responsible for her. They'd been seatmates on an extended flight. Period. Yet he felt invested. He felt…drawn to her. He felt…protective of her. For whatever reason escaped him in the moment, Daryl knew on a gut level that Imogen needed him tonight. That however capable she might normally be, tonight she was rattled. She was alone and vulnerable. And he swore to himself that he would keep her safe until she sent him packing.

Chapter 4

Kara huddled on the seat next to Daryl, feeling numb as she tried to sort out what had just happened. Had the man who kidnapped her been working for Ian? Surely not. Ian hated her and had shouted that he'd ruin her for the choices she'd made, but this? Could he have learned she'd fled the country already? Could he have put someone in place to terrorize her, humiliate her, hurt her so quickly?

She shuddered thinking about the threats the gray-bearded man had made. Nude pictures. Having some "fun." Even in American English she knew he didn't mean they'd be playing Tiddlywinks.

Without turning her head to verify, she sensed Daryl's steady, concerned gaze on her. She allowed her brain to replay his kindness on the airplane, his gentle smile and soothing tone, reassuring herself he was good, safe. Only then did she rewind to the moment he'd smashed the driver's window, punched the bad man in the face and appeared at her car door like an avenging angel. Daryl didn't fit the classic image of a winged cherub, but in primary school, the nuns had taught them that angels could be warriors, fighting God's battles with flaming swords and mighty power.

A wry, silent laugh escaped her when that random

memory from childhood crept through her head. As a child, stories of angels with fire and wrath had haunted her. Now, casting a brief glance at Daryl, the idea of a warrior angel seemed more reassuring. A relief. A comfort. At least when that angel wore blue jeans on his long legs and had thick, wide shoulders under his button-down shirt.

Daryl cleared his throat, and his rich baritone voice flowed over her as he said, "You're safe now, Imogen. I won't let anything happen to you."

Imogen. A prick of guilt stabbed her that she'd lied about her name to a man who'd risked so much to save her from her kidnapper. Daryl had had the awareness to realize from the moment she'd entered the bad man's car that something was wrong. And had rescued her.

She opened her mouth, prepared to correct him on her name, but hesitated, flicking a glance to their young driver.

"Did you know that man? What did he say to you that convinced you to go with him?" Daryl asked, his eyes pinched in curiosity and worry.

"He…he knew my name." Her *real* name. But he could have just recognized her where most everyone else in the airport had not. If he followed the Knights, he had certainly seen her face splashed in media reports about the team's star player. "And he didn't give me a chance to object or verify his credentials or—"

"Yeah, I saw him manhandle you and all but push you into his car. That was the first thing to trigger alarms for me."

She met Daryl's gaze fully now. "You saw that? You were watching me?"

He wrinkled his nose and rubbed a finger under his eye before saying quietly, "I was. But only because I'd just talked to the jerk, and he'd said he was waiting for his brother. So...when he grabbed you, I was...curious. When he didn't go toward town and your hotel, I figured something was up."

She sighed heavily. "Yeah. At first I thought maybe he was the ride that Im—" She caught herself. "That my assistant had arranged for me. I mean, he knew my name and I—"

But how many Americans really knew her? Why hadn't she been more alarmed by that man recognizing her?

Imogen had sworn no one knew Kara was leaving London, flying to America to stay out of the media spotlight until things settled down. Her assistant had promised to protect Kara's identity for as long as Kara needed to hide. That was the whole point of this trip. If she couldn't trust Imogen, she had no one left. She couldn't even call her parents for fear of what the paparazzi might do to wheedle information from her elderly mother and father. The media's harassment of them earlier in this debacle had so stressed her father he'd had a cardiac event that sent him to hospital for three days.

Their driver had reached the main motorway and slowed, casting a glance to the back seat. "Which hotel are you going to, ma'am?"

A fist of panic closed around her heart at the idea of being dropped at a busy metropolitan hotel, navigating the lobby, staying alone in the sterile room and then catching another taxicab or private car back to the airport at the crack of dawn.

"I, erm..." Her voice rasped, and her pulse fluttered in her throat.

When she didn't answer, Daryl prompted. "It was the Marriott, wasn't it?"

Her mind spun, and the terrifying moments in the bearded man's car echoed in her brain. The reckless speed. His cackling threats. The cold loneliness. And the relief and sense of safety when Daryl had arrived. *Daryl...*

"Well, yes, but..." She swallowed hard. "I don't... I don't want to go there any longer." She turned to Daryl, shocked at what she was ready to admit as she pitched her voice softer. "I don't want to be alone tonight."

His dark eyebrows shot up, then drew down in a wary frown. "You're sure? I think you'll be plenty safe there. I'll even walk you up to your room if you want."

Kara bit her bottom lip and wiped damp palms on her yoga pants. In the past three turbulent months, the only time she'd felt safe, felt calm enough to actually laugh, felt reassured was with this man beside her. He was a stranger, but...her soul seemed to know him. He didn't recognize her, didn't want anything from her, yet he had gone out of his way to soothe her fears on the plane, to protect and rescue her from her kidnapper. And so Kara had no qualms in her stomach when she said, "Where are you staying tonight? I... I'd rather go with you."

Daryl blinked, startled by Imogen's announcement. "Uh, I booked a cheap motel in the boonies. Because of the storm, everything close to the airport was booked. It's very basic." He tugged up a corner of his mouth. "They don't even serve free breakfast. Not sure it's what you want."

His description of the second-rate motel didn't seem to dissuade her. Rather than turned off by the idea of a cheap place, she looked disappointed he wasn't readily welcoming her to join him. Maybe he'd underestimated how deeply the scare with Rude Dude and the turbulence and whatever had her flustered to begin with were troubling her. Compassion swelled in him as he studied her pale, lightly freckled face in the dimly lit car. Even without the bright light of day, he saw the smudges like bruises under her eyes. Having napped on the plane or not, this gal was worn out, worn down by life.

Who was he to tell her "no"? If she wanted to accompany him to the low-rent motel, she could. He flipped up a palm. "All right. Your call. Teddo, it sounds like we're both headed to the Meadow Lark Motel, if you'd please?"

She sent him a watery smile as she pushed her dripping hair from her face. He returned a grin, happy that she felt comfortable enough with him to stop hiding behind her hair, amazing as it was.

His fingers twitched on his lap, wanting to comb his fingers through the thick auburn hair, even soaked as it was by their dash through the downpour. Already her hair was starting to curl as it dried, and he could imagine it in springy coils, a russet cloud around her shoulders.

Daryl caught his breath and snapped his gaze away, suddenly self-conscious about how he'd been ogling her. Not that there was anything wrong with admiring a beautiful woman. He just felt a tad uneasy with how much he was attracted to her considering how vulnerable she seemed. Honor would not allow him to act on his interest in her. She needed a protector tonight, not someone making moves on her.

They arrived at the small motel fifteen or so minutes later, and Daryl fished out his wallet, prepared to give Ted a large additional tip beyond what he'd already prepaid through the rideshare app. The guy deserved it after successfully chasing down Imogen's kidnapper. She saw what he was doing and laid a hand over his.

"Oh, please, let me pay. After everything you've done, I insist."

Daryl demurred. "Naw, I've got it."

"But—" Imogen hesitated as she dug in her backpack. "Oh, bugger! I don't have American cash yet. I planned to get it in the morning from a cash machine." She leaned forward, directing her question to Ted. "Can I pay you with a credit card or money app?"

Ted flashed her a smile. "Sure. Let me get you my deets." He fumbled in a pile of papers in the center console and handed both her and Daryl a business card. "That's got all the payment forms I accept. And if you call me in the morning, I'll be happy to take you guys back to the airport."

Imogen nodded assent, and the three arranged a time that would accommodate both Daryl's and Imogen's rescheduled flights.

Leaving the engine idling, Ted climbed out and helped Daryl retrieve their bags.

"Hey, okay if we take a selfie to commemorate our adventure? It's not every day I get to rescue a damsel in distress," Ted asked, his phone out and ready.

"Why not? Imogen?" Daryl put an arm around her, and Imogen resisted.

Her hand flew to her hair, and she stammered, "Oh, I don't know. We're drenched! And I—"

"You look beautiful," Daryl said with a chuckle, waving Ted closer as he mugged for the camera. "And the drenching is part of the story."

Daryl and Ted leaned in, and as the flash went off Imogen turned her face away. Daryl frowned, realizing belatedly that Imogen's reluctance could have been more substantial than concern for wet hair. He felt a tug of guilt for his insistence and swore to be more conscientious going forward.

After encouraging Daryl to check in first, Kara feigned interest in a rack of dusty brochures about Atlanta attractions, then kept her gaze lowered as much as possible while checking in. Their rooms ended up being on opposite ends of the long single-floor building.

Daryl bounced his key in his hand as they exited the office and paused under the awning to stare at rain that had slackened to a dribble. He seemed to be debating what to say, as she was.

What do you say to a handsome stranger who, in your brief acquaintance, has shown you nothing but kindness, understanding and bravery? Whose keen observation and decisive action saved you from a man with vile intentions? "Thank you" seemed so paltry, so insufficient.

Yet those were the words on her lips, when he turned to her with one of his charming grins and said, "Well, good night. My room is this way." He hitched his thumb over his shoulder. "If we're sharing a ride back to the airport, then I guess I'll see you in the morning."

"Yeah." She dragged up a smile for him despite her soul-deep fatigue, discouragement and, yes, fear. She'd been kidnapped tonight, after all. And she was a long way from settling the disaster with Ian. And she truly had no idea what she would do with herself with the next several weeks, even months, here in the United States. Alone.

At least until Imogen found a way to visit without the tabloids figuring out Kara's location.

"So since this place doesn't do breakfast," Daryl said, drawing her out of her glum thoughts, "why don't we meet over there." He pointed across the street to a restaurant with dark windows and neon lights advertising daily breakfast and lunch.

"Betty's Diner," Kara said, reading the name on the lighted sign over the front door. "All right."

They chose a time, and with a nod of agreement, he turned to go.

"Only..." she blurted without knowing why except she wanted to stop him, call him back. She tried to sort out the jumble of emotions bobbing inside her like a boat on choppy water.

He pivoted to face her, his expression open, expectant, curious.

Her mouth dried. "I just—well, earlier, when I said I didn't want to be alone..."

One raven eyebrow shot up, and his expression slowly morphed to one of worry, then more quickly to awkwardness. "Imogen, are you saying—"

She realized he thought she was looking to hook up, and her face flashed hot. "No!"

He chuckled at her quick and strident denial, lifting a hand as if in surrender. "Okay. Easy. Just clarifying."

She bit her lip and closed the distance to him, even though it exposed her to the mizzle. "I'm not saying you're not attractive. You are! Very!" She huffed and shook her head. "Bloody hell, I'm making a mess of this."

When she lifted a hand to wipe rain from her face, he caught her hand and pressed it between his. His grip was warm, calming and just what she needed at the moment. Stooping a bit to look into her eyes, he said, "Tell me what you want. You don't have to dress it up or make it pretty. Just say it."

She swallowed. Opened her mouth. And nothing came out.

He tipped his head to the side, his eyes narrowing a tad. "You don't have to be scared now, Imogen. Not with me."

The sound of a name, not hers, on his lips struck her differently this time. Daryl deserved more from her. He deserved honesty.

"Kara," she said. "My real name is Kara."

Chapter 5

Daryl blinked and had to take a beat to catch up to the left turn in the conversation. "Um, so not Imogen?"

She shook her head and peered at him with a hangdog expression. "Imogen is my assistant. It was the first name I thought of when you asked. I'm sorry I lied."

Puzzled by her fib, he twisted his lips as he considered her admission. "Okay. But why would you lie about your name?"

She hesitated, as if deciding how much of her story to tell him. All the while, they stood in the rain getting wetter and colder.

"Hang on. What if we got out of the rain to continue this conversation? My room's just there." He jerked his chin toward the door with a number four painted on it. He moved his hand to her arm, encouraging her to follow.

She bit her bottom lip and, with a nod, finally fell into step beside him. As he keyed open the door, her words from earlier replayed in his head.

I don't want to be alone tonight. But her fervent denial that this was a booty call left him with the picture of a frightened woman who needed a friend tonight. A foreign visitor to the US, whose welcome to the States had been a kidnapping and terrifying race down I-75 and dark country roads in a rain storm.

Stepping into the musty motel room, he found the light switch and strode to the bathroom to retrieve two threadbare towels so they could dry off. When he returned, Imog—*Kara*—was standing in the middle of the floor, her gazing taking in the shabby room. Without her raised hood or the night's darkness obscuring his view, he finally had a clear view of her exquisite face. Freckles trailed across a pert nose and high cheekbones, and her almond-shaped eyes were even greener than he'd first thought, like emeralds set in her heart-shaped face. And the lips she kept nibbling? Daryl tore his gaze away from the ravaged bow mouth before his imagination could drift to kissing those lips. No kissing. He was a gentleman, and she'd clearly laid out that this evening, her needs were not about sex. He noticed the tiny furrow in her brow as she took in their accommodations.

"I told you it would be basic," he said, giving her a grin and one of the towels.

She returned a shy smile. "It's fine. I'm not nearly as posh as most people believe. In Ireland, where I grew up, my family was far from rich. Our farmhouse was more than one hundred and twenty years old and was very *basic*, as you say." Her face brightened, and when her gaze drifted away, she seemed to be recalling fond memories of that house. His guess was confirmed when she added, "Luckily, my parents had upgraded to add indoor plumbing by the time I was born."

He laughed as he swiped the towel over his head and down his neck. "Definitely one of my favorite modern conveniences, too."

Her gaze landed on something behind him, and he turned to see what had caught her eye. On top of the small dresser was a single-cup Keurig coffee maker, a small selection of pods and two paper cups. "Can I fix you some coffee? Something warm to drink sounds pretty good to me right about now."

"Is there cream?"

He checked. "Um, the powdered kind and a couple of these creamer doohickeys."

She snorted a little laugh, drawing his gaze back to her.

"What's funny?" he asked.

"Doohickey? What does that mean? Is it even a real word?"

He lifted a hand and shot her a teasing look that said the answer should be obvious. He poured a little extra Southern drawl in his voice when he said, "Around these parts and where I grew up in North Carolina, it is most definitely a word. It means thingamajig or whatchamacallit."

Now she gave him a full-fledged laugh, the sound reminding him of birdsong, or a babbling creek, or the joyful noise of his sisters at Sunday family meals. He noticed a spark of life in her green eyes that he hadn't seen since he'd made a joke on the plane. In that moment, Daryl wanted nothing more than to make Kara laugh for as long as she'd let him.

"Now you are making up words!" She gave him a mock scowl. "Don't tease me."

He slapped a hand over his heart and stood straight and stiff. "I swear on the honor of the US Army and my beloved Nanna's grave, they are real words. They all mean a random thing you don't know or can't remember the name of."

Her face lit, and her russet eyebrows lifted. "An oojah!"

A chuckle rolled from his chest. "Now who's making up words?"

Imitating his stance with her hand over her heart, she sobered her expression. "I'm not. It means thingummy or yoke."

They held each other's gazes, playfully serious, until they cracked at the same time with spluttering and giggles. He turned back to the Keurig machine. "Was that a 'yes' on the coffee then?"

She tousled her hair with the towel, still beaming at him. "Please." She gave a light sigh and stooped to unzip her bag. "What an elegant and mercurial thing the English language is. It can be the same and yet so different from one country to the next. Australia, Ireland, Canada, New Zealand…" She pulled dry clothes from her suitcase and stood. "May I use your lavatory to change?"

"Be my guest." He started the first cup of coffee brewing. "I'll change, too, while you're in there." Once she ducked into the bathroom, he stripped off his own wet shirt and jeans and had donned dry khakis and briefs when he heard the bathroom door open.

"Are you decent?" she called.

"Yep."

She stepped back into the bedroom and stopped, staring at him. Her mouth worked wordlessly, and color rose in her cheeks. Daryl glanced down to be sure he'd zipped his fly. Check. Was she unsettled to see him shirtless after he'd promised no funny business? Maybe. Snatching his dry T-shirt from the bed, he whipped it on and moved to the coffee maker without comment.

Kara fetched a brush from her bag and climbed onto

one of the two double beds to lean against the headboard. She crossed her legs at the ankles as she brushed out her curling hair.

"Do you ever wear your hair with the curls or do you always straighten it?" he asked. "'Cause I think the curls are pretty."

She paused in her brushing and looked up at him. "You do?" Then, shaking her head, she amended, "I mean, thank you. Ian never liked it curly."

"Ian?" He carried the first cup of coffee over to her. "Who's that?"

She narrowed a strange look on him, studying him hard. "You truly don't know?"

He snorted. "Why would I? I'd guess he's a boyfriend or something, but I don't like assuming anything."

She seemed to consider his reply, and slowly a smile bloomed on her face that sent his pulse scampering. All too soon, a serious look returned as she said, "Yes. My boyfriend. Or rather...now ex-boyfriend, I suppose."

She frowned, and he instantly regretted the mention of her ex. If this Ian character was the source of the dark smudges under her eyes and the anxiety or grief in her emerald gaze, then he wanted no part of discussing him or reminding her of him in any way.

Turning back to the Keurig, he started a second cup. "I guess the question is how do *you* like to wear your hair?"

She heaved a weary sigh. "Whatever is easiest most days. Pulled back in a bunch or plait if I'm not working."

He glanced over his shoulder at her. "The children's charity, right? Acting out their traumas, you said?"

She looked confused for a minute, then smiled and nodded. "Oh, right."

"That *is* what you said on the plane, right? Did I get something wrong?"

"No, that's what I said. But I, erm…only do that work part-time. The rest of my time, most of my time, I'm…" She twisted a hank of hair around her finger and appeared to be weighing her words.

He chuckled. "What? Is your work some kind of secret?" He pulled an exaggerated mask of shock. "Are you a spy? Are you here on a mission for MI6?"

A laugh tripped from her, and when her coffee sloshed, she set it down on the bedside stand. "If I were, would I tell you?"

He shrugged. "Good point. So I guess that's a *yes*. Kara the spy." He snapped his fingers and pointed at her. "That's why you used an alias, isn't it? It all makes sense now."

She laughed harder and raised both hands in surrender. "You caught me. First day and my mission is banjaxed already."

Daryl reveled in her laughter, relieved to be pulling her out of whatever darkness had been weighing on her. He knew one or two moments of levity didn't fix problems heavy enough to have had her so downcast and anxious, but if he could spare her even a moment of grief, he would.

He considered the second bed, but opted for one of two padded chairs angled around a tiny table at the window. He sipped his coffee and savored the warmth filling his belly. Her avoidance of the question concerning her career puzzled him, but he wouldn't pry further if she was uncomfortable talking about it. "So you grew up in Ireland, then? Was it as great as it sounds to this American?"

"It was. I have a lovely family, and I had good friends."

Had good friends. He made a mental note of the past tense.

"But while I'm admittedly biased, I do believe it is the most beautiful place on earth, and I love my homeland."

"My grandmother used to say Scotland was the most beautiful place on earth. But for my money, you can't beat the Smoky Mountains around my home in North Carolina. Especially in fall when the trees are ablaze in oranges and yellows and reds." He waved a hand as if painting a picture for her. "It's breathtaking."

Her mouth curved contentedly as if she were picturing the scene. "I'd love to see it sometime." She glanced down at her coffee, then muttered, "I might, in fact, if I'm still over here in six months."

Before he could ask what might keep her stateside for so long, and what her sabbatical involved, she pinned an earnest green gaze on him, asking, "What was it like growing up in North Carolina? Tell me more about your family."

So he did. He told her about being the adopted youngest of five, about the family's idyllic property called Cameron Glen, about his Scottish grandmother who lived with them until she was 101 years young.

"My siblings are all married, and I have a bunch of nieces and nephews. I even have a niece who's older than me. When we all get together, it's chaos. No other way to describe it, but it's a blast, too, and I wouldn't have it any other way."

She finished her drink and set the cup aside. "So you're the only one not married? Was that a choice or have you not found the right one yet?"

"I'm not opposed to marriage. But I've been moving

around a lot with the Army and—" he shrugged "—guess I have kinda high standards. All the women role models in my life have set a pretty high bar for the woman I marry." He raised his coffee cup and pondered the point as he drank.

She arched a burnished copper eyebrow. "So you're looking for someone like your mother to marry?"

He sputtered so hard, he literally sprayed coffee across the small table. Coughing as he gathered himself and wiped up the mess with his sleeve, he shook his head and chuckled. "Gosh, no! I didn't mean that. I mean, my mom is wonderful and all that, but... I only meant my mom and sisters are such kind and generous people. They've got great marriages and kids and careers and integrity and make it all look so easy."

She twisted her mouth as if dubious of his perspective. "I bet if you ask them, they'll say it's far from easy. Do their husbands help with the kids?"

"Oh, yeah. And everyone pitches in to trade babysitting and spend-the-night parties and general support."

She nodded, yawned. "Tell me more."

"Really?" he said with a humored snort. "That yawn says I'm boring you."

She shook her head. "That yawn says I'm finally relaxed. Say more things. Did you say you rent rooms at Cameron Glen?"

"Cabins, yes. The property was created to be a vacation retreat by my great-grandparents."

He launched into a description of Cameron Glen's rolling hills, Christmas tree crop, fishing ponds and array of wildlife. He spoke of the refurbished cabins, summer swimming parties and winter sledding. Of his mother's garden, his sister's pet goats and fishing with his brother. If she thought he was rambling or boring, she gave no indication, and Daryl relished the walk down memory lane. "I'm on my way back there now, as a matter of fact. I didn't make it at Christmas, so I'm taking advantage of the days before my speaking engagement at Duke to visit my parents for a few days. Then it's back to California and the regular job."

"Oh, I know your mother will be so happy," she said around another yawn.

His stomach growled—loudly—and Kara giggled.

Rather than dismiss his stomach's grumbling, he stood and rubbed his ribs. "Are you hungry? I'm hankering for something salty about now."

Her expression perked up. "I am rather. Don't forget, I slept through the meal on the plane. But what is open and in walking distance this time of night?"

His shoulders dropped. "Not much, but…wasn't there a vending machine in the lobby?"

She swung her legs off the bed and paused. "Ugh! I still haven't got American cash." She sent him a sheepish glance. "Do you remember if the machine takes a credit card?"

He waved a hand. "My treat. Besides, it's still raining. No point in both of us getting wet again. Whatcha want?"

"Crisps, please. But I will pay you back. Case closed."

"Got it. Chips it is."

"No, crisps," she said.

"That's what I said," he teased. "Chips."

Flattening her mouth, she rolled her eyes. "Stop, Daryl. I'm far too knackered to remember where I am or what confusing word you Americans use for snack foods."

With a chuckle, he scooped the door key off the table and sent her a wink. "Back in a jiffy."

In the lobby, the desk manager gave him a startled look when he came in, and Daryl nodded a greeting. After selecting a variety of crackers, chips, candy and nuts, he headed back to the room with his arms laden with the bounty and fumbled to open the door.

"I got a smorgasbord of—"

He fell silent when he glanced at the bed. Kara was asleep, the golden light from the lamp catching copper highlights in her gently curling hair. Her face was so peaceful, so relaxed, he hated to wake her. He picked out a couple bags of chips—potato and corn—to set next to the bed, then added a chocolate bar.

Rather than wake her, Daryl found a small motel notepad in a drawer and scribbled a note. Taking the key to Kara's room from the bedside table, he turned out the light and silently left.

Chapter 6

When Kara woke hours later, the first thing she noticed was the mustiness that filled her nose, then as she puzzled over the odd scent, she peeked out at the stale room and was swamped by confusion. She bolted upright on the bed and needed several staggering heartbeats to blink away the fog of sleep and recall where she was and why.

Daryl. Her chest tightened when she thought of having slept in a stranger's room, but when she cast her gaze to the second bed, it was empty. Was she relieved...or disappointed?

"Daryl?" she said tentatively, as she searched the room for evidence of him. Spying the crisps and a candy bar on the bedside shelf, she scooted across the mattress to examine his offering. Beside the snacks was a small note that read simply, *Sleep well. See you at breakfast. D.*

Breakfast! Not only did the notion of hot food make her mouth water, the promise of seeing Daryl again brought a smile to her face.

Her pulse kicked. Criminy, what time was it? She hadn't set an alarm before she'd fallen asleep. She scrambled to find her phone—which she'd not set up to charge—double criminy! She discovered it was 10:47 a.m.—almost eleven! No, wait. That was London time. Her phone hadn't reset to local time, because she'd purposely kept her GPS locator off. She didn't want anyone knowing where she was. She clapped a hand to her chest, relieved she'd not missed breakfast with Daryl, much less her rideshare and her rescheduled flight. But counting back five hours, she gasped. She had less than ten minutes to wash off airplane grunge and redress in clean clothes before she was supposed to meet Daryl across the street at the restaurant.

After the world's quickest shower, Kara combed out her hair and grabbed her portable charger from her backpack as she snatched up the room key and dashed out of the room.

The motel parking lot was still dark, but last night's rain left a fresh scent in the air, along with a chilly dampness. She held her jacket closed at the throat as she jogged toward the lit windows and neon signs of the building across the street. A set of headlamps pierced the early morning on the highway, and as she waited for the auto to pass, she shivered remembering the harrowing events of last night...the high-speed chase, her driver's ill intent. If not for Daryl...

She pulled on the heavy glass door to the restaurant and was greeted with the enticing aroma of frying meats, coffee and something sweet. A chorus of voices, heavy with Southern American accents called out, "Mornin'!"

A stout woman with an apron added, "Be right with ya, darlin'. You can seat yerself."

She turned to scan the small dining room, and when she spotted Daryl, a little butterfly flapped in her chest. He stood from the table where he'd been waiting, his face all boyish grin, freshly shaven and too handsome by half. "You made it."

"Barely. I forgot to set an alarm. So sorry to keep you waiting." When she reached their table, he pulled out her chair for her and helped her remove her jacket. She accepted the gestures as the good manners she knew them to be in the United States. Once she was settled, she lifted the sticky plastic-covered menu and studied the offerings. "On my only other trip to the US two years ago, I stayed in New York and usually skipped breakfast or had a yogurt. Today I'm famished. I want all of it. A full American breakfast. What do you recommend?"

"Well, if you want traditional Southern fare, grits is the way to go."

"Grits?" She gave him a skeptical frown.

"Or biscuits and sausage gravy. Eggs, of course, probably scrambled or fried. Bacon, which is different here and a must." He imitated an Italian chef kiss with his fingers, then added, "But you can't go wrong with pancakes or waffles. French toast."

She laughed. "Now you're just reading the menu to me. You're no help."

He flashed a playful grin. "What can I say? Southerners know how to do breakfast right. Why don't we get a little of everything and you try it all? If you've never had American diner food, you owe it to yourself to experience it all." He pressed a hand to his chest. "And I would be shirking my duty as a Southerner if I don't introduce you to the wonders of our cooking."

She giggled and laid the menu on the table. "Well, if that's the case, how can I say no?"

His face lit with such pleasure at her agreement that his brown eyes seemed to sparkle. He clapped his hands together, rubbed them briskly and with a wink said, "Awesome."

When the stout woman appeared tableside a moment later, coffeepot in hand, she flipped Kara's cup over and poured without Kara asking. Dividing a look between Kara and Daryl, she asked, "Y'all ready to order or do you need a minute?"

Daryl lifted the menu with a flourish. "Get ready. This might blow your mind a little."

The waitress twitched a grin. "Lay it on me."

Daryl rattled off a list of foods that boggled Kara's mind if not their server's, and when he was through, he pointed at the coffee carafe. "And you can leave that here. There will be much coffee consumed this morning." He handed the sticky menus to the woman, adding, "Please and thank you."

The stout woman nodded once and clicked her pen closed. "Comin' right up! What flavor jelly you want for your biscuits?"

Daryl waved a hand, deferring to Kara. She blinked and raised a baffled look to the server. "Surprise me."

The waitress winked at her. "Will do, darlin'."

Kara gave Daryl a wide-eyed look. "What have I just signed up for?"

He threw his head back, his laughter deep and rich and so full of pure joy that it reached her core. Something shifted in her chest, in her bones, in her soul. This man was healing for her, she thought with a start. His mood was infectious, his warmth enough to chase the chill that had encapsulated her for too long. She'd almost forgotten how to be cheerful, how to embrace the possibilities of each new day. But Daryl's eyes, his smile shone with a genuine love for life that she could draw hope from.

"Your expression is priceless," he said. Then to her surprise, he reached across the table and covered her hand, saying, "Trust me, Kara. You are going to love me for this."

She glanced down at his large brown hand on her pale one, and a sweet tingle chased through her. Meeting his gaze, she tugged a lopsided smile. "I do trust you, Daryl."

His own smile slipped a tad, as if he'd heard the double meaning behind her assurance. He'd proven himself trustworthy. Thoughtful. Brave. If she didn't love him for the breakfast experience he'd offered, she might have fallen a wee bit in love with him for the character, kindness and humor he'd shown her in their short acquaintance.

He gave her fingers a quick squeeze before removing his hand and glancing away and asking, "Did you sleep okay? You were pretty out of it when I left last night."

She ducked her head. "Sorry. And in your room. How rude of me!"

He chuckled again. "The rudest! But one room at the Meadow Lark Motel is pretty much the same as the next, so it made no difference to me."

"I was enjoying your stories about your family, though. Will you tell me more? You said the Camerons have had a number of challenges in the past, close calls with dangerous people. What did you mean?"

He leaned back in his seat, idly twirling his coffee spoon on the tabletop. "Hoo-boy! We have indeed. How many days do you have? I couldn't possibly tell you everything in one breakfast."

I have all the time in the world, she wanted to say.

She had only the rental house in Kitty Hawk, where she planned to stay out of public view for as long as it took to feel safe again, to let the wrath and accusations and vitriol die away. "Then tell me the most recent brush with danger." A dark thought sprang to mind, and she sat taller. "Was your life ever at risk?"

"Hmm, not really. A lot of the really bad stuff happened when I was a teenager. Remember I said I'm a geek? I was a gamer, safe in my bedroom fighting aliens and playing sports on my computer." He paused and scratched his chin. "But I was there when my brother almost bled out once. A metal spike pierced his leg in a freak fishing accident about twelve years ago. I helped staunch the bleeding until the ambulance arrived. I was sixteen at the time, I think, and pretty scared Brody would die."

"How horrible!" Kara sipped her coffee, shuddering as she imagined the situation.

Daryl shrugged. "Yes and no. He has a nasty scar for a keepsake but also met his wife that day in the ER. Anya's a nurse, and they hit it off right away." He laughed again. "He was doped up on painkillers and even proposed to her from his gurney." Daryl shook his head, his mouth still hiked up in a grin. "We love to remind him of that whenever their anniversary rolls around."

"Poor Brody!"

He raised a hand, his expression sobering. "That was a cakewalk compared to when he and Anya were trapped underground by a landslide and later fought a serial killer for their lives."

"You're lying!" she said, eyes wide and tone aghast.

"Swear on my Nanna's grave, I'm not."

Her pulse was thundering as if she were the one in danger. "How did they get trapped? For how long? And... how did they escape a *serial killer*?"

He cocked his head. "Wouldn't you rather talk about something more pleasant? For instance, you haven't told me much about your family or growing up in Ireland. You lived on a farm, right?"

"Well, yes. We raised sheep and cows and had a small crop of rapeseed that we sold for processing."

"Mother, father, siblings?"

"Yes. They're both still alive and well in the same home. I have a younger brother and an older sister, Irene, who is married with a baby girl."

His smile twitched mischievously.

"What?" she asked.

"I'm just savoring your accent. 'A bebee gull.'"

She snorted a laugh. "My accent? You're one to talk! 'Hey, y'all, ah like ah-ce tea.'"

He gave her a serious nod. "True. That was pretty good. But slow it down more. Southerners don't get in a hurry when we talk." He looked past her shoulder and sat straighter, rubbing his hands together. "Oh, yeah, here's our food."

Their waitress appeared with a tray laden with savory smelling delights and baked goods that still steamed from the oven. Once she'd spread the bounty before them, Daryl waved a hand toward the offerings. "Pick your poison. Start with some grits and bacon?"

"If you say so. I am your student. Teach me the wonders of an American breakfast."

For the next several heavenly minutes, he did just that, introducing her to biscuits, the fluffier, more buttery version of a British scone; sausage gravy, peppery meat in a white sauce; grits, best if cooked in milk with salt and plenty of butter, cheese optional, according to Daryl; and American bacon, smoke cured and fatty, but cut thin and cooked until crisp. Each food was better than the next, and she was relishing it all, filling her stomach and enjoying Daryl's chatty banter and teasing as much as the meal.

He regaled her with more stories of his life at Cameron Glen, playing football in high school, his years at West Point, his new tech job in California.

"If you work in California and your family is in North Carolina, does that mean you were in Europe on vacation?" she asked.

"Sort of. I had a buddy who got married in Vienna." He chugged his orange juice then said, "But enough about me. Tell me more about you. Your family. Your sabbatical plans."

She dismissed him with a wave of her hand. "I'm sure you'd find me dull."

"I'm sure I wouldn't," he countered, swiping his scone…erm, biscuit…through the white gravy on his plate. "Is any of your family or a friend joining you while you are in the US?"

She lowered her gaze. She'd intentionally not told her family where she'd be so they didn't let anything slip by accident. "Well…no."

He made a sad sort of humming sound in acknowledgment. After a beat he said, "My Scottish grandmother used to tell us stories of her life in Scotland, growing up on a sheep farm before the Second World War. How long has your family had its farm?"

She relented. As long as she could keep him focused

on her early years in Ireland, maybe she could deflect from her current circumstances without lying outright. "At least three generations. Before that it gets murky, and I haven't really asked. But my mother's grandfather worked in the shipyard in Belfast."

Their waitress appeared tableside, placing a paper ticket between her and Daryl. Kara grabbed it. "This is mine. You've done so much for me. I must insist on buying your meal."

Daryl opened his mouth to protest, but their server cut him off. "Don't argue with her, honey. Gals these days want to pay their way fair and square."

He raised both hands. "All right. I know when I'm beat." He nodded to Kara. "Thank you."

Their server faced Kara again and cocked one hip out as she stared at her. "Do I know you? You look real familiar to me."

Kara's breath stuck in her lungs. She prayed silently the woman wouldn't guess her identity, wouldn't give up her secret to Daryl. Or worse, that she wouldn't spread the word in her community that a British movie star had been in her diner, such that her presence in the US leaked to the media. "Um, I don't think so."

"Hmm," the woman said, tipping her head to the side as she studied Kara. "Are you sure? Who are your people?"

Kara blinked. "My people?"

"Your family," Daryl supplied, then turning to their waitress, added, "You must know her doppelgänger. She's just here visiting for a while."

The waitress bobbed a nod. "Yeah, I thought I heard something in your voice. An accent. Should've guessed you weren't from around these parts. Well, enjoy your visit. Ain't no place in the world like the US of A."

Kara fished out her credit card and handed it to the woman, who shuffled off with a promise to be right back. Sighing with relief, Kara returned her attention to her meal. She'd just doused a cinnamon waffle in maple syrup—or *sirp*, as Daryl pronounced it—when his gaze flew to the large front window.

He dug his phone out and checked the time, muttering, "Geez, it's already seven. Ted just pulled up at the motel to take us to the airport."

Kara's heart sank. She wasn't ready to end this meal—or more specifically her time with Daryl. She took a last gulp of coffee and dropped her napkin on her plate.

Daryl peeled off some cash that he dropped in the center of the table. "I've got the tip."

Rising from her chair and collecting her backpack, Kara made a mental note to research American tipping customs, which she remembered were quite different from much of Europe. She retrieved her credit card at the front counter, scribbled a half legible signature on the slip and hurried out of the diner behind Daryl. Together they trotted back across the road to the motel, and, with stops to retrieve their belongings from their respective rooms, met Ted at his car.

Conversation on the ride to the airport centered around Ted reliving the race through the rain last night and how he'd shared the picture he'd snapped and the tale of their adventure with his mates.

Once at the airport, they crept through traffic at the drop-off for their airline and waved to Ted as they made their way inside the airport lobby.

"My gate is that way," she said, pointing to the left. Her flight to Norfolk left from a different concourse.

"Well, I guess this is where we part, then," Daryl said. He pointed to a sign directing passengers to a different security entrance. "The gate for Asheville is that way."

She nodded and faced him, battling a lump in her throat as she tried to find the words to express her gratitude for all he'd done for her and her appreciation of his friendship, steadiness and courage. Instead, when emotion clogged her voice, she stood on her toes and pressed a quick kiss to his lips and rasped, "I'll never forget you."

He gave her a stunned look, then a gentle smile as he stroked her cheek. "Same. Goodbye, Kara."

His fingers on her cheek washed a balm of sweet longing to her core, but she tore herself away, flicking her hood up as she turned away.

"Hey," he called, and she glanced back. His brown eyes were bright with resolve. "You're going to be okay."

With a sure nod and a wink, he pivoted and walked away, leaving her goggling and teary-eyed. Huddling beneath the shield of her hood, she clung to his words of reassurance as she made her way through the crowded airport, on her way to her isolated beachside hideout.

Chapter 7

"Daryl!" Grace Cameron cried happily as she wrapped her adopted son in a tight embrace. "We were expecting you last night! What happened?"

He cringed. "Oh, man. I'm sorry, Mom. There was bad weather in Atlanta last night, lots of lightning. I meant to call when my flight was canceled, but things got crazy pretty fast and after that..." He shook his head. "Well, it's a long story."

"Define crazy," his mother said with a worried knit in her brow.

Daryl scratched his chin, deciding what details to exclude for his mother's peace of mind. "Long story," he repeated.

"You're here now, though, and that's what matters."

Behind his mother, a crowd of faces, young and old, appeared, each person jockeying to be the next to hug him, draw him into the living room or carry his suitcase.

As his family gathered around him with warm greetings and eager smiles, Daryl couldn't help but think of Kara. By herself. No family or friends meeting her or sharing her time in the States.

I don't want to be alone tonight.

He tried to push aside the nagging concern about her.

He'd never see her again, and since they hadn't exchanged contact information, he had no way to check up on her, so…he needed to forget her and move on. She'd be fine. He'd meant that when he told her the same, trying to buoy her before they parted. But did he still believe it? His own boisterous welcome home made his chest tighten when he thought of Kara not having the same support.

His youngest nephew, Joey, tugged on his arm. "Hey, Daryl, guess what? I made three goals at my soccer game on Saturday!"

"Three! Wow! That's great!" He offered his nephew a high five.

All speaking at once, his other nephews and nieces all shouted their own brags and stories. He tried to catch relevant snippets of each and respond appropriately, until Brody whistled loudly and sent the kids to wash up before dinner.

When the kids were down the hall, noisily vying for the bathroom sinks, Brody clapped his brother on his shoulder. "Good to have you home, D. Now that you're working stateside again, will we see more of you?"

"One can hope," Daryl returned.

"And Nathan's wedding? How was it? Beautiful, I bet," his mother said.

Daryl nodded. "Very." He elaborated on the historic church, the festive reception and touching ceremony as he cleaned up and helped carry the meal to the table. As the family gathered in the large dining room, his oldest sisters, Cait and Emma, asked to see pictures of the bride's wedding dress and the interior of the old church.

Daryl shook his head. "Didn't take any. You know that's not my thing."

Emma's mouth dropped open.

Cait slugged his shoulder lightly. "You've got to start taking pictures, Daryl! Your life events are passing you by undocumented. That's...unconscionable!"

He smirked at his sister and tapped his temple. "My pictures are here."

"Yeah, but here—" she poked his head "—doesn't help here." She pointed to her eyes.

"If you didn't take pictures, did it really even happen?"

The new teasing voice came from behind him, and he turned to find his niece Fenn—who was more like his cousin since they'd grown up together—grinning at him.

"Hey, hey! Look who the cat dragged in! I didn't know you would be here!" He opened his arms for a hug, and she gave him a tight squeeze.

"What? And miss seeing my favorite uncle on one of his rare appearances?"

"Hang on. You told me I was your favorite uncle," Brody teased with a mock scowl, and Fenn winked and shushed Brody with a conspiratorial grin.

Daryl took his usual seat, savoring the playful banter. The good-natured teasing and shared sense of humor was one of the things he loved most about his family.

A blessing was said over the food, serving bowls were passed and his mother turned the conversation back to his delay getting home. "We have time now for your long story. What was so crazy about your canceled flight last night?"

Daryl looked up from his plate and found all eyes on him. "Um..."

"Um?" Brody said, arching one eyebrow. "Oh, this is going to be good."

Brody's wife elbowed him. "Shh. Let him talk."

"So I met a girl on the flight from Amsterdam," he started.

"Would this 'girl' be older than eighteen?" Fenn asked, and Daryl knew immediately she wasn't actually asking about her age.

He rolled his eyes and started again. "I met a *young woman* on the plane. She was Irish, living in London, coming to the US for a sabbatical." He summarized the bullet points of the trip, leading up to his suspicions that the car she'd gotten into at the public transit exit wasn't legit. "Kara seemed wary of the guy, yet he all but forced her into his car."

"Oh, dear!" his mother gasped.

"Oh, no," Emma and Fenn said simultaneously. The mother and daughter had worked fighting sex trafficking together for the last thirteen years, so it was obvious where their minds had gone.

"So I had my driver follow her," he continued, leaving out the part about the high-speed chase and the violent storm that made the conditions all the more dangerous. "We were able to catch up to him and rescue her after several miles. Kara was understandably shaken, but unharmed."

A collective sigh of relief sounded around the table. He sent Emma and Fenn silent looks that confirmed the kidnapper had had unseemly intentions for Kara. He detailed how Kara had not wanted to go to the downtown hotel after the kidnapping attempt and had spent time talking with him in the run-down motel.

"Just talking?" Brody asked, curling his mouth in an impish grin.

"Mixed company," Cait said, covering her daughter's ears.

"Just talking," he said, nodding to his mother. "Mom raised me to be a gentleman."

His mother beamed at him.

"Even so…" his sister Isla said, eyeing him with suspicion, "I get the feeling there's more to this story. You liked her, didn't you?"

Daryl's stomach flip-flopped, and his mouth opened and closed like a fish out of water. His sister had an eerie sixth sense about things that had always unnerved him, especially when it was focused on him. "Um…"

"There's that 'um' again," Brody said in a lilting tone.

Daryl shot daggers at his brother with his gaze.

"Ooh," Fenn said with a knowing smile. "I see."

His older nephews and nieces caught the drift of the conversation and chimed together, "Ooooh." Or made kissing sounds.

Cait's daughter Cece sang, "Daryl and Kara, sitting in a tree," until her mother hushed her with a look.

Daryl shoved his peas around on his plate. "She was nice. And pretty. And we had a good rapport. But that's it. I doubt I'll ever hear from her again. We didn't trade info. End of story."

Isla tipped her head and narrowed an intense stare on him. "Mmm. But is it the end of the story?"

"Mom, dinner is delicious," Daryl said, changing the topic. "Are the green beans homegrown?"

Isla exchanged a smug look with Cece and Cait, who both sat across from her, but the conversation turned to Fenn's latest work as director of the nonprofit her parents had started years earlier.

While his family asked Fenn questions about the fundraiser she was initiating, Daryl dwelled on Isla's implication that his relationship with Kara might not be over after all. Did he believe his sister's unexplainable predictions?

She had a pretty good track record, including having recognized her own husband as her soulmate when they first met. He thought of Kara—the quick but earthshaking kiss she'd given him, the light in her emerald eyes that bore to his marrow, the deep connection he'd felt with her. And he hoped, privately, that he would somehow hear from Kara again, even if only to know she was okay.

After dinner, Daryl retreated into the living room with all of the family except the few kids selected to help their grandmother with clean-up duty.

One of the younger boys found a football and threw it to his brother. "Daryl, want to play catch?"

"Outside," Isla said.

Emma's husband groaned and rubbed his stomach. "I'm still digesting."

Brody intercepted the next illicit indoor pass and tossed the football from one hand to another. "Forget digesting, old man. It's football time. Daryl? Eric? Are y'all in?"

Daryl glanced at Eric, who'd been more brother to him through his teen years than whatever other tangled, technical relationship marriages and adoptions dictated. "I'm game. How about it, man?"

Eric handed his adopted daughter to his wife and tousled the toddler's hair lightly. "Let's do it! Old guys versus the young guys."

"Hey!" Eric's father groused. "Who are you calling old?"

Daryl flashed a wide grin as he aimed a finger at his brother-in-law. "You, grandpa. Ravi, Brett," he called as he moved into the living room where his nephews were bickering with the nieces. "What do you say? Wanna help us kick your dads' tails at football?"

"Yes. Please!" Brett said with a dramatic groan. "Anything but staying in here with the girls. They want to watch some chick movie about old-timey women chasing husbands."

Daryl caught Brett in a headlock and lightly rubbed his knuckles on his nephew's skull. "Ack! Not a chick flick! Save me, Daryl."

Brett battled his way out of the headlock and scoffed at Daryl's teasing. On the television, orchestral music swelled and a bucolic scene lit the screen, which the subtitle announced was near York, England, 1846.

"Can I play on your team?" Cece asked. "I've seen this movie before."

Daryl made a wide sweeping motion with his arm. "Sure. The more the merrier. Anyone else?"

The men and their children began filing out, and Isla said, "Let Cece play with the old guys. They'll need someone who can catch."

Isla's husband, Evan, gave her the stink eye. "Excuse me?"

Daryl chuckled and cuffed Evan in the shoulder with a playful, "Ooooh, burn!"

Before following the crew, already tossing the ball back and forth as they filed out the front door, Daryl glanced at the TV. Three young women in period dress were strolling, arm in arm, across a grassy field.

"Ya'll enjoy your movie." He tugged niece Prisha's braid, and as he headed out of the room, he did a double take at the women on the screen. One blonde, one brunette…and one freckled, with waving auburn hair. His heart lurched. He squinted at the screen, not really believing his eyes. But yes, the longer he watched, the more the camera took close-ups of her face, the more he listened to her voice, the more certain he was. *Kara!*

Adrenaline dumped in his system with no particular outlet other than to make his pulse race and his hands tremble. He snatched up the remote control and paused the movie when Kara came on-screen again.

His nieces and sisters groaned and protested. But as choruses of "Hey!" and "Uncle Daryl!" and "Ugh, D, stop it. Go play football!" sang around him, he only gawked at the television, stunned. He mentally replayed everything Kara had told him about her career, her life. Or more specifically everything she didn't say, the answers she'd artfully dodged. He'd not pushed, deciding it wasn't his business, that it didn't really matter. He'd never see her again. They'd been two proverbial ships that passed in the night. Except…

He'd really liked her. He wanted to stay in touch with her. He'd sensed a mutual chemistry—

"D, what's wrong?" Cait pushed off the couch and put a hand on his arm. "You look like you've seen a ghost."

"I kinda have." He blinked hard and gave his sister a quick glance before pointing at the screen. "Who is that?"

Cait looked at the TV then back at him.

"What?" his seventeen-year-old niece Lexi said with a laugh. "You don't know? Good grief, D, what rock have you been living under?"

Lexi's mother chided her with, "Easy, Lex. Not everyone spends half their life following pop culture like it was gospel."

"Daryl!" Brody called from the foyer, "Come on, man! We're waiting on you!"

"Um...start without me. I'm..." He was what? In shock? Transfixed? Curious as hell to watch the movie and see Kara in action? "So who is she?"

"That's Kara O'Quinn," Cait said. "She's been in British movies and television for about five years and wasn't super well-known until she started dating Ian Stafford, the soccer star for the Knights."

Ian. She'd mentioned her ex. The man who'd put fear and sadness in her eyes.

Cait continued, her tone soft as she broke the news. "And their relationship was all over the British media. Even more so now since this whole doping and drugs scandal hit."

Daryl ripped his gaze from the screen and snapped a frown toward his sister. "What drug scandal?"

Lexi chuckled and flopped back on the carpet. "Oh, Uncle Daryl, you really should get out more. Maybe pick up a newspaper? Figuratively speaking, of course, since news is all electronic now days."

"Lexi," her mother said, "why don't you go help your grandmother with the dishes instead of ragging on your uncle, huh?" Emma followed the suggestion with a look that said it was not a mere suggestion, but a directive.

Rolling her eyes, Lexi pushed off the floor and traipsed into the kitchen.

Nine-year-old Prisha stood, too, and pried the remote from Daryl's hand. "Can we watch the movie now?"

Numbly, he took a seat on the couch next to Emma, who patted his leg.

"You okay there, sport? Why is Kara O'Quinn a big deal to you?"

Isla gasped, her expression knowing. "Noooo!"

Cait caught on next. "Hang on! Is she—" she pointed at the television "—the woman you rescued? The lady from the plane and the one-night stand?"

Daryl scowled at Cait. "I told you it wasn't a one-night stand. Not the way you're implying."

Cait sat forward, clutching at his arm, her eyes wide. "But you're not denying it was her. You met Kara O'Quinn! It was her, wasn't it?"

Prisha paused the movie again and gaped at him. "You met Kara O'Quinn?"

Lexi appeared in the doorway again. "Holy cow, D! Did you?"

He dragged a hand over his mouth, processing what he was learning, questioning what it meant, deciding how he felt about Kara hiding her identity from him.

I do trust you, Daryl, she'd said. But if she'd really trusted him, why hadn't she told him the truth? The whole truth?

His mind spinning, his heart racing, he glanced from one giddy, stunned female face to another and admitted, "Yeah, that's her. That's the Kara I met."

Chapter 8

"So this soccer player, this Ian Stafford, tell me about him," Daryl said. Once it was known he'd met the Irish celebrity, a selection of his siblings and nieces had assembled to fill him in on the pop culture stories he missed. Even a couple of the men left the football game to join the conversation.

"Well, he's about the hottest thing to appear on the British soccer scene since David Beckham," Cait said. "He's good. Like *really* good."

"And he's not just hot as a player," Lexi added. "He *hooot*." Her exaggerated tone and swooning expression let Daryl know exactly what his niece meant. He gritted his teeth, trying to shove down the prick of…what? Jealousy? Why should he be envious of this handsome and talented British sports icon?

"When he and Kara started appearing in public together, the media gave them the couple name 'Kian,'" Lexi added, pulling up a photo on her cell phone to show him.

"Couple name?" Daryl repeated with a wrinkled nose. "Wha—"

"You know, like Bennifer. Or Brangelina."

Daryl glanced at the image Lexi showed him, and the

gnawing jealousy spiked. His stomach roiled seeing Kara beaming at the ruggedly handsome man beside her at some formal occasion.

But yesterday, she'd called Ian her ex. So he had no reason to be envious. Daryl snorted. *As if I have any claim to Kara to begin with...*

"She hadn't been a big star in her own right really. She did mostly smaller roles and was only beginning to come into popularity when she starred in a hit British drama last year. So I can see why you'd not heard of her before last summer. But when they started dating—" Cait wagged a finger toward Lexi's phone, which still glowed with the image of Kara and Ian "—they were everywhere in the news. Even here in the States people were following them. They were the *it* couple. As big as Taylor and Travis in the US."

Kian. Daryl turned the phone over and suppressed the urge to growl.

"Especially after rumors about the drug use and their breakup leaked," Brody said.

Daryl frowned. "Again, what drug use? You never answered before."

Lexi groaned and rolled her eyes.

Cait put a hand on Lexi's knee. "Okay, now. Give him a break."

Brody cleared his throat. "I don't know all the details, but news was leaked to the media that Ian was not only taking performance-enhancing drugs, but other illegal substances, as well. The story goes that not only Stafford's personal handlers and coaches knew, but his team's management did as well, and they covered it up. Denials, cheating on drug tests, counter stories to shift the blame and suspicion away from Ian."

Daryl scowled. "Counter stories? What do you mean?"

Cait cringed. "Well, it came out that Kara was the one who leaked the story. She says she didn't, but…"

Daryl's skin prickled with heat as anger stirred in his belly. "But?"

"But the team insisted the real story was Ian was the one who caught Kara with drugs, and she spread lies about him to preempt any fallout that would cast her in a bad light. That she was manipulative and spoiled and threatened privately to destroy Ian's career when he wanted to quietly break up."

"So the 'he said,' 'she said' battle began, and most of the public, being adoring fans of soccer, sided with Ian," Lexi explained. "The team had the money to defend Ian, to protect their asset and really cast Kara in a bad light. She became public enemy number one and basically went into hiding to avoid all the negative publicity and hate being spewed at her."

Daryl could only gape at his niece, a sick feeling churning inside him. He thought back to the way Kara had kept her head down, her shoulders hunched and the large hood up shielding her face. Her mysterious sabbatical. Her use of a fake name. Her generally stressed and frightened demeanor. All of it made sense now, and he wanted to scream at the unfairness and cruelty she'd faced.

She'd said she trusted him, yet she hadn't told him any of this information about her situation. Then again, why should she have? She didn't know him from Adam. She clearly was trying to keep a low profile. So why would she tell a random stranger who she was and the tawdry details of her personal trauma when she'd already been publicly humiliated and lambasted? She hadn't told him because she hadn't wanted him to know. As simple as that.

When a new thought occurred to him, Daryl shot Brody, Lexi and Cait a sharp panicked look. "Hey, y'all can't say anything about this to anyone! Promise me." He singled out Lexi, who looked crushed by his request. "I mean it, Lex. Kara didn't want anyone to know who she was or where she was going. She was scared and hiding. This has obviously been devastating to her, and she came to the States looking for privacy. You cannot tell anyone I saw her or where we were. Nothing!"

Brody and Cait nodded, their expressions understanding and solemn. Cait turned to her niece. "Lexi?"

"I understand," she said with defeat in her voice. "Damn it. I'm sitting on a twist in the biggest celebrity story of the year, and you won't let me even tell my friends?"

"Especially not your friends," Daryl said.

"They can keep a secret," Lexi said, even though a warble in her voice said she didn't really believe it herself.

"But can they? Really?" Brody asked. Lifting his gaze to Daryl, he said, "You'd better get out there and tell my daughter and the others who heard who your new friend is to keep their mouths shut, too. My permission to threaten them with extra chores or no dessert for a year if they squeal, too."

Daryl dragged a hand down his cheek, still goggling at the enormity of the situation. And how powerless he was to change anything for Kara. By her design, he didn't know how to reach her or where she was going to be living for the coming weeks. And maybe it wasn't his job to do anything for Kara other than keep her secret. He could protect her seclusion and hope she found happiness down the road.

As small as those things seemed to him, they were all he had, all he could do. They had to be enough.

Chapter 9

Six months later

Kara was sitting on the balcony of her small beach rental condo, drinking her morning tea and enjoying the September sunshine, when her phone pinged with a text message. Since she'd gone silent with everyone but Imogen, trusting her assistant to relay messages to update her family that she was still safe and doing all right, she knew who to expect when she glanced at the new message. What she hadn't expected was to see a picture of herself, looking bedraggled and scared and captured in the image with a man she barely remembered.

And a man she couldn't stop thinking about.

The next text read, Have you seen this? It's blowing up the internet at this very moment.

Kara's heart lurched. She set her mug of tea down with a thunk on the glass-topped patio table. She stared at the photo, her mind reeling and finally texted back, I remember the guy taking the picture, but... How did this happen? Why now?

Instead of a returned text, she got a call and swiped to answer it. "Tell me everything."

"It can be traced back to some guy in Georgia, who

realized who you were, apparently, and shared it on his Instagram page. His friends shared it again, and so on, and boom. It's exploded in the last few hours. People are guessing about what it means, who the other people are in the picture. The OP has done an interview with *Entertainment Tonight*, telling a story of rescuing you from a kidnapping and…sheesh. I thought you said you trusted that guy who you spent the night with. How could he do this to you?"

Kara appreciated the outrage on her behalf in Imogen's voice but quickly corrected her thinking. "The guy who took the picture and obviously shared it around was the driver. Daryl is the other one in the picture."

The sweet, good-looking one, she almost said. Her heart twisting, she studied the poorly lit photo, focusing on Daryl's half smile, as if the driver had snapped the picture before Daryl could flash his full wattage grin. How could she miss someone so much who she'd only known for a few hours? Barely one day. Yet she found herself reliving those hours in her mind and experiencing a bittersweet tug of longing every day. When she watched the sun rise over the ocean, she wanted to share it with Daryl. When she found herself getting upset or stressed, she imagined Daryl holding her hand on the airplane and calming her during the turbulence. She remembered his smooth voice saying, *You're going to be okay,* as they parted at the airport. When she made herself grits, trying to recreate the Southern breakfast they'd shared, she heard him saying, *My mom cooks grits with milk, salt and plenty of butter, and I like to add cheese.* In the past few months, grits had become a staple of her American breakfasts.

"I don't think anyone has figured out where you are, but this picture has certainly renewed interest in your disappearance," Imogen said, drawing her attention back to the problem at hand. "This sighting in Georgia has put people on your trail. Speculation is rampant, and largely way off base, but…if someone really wanted to find you, say the tabloids or…"

"Or Ian and his cronies?" Kara supplied, not hiding the frustration in her voice. Her stomach rolled at the notion that if Ian or the powers that be with the Knights organization wanted to find her, they might have just been given the clue they needed to start tracking her down. She shivered remembering the kind of threats that had been made, the ways the team's lawyers and owner had sworn to ruin her, even harm her if she didn't do their bidding. She recalled all too clearly the ire in Ian's face, the sense of danger she'd felt in the presence of the team representatives when she'd refused to take the blame or recant her story in order to make Ian appear the victim and salvage his career. Ian was ready to trash her reputation, her livelihood, her life to save himself. That betrayal had been just one of a hundred cuts that had left her heart and soul bleeding and her world in tatters this spring.

She'd just begun to feel herself healing, putting a new plan in place. Now her secret location, her refuge from the storm was at risk. Did she relocate? Would a move now help or expose her?

"And people want to know who the other man in the picture is." Imogen's comment shook her from her frantic musing. "Guesses have been all over the place, from your secret lover to—keeping to the lie that you were the junkie instead of Ian—your drug dealer. Some think he's the guy who kidnapped you and that you're being held hostage somewhere."

Her chest tightened. Daryl…

"People will believe anything, won't they?" Kara snorted her derision. "Nothing could be further from the truth. Daryl kept me safe. He kept me company. He kept me calm when I was ready to fall apart. He was my guardian angel."

"Well, it's just a matter of time before someone recognizes him and his identity is splashed across the internet. I hope you *can* trust him. He's going to have people asking him a lot of questions very soon."

She could trust him, couldn't she? He'd been quiet for all these months. But was his silence because he was protecting her secret or because he'd not recognized her? Because he hadn't known the media blitz that she was dodging and how much money the paparazzi were offering for information about her whereabouts or a candid photo? The real test of Daryl's trustworthiness, it seemed, was coming in the next few days, when her fame, her disaster back in England, found him.

Daryl's phone rang as he was walking from his car into his office at the small Silicon Valley startup, and he arched an eyebrow when he saw who was calling. "This has got to be a butt dial. There's no way I believe you actually deigned to *call* me instead of texting."

"Not a butt dial. This was too important for just a text," Lexi said.

His phone buzzed, indicating an incoming text. From Lexi. He chuckled. "And yet you did just text me. So what gives?"

"Look at what I sent you," she said, and he didn't like the tension in her tone.

"Hang on," he said, hastening his step to get out of California's overbright September sun and swiping to check the incoming message from his niece. She'd sent him a picture, and he squinted at the dark photo, waiting for his eyes to adjust to the dimmer light of the office building before he could focus. Before he recognized who was in the picture and when it had been taken. The rideshare driver, Daryl...and Kara. His pulse thumped harder seeing her face again. Her head was angled away from the camera, catching her in profile, but he remembered the shot being taken in the motel parking lot.

"Damn, Lexi! Where did you get this?" he rasped, stunned.

"Same place everyone else in the entire world is seeing it. The internet. The driver who took the picture, or maybe one of his friends, figured out who she was and the gold he had in his possession. It's been circulating on social media for about two days, and the questions and speculation are ramping up. I knew you weren't likely to know about it, seeing as you live under that rock of yours—" she was interrupted by his snort for her sarcasm "—and I thought you should be warned."

He was already making mental calculations and speculations of his own about how this leaked photo would impact Kara, when Lexi's word choice registered. "Warned?"

"People aren't just looking for Kara. They're looking for *you*."

"What?" His throat grew dry, and his heartbeat raced with anxiety and shock.

"The public wants the story behind the picture. I'm surprised you haven't already been barraged with calls and pursued by paparazzi."

Daryl cast a glance around the office lobby, where his coworkers were arriving for a new work day and chatting at the coffeepot and around the daily tray of pastries. One of the administrative assistants made eye contact and smiled as she called, "G'morning, Daryl."

He lifted a hand and tried to smile back. Then, turning his back to the room, he hurried to his office where he could shut the door and finish his conversation with Lexi in private. "What has been said about Kara? Have they found her? She's the one who needs to be warned."

"I don't think they've found her, but they're putting the pieces together. She fled the UK and was in Georgia this spring when the photo was made, hasn't been seen since. The driver has said he took her to the Atlanta airport the next morning, so she could have flown about anywhere. But, Daryl..." When Lexi paused and took a breath, his gut tensed. "People are saying they're looking at airline schedules and manifests, trying to access flight logs from back in March. They could figure out where she is, or someone who's seen her over the summer will talk. A store clerk or delivery guy or hotel maid..."

Daryl dropped heavily into his desk chair and rocked back, his free palm rubbing his temple. "Damn it, why can't people just leave her alone? It's none of their business where she is or what happens in her private life."

"It's part of the territory when you're a public figure, but..." He heard Lexi sigh again. "It's you I'm worried about, D. You're part of the story now, and your life will be turned upside down, I'm afraid."

Daryl considered her point, a quiver of unease rippling through his core. For an introvert like him, the notion of being in the public eye and his privacy invaded gave him chills. "I'll manage. Forewarned is forearmed, huh?"

"I guess. So...what do we say if someone calls here at Cameron Glen?"

"Nothing. Say nothing about me, my relationship or lack thereof with Kara, and nothing, absolutely nothing, about Kara. No comment. No comment. No comment. Just hang up. Don't answer."

At that moment, someone knocked on his door, and the front desk receptionist peeked into his office. "Excuse me, Daryl, but there's a reporter from the *National Inquisitor* here to talk to you. Should I—"

"No. Get rid of them. I'm not here, not talking to anyone from the press." Daryl cursed under his breath. "I gotta go, Lex. The Trojans are at the gate."

Kara's head spun and her chest ached as she carried her tea mug back into the kitchen. How long did she have before someone found her and spilled her location to the press? To Ian and the Knights organization?

She rinsed her cup in the sink and set it in the rack to dry, and as she turned toward the living room, a bulky figure moved from the entry hall into view.

"Hello, Kara. It's been a long time," the man said.

She tried to scream, but fear jammed her throat and stole her breath.

Instead, she backed deeper into the kitchen, simply wanting distance from the man in the tailored blue suit. She couldn't instantly remember his name, but she remembered his face and his position with the Knights organization. He might not have an official title, but he'd been clear six months ago that he was the team owner's fixer. A goon willing to do whatever it took to get the result the team owner wanted. *Whatever* it took...

Straightening her back, she tried to infuse her voice with more starch than she felt. "How did you get in here? It is just as much against American law to break into someone's residence uninvited as it is in the UK. Leave now or I will call the police."

Only after she made the threat did she realize she'd left her phone on the balcony.

The man in the suit gave her a false, patronizing smile. "The bobbies won't be necessary. I only came to talk... and collect your signature on this."

He drew a printed document from his breast pocket and unfolded it.

"What is that?" The question had been reflexive. The contents of the document didn't matter. Besides the fact that she knew better than to sign anything without her lawyer reviewing it, she refused to capitulate to any of the football club's self-serving demands.

But would protecting her own interests and career mean risking an even nastier media campaign and flood of lies from Ian's people? Could she even be jeopardizing her safety? This goon had certainly insinuated as much six months ago when he'd dragged her down to the Knights' business office and thrown his weight around enough to scare her into fleeing the country.

The man took a seat on the couch and crossed his legs. "Just a simple agreement that ends all this bad business, so that Ian can remove this albatross from his back."

She grunted and folded her arms over her chest, as

much to hold her composure together as to indicate her defiance. "To remove me from the Knights' business interests, you mean. You only care about Ian as much as he can make money for the team and Mr. Knight," she said, referencing the team's multimillionaire owner.

The man—Reginald Holt, the name finally popped into her head—waved a dismissive hand. "It's true that your little stunt has cost the team quite a lot of money and continues to as long as questions surround Ian. He's our star, and we take slander against him and rumors that jeopardize his value as a player seriously." He pulled out a pen, uncapped it and slapped it down on top of the papers he'd placed on the coffee table. "So this agreement, in which you take full responsibility for the lies you leaked to the press and—"

"I didn't leak anything! I've told you that! I told Ian and Mr. Knight as well. Someone else let the information out to the media. I worked hard to keep it private. The only reason I said anything to anyone is because I was worried about Ian. I wanted to get him help, and the team doctors and coaches turned a deaf ear!"

Her impassioned argument clearly didn't faze Mr. Holt. He gave her a bored look and aimed a finger at the papers he'd brought. "You will release a statement to news organizations of our choosing, saying that you fabricated the story of Ian's drug use out of bitterness and vengefulness for his career overshadowing yours. That you were, in fact, the one using illegal drugs and not in your right mind when you made the false statements."

"But none of that is remotely true!"

"Furthermore, you will then disappear from public view again, in a location of Mr. Knight's choosing, where we can be assured you will not speak to the press or other authorities again."

"Disappear? You want to hold me hostage to keep me quiet!" She barked a sour laugh. "There's no way I'll agree to any of that! Not only is it all lies that will ruin my career—" *assuming that isn't already the case* "—but I will not be kept a prisoner!" And yet…wasn't she already essentially a prisoner here in her rental house by her own choosing? Hadn't she withdrawn from life to protect herself and hide from public scrutiny and backlash?

She shoved her recriminations aside to focus on the more immediate threat. Ian's people, or more specifically, Mr. Knight's people had found her and were prepared to destroy her.

Holt heaved a deep sigh. "Miss O'Quinn… Kara…"

She cringed at the smarmy, faux-reasonable tone and stiff smile he used as he addressed her.

"The thing is, Mr. Knight must have your cooperation and your future silence. This is nonnegotiable. I've been authorized to use any means necessary to obtain your signature on both the media statement and the binding nondisclosure agreement." His eyes grew icy as he added, "As well as any other measures needed to ensure your silence."

His meaning was clear, and a chill raced down her back even before he narrowed his gaze and repeated slowly, *"Any means necessary."*

Be strong. Be brave. Stand your ground. She hadn't been raised to compromise her values, and lying, capitulation and injustice were not things she could agree to, even to save her own skin. Hadn't her great-grandfather, a participant in the Easter Rising, stood up to injustice?

Hadn't her grandmother been part of the resistance during World War II? Her parents might be farmers now, but in their youth, they'd vocally stood up to hatred and violence that tore Ireland apart. She had a legacy of moral strength to uphold.

Pressing a hand to the swirl of acid in her stomach, Kara firmed her resolve and lifted her chin. "You'll not intimidate me. I've done nothing wrong, and I will not sign anything saying otherwise."

Mr. Holt rubbed a hand on his mouth and made a low rumbling noise from his throat. "I didn't come today to walk away empty-handed, so…it seems we are at an impasse. Perhaps you'd rather sign a suicide note. You were so despondent and plagued by guilt over what you did to Ian that you took your own life."

Ice sluiced to her core. If she'd had any doubt these criminals were willing to kill her to protect the money Ian stood to earn them, his cold eyes removed that question. A lethal glare pinned on her, he stood and strolled toward her.

Her heartbeat quickened, and she cast her gaze about for a weapon. Unfortunately, the rental house's kitchen had been woefully short of tools and cookware. The plastic spatula in the sink was hardly a weapon.

The goon was upon her in seconds, grabbing her wrists and twisting her arms painfully behind her back. He slammed her against the counter, causing her breath to whoosh from her lungs. As she gasped for air, he pinned her with his sizable body.

"While I won't break your right hand until you sign, I have no problem breaking your left." He wrenched her left arm down, and before she could figure out his ploy, he'd slammed a drawer on her left hand. She did scream, then. Pain ricocheted up her arm and made bile climb her throat.

Digging deep for strength and clarity of thought, she thrashed and bucked. A scene from the last movie she'd filmed came back to her. Her character had been in a similar situation, in the grips of a killer, fighting to get away. She conjured the techniques her character had used, praying the script writers had some basis in fact for the moves her character had employed. She rocked her head back hard, crashing the back of her skull into Holt's face. He howled in pain but didn't release her.

Next she kicked backward with her feet, aiming for his knees, his instep. The move only further enraged him, and he slammed her face into the countertop. Then, tangling his fingers in her long hair, he dragged her to the kitchen sink, turned on the water and shoved her face under the fast-flowing stream from the tap.

Kara sputtered and coughed, unable to get a breath without choking on the water.

Despite the thrum of adrenaline and rushing water filling her ears, she heard Holt growl, "Ready to sign the agreement now? Or would you rather have your hand slammed again?"

He shut off the water long enough for her to sputter. "N-no! I won't lie!"

The water came on again, but, anticipating the fresh assault, she gulped a breath of air, held it. Lifting her foot, she again stomped hard on Holt's foot, then, as he yelped and shifted his weight, she aimed her foot backward into his kneecap like her family's milk cow, Georgette, when she was in a bad mood.

The kick destabilized her assailant. She seized the precious seconds to turn to face him, even though the move made his grip pull harder on her hair. Curling the fingers of her right hand, she dug her fingernails into his face, scratching his eyes.

He howled in pain and released her hair. As he swatted at her hand, stepping back from her, she ran. He was on her again in a few steps, knocking her to the floor and pinning her with a knee in her back. Kara refused to give up. She had no doubt she'd only had a taste of the measures Holt would go to in order to exact her compliance.

Bile and the tea she'd just finished rose in her throat. Swallowing hard, she mustered her strength and bucked hard. Squirmed. Thrashed.

Finally she felt his hold ease as he shifted position, trying to gain a firmer hold on her. With a hard twist, she managed to roll over, and she battled him with everything she had. She slapped, kicked, bit, clawed—full trapped animal mode. The instant he shifted to gain distance from her, she scrambled to her feet.

Grabbing the first thing her hand found, she flung a large vase at him, then a decorative shell from the end table, the television remote, a dirty wine glass she'd left by the couch...one missile after another. He ducked, raised an arm to ward off the flying objects and shouted curses at her.

The tactic worked well enough to slow his pursuit, holding him off long enough for Kara to flee through the front door. She had nothing with her. Not her phone. Not her purse. Not any idea where she would go.

But she ran.

Chapter 10

Kara heard the heavy footsteps of Reggie Holt behind her as she darted down the steps toward the car park. Without a car, she couldn't just drive away. Could she hide? Was anyone around who could protect her?

Daryl.

His name popped into her head, and her heart gave a painful throb. She shoved the thought aside, needing to focus on the current danger. She didn't have time to knock on neighbors' doors.

Reaching the ground floor, she spotted a utilities closet and tried the knob. Locked.

She headed around the corner of the building, out of view of the stairs. There was little on this side of the condominiums except the two skips, or dumpsters as her American neighbors called them. She had no time to weigh the notion of what filth might be inside. Kara simply grabbed the open edge and hoisted herself inside. The reek of rotten food and buzz of flies greeted her instantly, but she clamped her mouth closed around the urge to groan or retch. She had to stay quiet, stay still, stay out of sight.

The thud of feet on concrete reached her, and she tried

to hold her breath, even as her lungs screamed for air after her bolt down the stairs. A large box had been tossed in with the other rubbish, and she slid it slowly over her head while she wiggled her feet beneath a plastic bag of a neighbor's trash.

The sound of his footsteps retreated, but she didn't move. Moments later, she heard someone return her direction, heard a male voice asking, "Have you seen a woman with red hair about this morning?"

"No, sorry," a woman answered after a brief hesitation.

"All right. Cheers," Holt said.

Outside the skip, she heard the shuffling of feet. When a new bag of trash thudded into the bin next to her, she gasped softly, startled. The person at the skip didn't leave, and after another moment, the box over her head lifted. The older woman who cleaned the condo next door peered down at Kara, her eyes widening. Kara shook her head, pressed a finger to her mouth to beg for quiet and pleaded with her eyes for the woman not to give her away.

The woman glanced toward the car park then back to Kara. "Stay here," the woman said softly, her gaze directed elsewhere. "He's going back upstairs toward your place. I'll be back in a few minutes when the coast is clear."

"Thank you," Kara mouthed.

The woman replaced the box and shuffled away, her shoes scuffing the ground.

Kara shut her eyes and tried to breathe through her mouth to block the odors wafting around her. As she waited, feeling a wash of humiliation to have been found hiding in a pile of refuse, tears pricked her eyes.

Daryl.

The name came again, and this time she let an image of the kind and brave man's face fill her mind's eye. She longed for the sort of comfort and reassurance his presence had given her months ago. Six months ago, when she'd needed rescue, Daryl had come through in spades. She needed that sort of protection now, because she knew Holt and his boss would not stop looking for her, would not stop trying to bring her down, even kill her. She battled back the despair that tugged at her. Giving up, giving in was not an option for her.

A rustling sound just outside the rubbish bin caught her attention, and she froze.

"Psst, miss?"

The box lifted off her head, and the older woman gave her a nod. "Come with me. He's inside your condo now. I'll take you to my car, and we can get you away before he knows what's what. Okay?"

The woman held out a hand, offering to help Kara climb out of the skip. With a nervous glance around the area to assure herself Holt was, in fact, not around, Kara clambered out of the bin while cradling her injured hand. "Thank you."

"Just giving a hand up like someone did for me when I fled my husband. The snarly guy, he your boyfriend or your husband?"

Kara snapped a startled look at the woman, and when she realized the woman had assumed she was in an abusive relationship with Holt, Kara balked. Deciding any other explanation would only draw more questions and unwanted attention to her plight, she said softly, "He's an associate of my ex-boyfriend."

The woman grunted and jerked a nod. Placing a hand

at Kara's back, she hustled Kara toward the car park. "I'm Sue, by the way."

Kara opened her mouth, thought of the picture circulating on the internet and said, "Imogen."

Thirty minutes later, Kara was at Sue's house wearing too-big fleece pants and a clean T-shirt while Sue laundered the rubbish stink from Kara's other clothes. She sat on her new friend's couch, cradling an ice pack against her aching hand, having refused to go to the emergency room. She gave only a fleeting thought to the possessions she'd abandoned, but going back to the condo was out of the question. Holt would have the apartment staked out. Her belongings—including her phone and wallet—were already in his possession.

She knew Imogen would help by wiring her money for a new phone, new clothes, new lodgings, but she cringed thinking of the hassle just the same.

She cast a frustrated glance to Sue, who sat across from her in a stuffed chair. "I ran out without anything. I don't have my phone or money or—"

"Don't you worry, honey. We'll get you sorted out. Do you have a friend or family member you can go to?"

Her chest squeezed, feeling the weight of her isolation. "I—not really."

But at the edges of her thoughts, a face teased her. She knew where she wanted to go, but she hadn't gotten Daryl's phone number or address. How did she contact him?

No, she needed to call Imogen and get funds sent to her for—

Her heart kicked hard, a new wave of dread spinning through her. If Holt had her phone, he'd be able to see that Imogen's number was the only one she'd used in the last six months. He'd know Imogen had been helping her. A tremor shook Kara. What might Holt and his bosses with the Knights organization do to Imogen in retaliation? She'd no doubt they'd hurt her assistant—her friend— in order to get information about where Kara had fled.

"I need a phone. I have to call my friend and warn her! They'll go after her, and she needs to hide!"

Sue gave her a concerned look but nodded. "You can use mine for now, and then we'll run up to the store and get you a new burner phone."

Kara nibbled her bottom lip and whispered, "Thank you. Once Im—erm, my friend wires me money, I can repay you for everything."

"Does your friend live close? I can buy you a bus ticket or drive you myself if it's not too far."

"No. She's...overseas."

Sue slouched back in her chair, and the twist of her mouth told Kara the woman was ruminating. "You need a plan, honey. I can take you to a shelter, if there's no place else safe."

Safe. There was that word again. Kara wondered if she'd ever feel truly safe again. "A plan..." she muttered quietly.

Daryl. Blimey, how she wanted him here now.

Sue pulled her mobile phone from her pocket and handed it to Kara. "Well, call your friend. Let's get that money wired as a start."

Imogen's voice was hesitant when she answered the call.

"It's me."

"Oh, thank God! Are you okay? I've been calling and

calling, and a few minutes ago a man answered your phone!"

"Holt showed up at the condo." Kara warned her assistant of the danger she could be in, advised her to leave London, be alert. "And I need cash to replace the things I left behind."

"Oh, bloody hell! Of course, Kara. I'll send the money right away. Where to?"

Once a Western Union location was arranged, with Sue the recipient since Kara had no ID at the moment, Kara again cautioned Imogen to be careful, thanked her profusely and followed Sue back out to her vehicle. Kara was silent as they drove to the local bank, her mind drifting back to the conversations she'd had with Daryl, the happiness she known over breakfast in the small-town diner, the courage he'd shown when he saved her from her kidnapper. His stories of his family and Cameron Glen—

She gasped. *Cameron Glen!*

If not Daryl specifically, she knew where to find his family. He'd said it was in western North Carolina. That they rented cabins. They'd have to have a public listing for their business somewhere. Surely they'd help her get in touch with him. And just like that, she had her plan.

Later that afternoon, once Kara had the money she needed from the wire transfer, she paid Sue for the petrol to drive her to the western side of the state. She'd looked up directions to Cameron Glen after admiring the beautiful pictures of the cabins and property on the retreat's website. Several hours later, well after dark, Sue pulled up to the property's office.

Kara approached the door and read the notice on the

office window explaining how to reach the manager after business hours. Using Sue's phone—she still needed to find a new burner phone to purchase—Kara had called the after-hours number.

The call was answered by a cheerful female who said her name was Cait. She remembered Daryl naming all of his siblings but couldn't specifically recall a Cait.

"Um, yes. I'm trying to reach Daryl Cameron. I'm...a friend of his and...well, I'm here...at Cameron Glen, you see, and I need—" Kara stopped for a breath when her voice cracked.

"I'm afraid Daryl isn't here. He lives and works in California now," Cait replied. "Is there anything I can do for you, Miss—" Cait drew the title out, clearly inviting Kara to fill in the implied blank.

Ignoring the unspoken question, Kara asked, "Could you help me get in touch with him? It's...important."

"Well, yes," Cait said slowly, then in an inviting tone added, "You said you were here at Cameron Glen? Whereabouts? I can come meet you. Or you could come to my place. We're the house just past cabin five. Our porch light is on. Blue Honda in the driveway." When Kara didn't reply right away, the woman added, "I'm Daryl's sister. I can help you until we get in touch with him."

Did she really have a choice other than to trust his family? She couldn't inconvenience Sue any longer. And his family was the only way she knew to reach Daryl. "I'll be there in a moment."

A couple of minutes after she'd bidden Sue goodbye, Kara stood on the front porch of a quaint log cabin–style house with large windows. When the front door opened, she gaped at the woman who answered her knock. And the woman gaped back at her.

"You're Kara O'Quinn!" the woman said, her eyes widening.

"And you're...*white*!"

Kara felt herself flush to the roots of her hair as Cait showed her into her home. "I apologize for being so... blunt. Crass. I just... I assumed Daryl's family was Black, as well. I didn't mean any offense."

Cait waved off her apology and grinned. "None taken. I am, in fact, white." Her voice held a note of humor. "As are most of the Camerons. Brody's wife, Anya, is South Asian. I apologize for my reaction to finding out who you are, too."

A teenage girl and handsome dark-haired man joined Cait in the living room. Cait motioned for Kara to sit down, offered her a hot drink and told the teenager to stop staring and introduce herself.

"I'm, um... Erin. I...love your movies!"

The man stepped forward offering his hand. "Matt Harkney, Cait's husband, also white. Nice to meet you." He twitched a cheek, flashing a teasing grin as he shook Kara's hand.

"Matt!" Cait scolded from the kitchen.

Kara perched on the edge of the overstuffed couch, clasping her hands in her lap as she sent furtive glances around the living room. Her attention stopped when she spotted a family portrait. The image was crowded with smiling faces.

So, yeah. Big family, she remembered Daryl saying, a smile lighting his face.

That same bright smile shone at her from the picture. Daryl stood between an older man—his adoptive father, presumably—and a pretty strawberry blonde, a few years older than he was. A sister, obviously. Her chest squeezed as she stared at the image of a much younger Daryl. He wasn't as tall or broad shouldered as he'd been when she met him that spring, but glimpses of the man he'd become were clearly there. The warm brown eyes. The engaging smile. The square jaw.

"Here you go," Cait said, drawing Kara's attention away from the portrait. She handed Kara a steaming mug of spiced tea. "I think I can guess why you're here. I've seen the posts on social media."

Kara clutched the mug between her palms, the warmth of the cup soothing to her injured hand. "Right. So…"

Cait lifted a hand, cutting her off. "You don't owe us any explanations." She pulled a cell phone from her back pocket and looked at the screen. "Let's call Daryl, what do ya say?"

"D, you need to come home, like ASAP."

Daryl stiffened at the worrisome tone in his sister's voice. "What's going on, Cait? You're scaring me. Is it Mom or Dad?"

"Well…no."

"Talk to me."

"I've been asked not to say over the phone. But…you need to come."

"This kind of cloak-and-dagger isn't like you, Cait," Daryl groused. But he was already pulling up the airline schedule and booking a flight back to North Carolina. If his sister said he needed to come home, he would go home, no questions asked. "The earliest I can get there is tomorrow afternoon. Good enough?"

"Good enough."

Twenty-four hours later, Daryl was pulling his rental car into the long drive of Cameron Glen, and a familiar feeling of home and comfort washed over him as it always did when he drove onto the property. Today a tension coiled in his gut, not knowing what Cait's summons was about. He'd played out all kinds of scenarios, from illness in the family to destruction of property. But why would those be kept secret? Was the media hounding his family the way they'd stalked him in recent days? He'd had to employ a degree of subterfuge and evasion to avoid the cameras as he came and left work and his home. He'd lost a tail on the way to the airport, faking a trip to work so that no one was any the wiser about his trip to North Carolina.

After parking his car in his parents' driveway, he climbed out and stretched his back. He heard the front door open as he swept his gaze around the yard, soaking in the brilliant fall colors of the hardwoods.

He met his mother's eye, a tick of relief at seeing her well registering before he saw her gaze shift down the hill toward the large fishing pond at the center of the property.

"Daryl!" a female voice called from a distance, drawing his attention to the pond. Turning, he took a few steps across his parents' yard. He recognized Emma and Lexi right away, but another woman was with them. Her hair shone coppery in the September sun, and he couldn't place—

Wait. The pieces fell into place in rapid succession, and his heart stilled.

* * *

Kara's breath snagged in her chest when she spotted Daryl. Even from a distance, he cut such a strikingly handsome image. She'd thought she'd falsely remembered him as more handsome than he really was, but Daryl was every bit as achingly attractive as she'd thought.

When he turned and started toward her, Kara walked quickly up the grassy bank to the driveway that wound through the property. He, too, hustled to the driveway, traipsing with increasing speed down the steep hillside from the house. When their feet hit the pavement, they ran to each other. She leaped into his arms, and he lifted her from her feet as they embraced.

Hot tears of relief and joy prickled her eyes, and she laughed at the sheer absurdity of caring so much for a man she'd only known for a day six months ago. But the tightness of his hug, the low hum of pleasure that rumbled from his chest and his reluctance to release her spoke of at least a similar happiness. Even after his sister reached them and greeted him with a lilting, "Howdy, D. Surprise," he held her.

"Are you all right?" he said softly, for only her ears.

"I am now." She leaned back in his embrace to gaze at him, blinking back the blurring moisture that gathered in her vision. She needed to see those kind, warm eyes that had given her so much comfort months before.

Setting her feet back on the ground, Daryl stroked both hands from her head, down her arms and gripped her hands.

She winced when he squeezed the hand Holt had crushed and cradled it against her chest. Frowning, Daryl carefully examined the hand. His expression darkened as he studied the bruising and swelling.

"Who did this to you?" An angry growl tinged his tone, and heat leaped in his eyes. When she hesitated, deciding how much she should tell him, he placed a firm hand on her shoulder. "I know who you are now. I know what has been reported about your relationship with Ian Stafford, and I know the media likely hasn't reported your side of the story."

She shook her head, her throat too tight with emotion to speak.

"I also know how scared you were of being recognized in March. How haunted your eyes were. I saw the fear and pain."

She closed her eyes and ducked her chin to her chest, a quiver rippling through her.

"But I want *you* to know—" he nudged her chin up with two fingers and drilled a bright stare on her "—that you can trust me, trust my family. You are safe here, and no one will betray you to the press."

A different shudder raced through her now. Relief. Gratitude. Faith. "Thank you," she rasped.

He pulled her back into his embrace and let her simply lean into him and settle her mind.

After a moment of silence, he said softly, "We should have your hand seen by a doctor. I'm guessing it's broken."

She yanked back from his arms. "No. I... I can't risk being recognized. Holt is here, in the States, looking for me. I barely escaped him yesterday, and he—"

"Hey, hey, take a breath. You're okay."

She swallowed hard, realizing how panicked she must have sounded. "I can't go to a doctor. I—"

"We have patient privacy rules here," he said.

"We already tried to get her to go to an urgent care. She wanted to wait for you. Meanwhile, I've been thinking..."

Kara had almost forgotten Daryl's sister and niece were standing just a few feet away until Emma spoke. She faced Emma, blinking away tears.

"Anya could help us sneak her in the hospital for an X-ray. She could ask people she trusts the most in the ER," his sister said.

"Good idea," Daryl said.

Kara lifted a questioning gaze to Daryl. "Who is Anya?"

"My sister-in-law. Brody's wife." He placed a hand on her cheek, gently cupping her face. "She's an ER nurse and very trustworthy."

"If you trust her then—"

He nodded confidently and drew her close again for another hug. "My rental car is at my parents' house. We can leave as soon as I call Anya and get everything set up."

She swallowed hard and ducked her head once in consent. "But I need to talk to you about something else, too. I didn't come here, didn't track you down because of my hand."

His mouth twitched in a lopsided grin. "I figured as much. Why did you find me?"

She shot a quick glance at Emma and wet her lips.

"Why don't I call Anya and set things up while you two have your chat?" Emma said. "Lexi and I will wait up at Mom and Dad's until you're ready. Okay?"

"Thanks, Em. You're the best." He flashed his sister a grateful smile, to which she returned a teasing look of smugness.

"I am the best. So glad you finally recognize that." Emma's playful grin and Lexi's dismissive groan loosened the tension in Kara's core. Daryl's loving, helpful family was just what she needed now, when she was so isolated, unable to see or talk to her own family for fear of putting them in jeopardy or compromising her location.

Once Emma and her daughter had strolled several feet away, headed up the steep hill to the older Camerons' home, Daryl ushered her back to the bench where she, Lexi and Emma had been watching the ducks.

He motioned for her to sit first, but instead of joining her he stayed on his feet. When she patted the bench, silently asking him to join her, he shook his head. "I've been sitting for hours between the flight and driving in. I'll stand for now. Unless—" His brow dipped as he regarded her, a question hanging between them.

"No. That's fine. And thank you again for coming so quickly. I had no right to ask. And I'll repay you for the airline ticket and all of your expenses—"

"Kara," he said, stopping her. "What's going on? Who is this man who hurt you? Why are they looking for you?"

She sighed and dropped her chin, staring at the grass at her feet.

He did sit next to her now, stroking a hand down her back. "I know a little bit of the backstory. Your split with Ian, the hounding by the press, the media uproar about the soccer star and accusations flying back and forth."

He paused then, waiting for her to fill in the blanks.

"The press is only telling one side of the story, the side Ian and his agents, the owners and management of his football team want the public to believe."

"That's easy enough to guess. But what is the whole truth? What is your version of the story?"

"There's time for that conversation later, but here's the crux. Ian is the biggest thing to happen to Knights football—or soccer, as you call it—in the history of the club. He's put them in a position to win championships and build a following that would rival Manchester United or Chelsea. He stands to earn the club millions, maybe billions of pounds. He's their golden boy, and they will do anything to protect him and his career. Not so much because they care about him, but because of the money, the business, the potential championships he represents. He's crucial to the team's success, and they will protect him at all cost. In their eyes, I threaten that empire, and I must be controlled. If not controlled, then silenced. Permanently."

He stiffened. "Hang on. Are you saying someone on Ian's team has threatened your life?"

She raised her injured hand. "This was just a warm-up. I barely got away from Holt. And he's not—" she bit her bottom lip, mulling her word choice "—officially with the team. They naturally want plausible deniability. But the team owner has the means to hire men to do his bidding."

"He's hired a hit man to come after you?" Daryl's tone was incredulous, and when she cut a side glance at him, his expression matched his disbelief.

"I know it sounds insane, but there is so much money, so much invested in Ian's success, the team's success..."

He shifted on the bench, dragging a hand over his mouth as he stared out across the pond where the ducks swam about idly. "Yeah, it sounds pretty cray cray, but..." He angled a worried stare toward her. "I believe you. And I hate that you're in this position. Really hate it."

He exhaled harshly. "So how do I figure in this picture? Other than our chance meeting six months ago and that picture circulating on social media right now. I don't see how I…why I…"

"That's why I'm here."

He cocked his head, his brow lowering. "What? The picture? I've had to dodge a few reporters, but—"

"No. Not the picture. Although I am so sorry that you got caught up in that."

He waved it off. "I'll be fine. It'll blow over. You're the one I'm concerned about."

She drew a deep breath, squelching the twitter of ill ease in her stomach and unsure why her ask bothered her so much. Was she afraid he would turn her down? Or anxious about what would happen if he accepted her proposal?

"The thing is… I want to hire you."

A skeptical V formed between his eyebrows. "Hire me?"

"Yes. I want you to be my bodyguard."

Chapter 11

A startled laugh burst from Daryl's throat before he could catch it. "Your bodyguard?"

She sat taller, her frown dark. "Why is that funny to you?"

He held up a hand intended to pacify her. "I'm sorry. It's not funny. I just… Kara, I'm not trained to be a bodyguard. I'm an IT geek."

"Who served in the Army as an officer and proved to have keen instincts, defensive skills and courage when you rescued me from the kidnapper back in March."

He shook his head. "That's different. I did what I had to when a need came up, but that doesn't mean—"

"You're strong and fit, and you know how to use a weapon, I'd wager. And probably some kind of hand-to-hand skills? Boxing or judo or Krav Maga?"

Daryl's head spun. As much as he wanted to make sure Kara was safe, he was hardly the man for the job. But how did he convince her when the pleading in her eyes cracked his heart? "Just because I've sparred with people in the boxing ring and know a little about defensive tactics doesn't mean I can protect you from a hit man. If you believe your life is in danger, you need to hire a professional. I could probably help you find a service that—"

"I don't want a faceless stranger or man for hire. I want *you*, Daryl. I trust *you*." She put her good hand on his arm, her expression imploring him, her wide green eyes full of unspent tears. "I *need* you, Daryl. You're the only person I've felt safe with in months."

"Kara, honey… I… I have a job already. A job I need to keep."

Her shoulders drooped, but she didn't relent. "I know it's a big ask. And I will pay you well. Name your price, and I will double it. I'll pay all your expenses and—"

He framed her face with his hands. "It's not about the money. I would help you if I could, but I'm not… I don't know how to keep you safe. I want you to have better protection than I know how to provide. I don't know what I'd do if anything happened to you on my watch, because I wasn't…enough."

A spike of something cold and prickly flowed through him when the last of his sentence tripped off his tongue. Where had that nudge of doubt and sense of not measuring up come from? Hadn't he excelled at everything he'd ever undertaken? Top grades in computer programming, high school football captain, officer training at West Point—the list of high achievements and successes was long, so the niggle of doubt caught him by surprise.

Shoving aside the uncertainty, he focused on the issue at hand and the dejection written in the lines creasing Kara's brow, the dark circles under her eyes, the obvious bruises and swelling where she'd so recently been battered by the henchman who—

Daryl fisted his hands as a cold rage overcame him for the abuse this unknown man had doled out to Kara. Given time alone with the creep, Daryl would—

He paused, realizing how strongly protective of her he felt. Was that the element of his character that Kara had sensed? The key factor that had drawn her back to him with her outrageous request? She knew the truth—that he cared about her enough that he would move mountains to see she was safe.

"Isn't there anything I can say to change your mind? Daryl, I don't want to be alone in this. I want you. I feel safe with you, if that counts for anything."

He leaned in and pressed his forehead against hers. He stroked a hand down the back of her head, then cradled the nape of her neck. "It counts for a lot. And while I'm still not convinced I'm the best man for the job, I'm not going to walk away and leave you exposed until I'm certain you're no longer at risk."

"Does that mean you'll take the job? That you'll protect me?"

"Of course, I'll protect you…until we find a better option."

He felt her sag as tension uncoiled in her muscles, heard the exhale that was almost a whimper of relief. "Thank you."

"My family and I will hide you here for now, but I think we should go somewhere else soon. That picture circulating on social media links you and me, and all too soon, the world will be knocking at Cameron Glen's doors."

"And I'm so sorry for that. If I could have stopped the guy from taking that picture—"

"Water under the bridge. Stop apologizing for things that are not your fault." He took a step back, letting his gaze drink her in. She hadn't been far from his thoughts for even a day since they parted in March. Seeing her again, touching her was a sweetness he'd not allowed himself to believe could happen. But…she was here. Here and…warm and beautiful.

Without debating or second-guessing, he dipped his head to lightly press his lips to hers. She gasped softly, then leaned into the kiss, opening her mouth to more fully draw on his. Her arms circled his neck, and she rose on her toes, angling her head and kissing him with a fervor that matched his. When she drew back, her breathing deep and ragged, she met his gaze straight on and gave him a modest smile. "Well. Now that we've established that…" A tear dripped onto her cheek. "I've missed you, Daryl. So much."

He returned a crooked grin, a drunken sort of happiness bubbling up in his chest. "Same here. It's really good to see you again. Even if—"

His mood sobered. Kara was in danger and needed his protection. He had to focus on *that*, not his infatuation with the beautiful British movie star.

He took a step back from her and lifted her injured hand to examine again. "First order of business is to get you seen by a doctor. After that, we'll strategize with the family about the best way to keep you safe."

"The family? But—"

He twisted his mouth and nodded. "This isn't our first rodeo. We've dodged more than a few bullets. Through our mistakes and successes, the Camerons have learned important survival techniques over the years."

She canted her head, her expression wary. "Dodged bullets? Is…is your family…"

He chuckled, guessing at her concern. "No. We're not

mobsters or criminally connected. We've simply had a bad run over the years of coming up against dangerous situations and people. But we've grown from each situation, and in some cases used the experience for good. Emma, for example—" he hitched his head in the direction his sister had just left "—started a nonprofit called STOP to fight sex trafficking. Her daughter Fenn also works with the organization now, and it's growing nationally."

Kara's face brightened. "That's fantastic! I... I didn't mean to imply I thought you or your family were—"

"An easy assumption when I use phrases like dodging bullets." He pivoted toward the house and slid a hand to the small of her back. "Let's get that hand seen and start making plans, huh?"

"She needs a disguise," Lexi said, her eyes bright. The seventeen-year-old was clearly intrigued by the cloak-and-daggers aspect of Kara's situation. "She should dye her hair or, better yet, lighten it."

Daryl winced internally at the idea of Kara changing her gorgeous auburn hair to any other color. But his niece was right. Altering Kara's appearance was a smart move, since her celebrity made her so recognizable.

He glanced at Kara, who nibbled a fingernail on her good hand then nodded.

"I can always dye it back red later, after all. I've darkened it for roles before." She dropped her gaze to the splint on her fingers. The X-rays that Anya had helped them get at the ER had shown she had a fracture in one finger but otherwise only deep bruising. "What about colored contacts? I've used those before, as well."

"Sure." Daryl propped his arms on his thighs as he

leaned forward. "We can arrange to get some, don't you think?" He aimed his gaze at Emma, consulting her.

"I don't see why not." Emma sat next to Lexi, idly fingering the silky strands of her daughter's long wheat-colored hair where it lay against Lexi's back. "More important, I believe, is where will you go? You can always stay here at Cameron Glen, but as you pointed out, thanks to that picture on the internet, a smart reporter only needs to follow a short crumb trail to track you here, Daryl."

"We'll deny she's here if anyone comes around," their father, Neil Cameron, suggested from across the living room. "It's the truth that you'd never met her before that night and parted ways afterward. We can just pretend that was the end of your connection and send snoops away. If she stays out of sight, surely speculation will die down, and they'll move on to other locales."

"We can start rumors online that she was sighted in New York City or Los Angeles. Or even somewhere back in Europe like Paris," Lexi suggested, her tone full of excitement. "Surely you can use AI to create a fake picture of her walking down Madison Avenue or ducking into a French café. Right, D?"

"Anything he created and posted would have his IP address on it and could easily be traced back to him." Emma's husband, Jake, glanced at Daryl for confirmation. "Am I right?"

Daryl rubbed his chin, mulling all the proposals flying around the living room. "Yes and no. There are ways to mask the source, so that it's not easily traced if you know what you're doing. And I could ask friends of mine in the business to make the posts without revealing why."

Kara frowned. "I don't like involving outside people.

The more people who know where I am, the easier it is for leaks to happen."

Lexi wrinkled her brow. "So the powers that be at this soccer team are really trying to kill you? That's so…dark, evil. Sports aren't like that in the US."

Jake cleared his throat. "Honey, when millions, even billions of dollars are at stake, every business, even American sports, has the potential for seedy elements to get involved. Money changes everything. And huge sums of money wield a powerful influence."

Lexi wrinkled her nose. "That's horrible."

Daryl shifted his full attention to Kara, whose pale face seemed all the more wan in the diffuse sunlight of his parents' living room. "What do you think? We could lay low here for a while, but I still think we need to consider a backup location, in case—"

"Fenn's apartment?" Lexi said, interrupting him. "I know she'd do anything to help, and she has that extra bedroom since her roommate moved out at the end of summer. And if you're willing to pay rent, all the better. She's kinda strapped, paying for the apartment on her own."

Kara perked up. "I can definitely pay rent. I wouldn't assume to do otherwise." Her gaze swung to Daryl. "What do you think?"

He nodded slowly, rubbing his chin as he turned the idea over in his head. "She might even be able to help us in other ways."

"How's that?" Kara asked.

"Fenn has connections with investigative reporters and police officers through her work with STOP," he said.

Kara's eyes widened, and she paled. "Daryl, no! I'm trying to avoid reporters, if you remember."

"You can trust Fenn," Lexi piped in. "One hundred percent. She's a Cameron first and anything else second." Lexi pulled an amused face. "Well, technically she's a Turner like me. But the Cameron blood is a strong influence, and we Turners are loyal and trustworthy, too."

Daryl raised his phone. "Should I call her? We can be at her apartment in Durham in a matter of hours."

Kara looked from one face to another, as if weighing whose ideas she trusted and liked the most. "Maybe we stay on the move? Here for a bit then with Fenn, back and forth? I'm scared of staying one place too long."

"Keep 'em guessing," Neil said, nodding. "Seems a good strategy to me."

Daryl flopped back on the couch, looking for a way to put into words the thing niggling in his brain. "Besides keeping Kara safe and hidden, what's our endgame here? The Knights will be a football club and Ian will be an eligible player for years to come. How do we end the threat against Kara and help her move on with her life?"

He rubbed both hands on his jeans, hating himself for the question sitting on his tongue. He sighed and angled a look toward her. "What sort of demands have they made of you? Is there a chance this could be settled with lawyers and a signed agreement?"

Kara's back stiffened. "Holt has already produced a document they want me to sign. But signing would mean saying I did things I didn't do, smearing my integrity and making me the villain in this scenario. Are you asking me to destroy my reputation and ruin my career? To compromise my principles and damage the trust that my fans have in me?"

Daryl held her gaze as the grandfather clock in the foyer marked the seconds with a loud tick, tick, tick. "No. I don't want you to compromise your values. I'm just thinking about your safety, long-term. I admire the fact that you're willing to stand up for truth and principles, but...you asked me to keep you safe. Right now, the path you're on is dangerous. We need options."

"I just wish it didn't mean inconveniencing you, as well." Her chin dropped, along with her gaze, her shoulders. "Possibly putting you at risk."

"Protecting your values is noble, a risk we can work with for now." At the edge of his vision, Daryl saw his father smile and nod. Having Neil Cameron's approval shouldn't still mean so much to him. Daryl was a grown man, raised well, taught right from wrong and instilled with self-worth. But knowing he was the adopted child, the plus-one in the family, Daryl had never quite shaken the impulse to prove himself and seek acceptance. His family had never given him reason to believe he was anything but fully loved and integral to the family, yet the tiny voice whispered to him, pushing him to always earn his place in the family's esteem.

"So..." Neil said. "Endgame, you said. Can we debunk the rumor mill and prove the allegations against your ex, this Ian fella, to clear your name? If the public knows you are innocent of the unseemly things you're being accused of—" Neil paused, his eyebrows drawing together. "What is it exactly that they're saying you've done?"

Kara's expression darkened, but she didn't speak.

Lexi took the silence as her cue to pipe up again.

"They're saying that out of spite, after a bad lovers' quarrel, she lied about Ian using performance-enhancing drugs and other illegal drugs. They say she made up the story that the soccer club knew about the drugs and buried it. They're saying the supposed fight was over the fact *she* was the drug user, and she was trying to shift attention away from her abuse and mental instability and smear Ian instead. It's his word against hers, and the press is taking his side because the soccer team is standing behind Ian, saying she has no proof."

The room remained quiet, except for grunts of dismay and frustration, until Kara added softly, "There's more. Other ugly twists to the tales to make me look unstable and deplorable. Infidelity on my part. Altered porno films that make it seem I was the star. Accusations of petty theft and venereal disease and just about anything that the mudslingers can dream up and throw to see what sticks. You know how internet trolls can be."

"Ay caramba," Emma muttered as she flopped back against the sofa cushions. "What a cl—" She glanced to her daughter and seemed to reconsider her word choice. "Colossal mess."

Lexi's side-eye and knowing grin told Daryl his sister hadn't fooled her daughter a bit.

"Well." Lexi slapped her hands on her legs as she shoved to her feet. "No time like the present to get started with your makeover. We still have a box of black hair dye left from last year's planned Halloween costume."

"And thank God you didn't go through with it! I can't stand the idea of you changing your beautiful hair!" Emma said, then seemed to immediately realize her gaffe. "Not that your hair isn't beautiful, Kara. And it's a shame… I mean I see the necessity… I just meant—"

But the comment clawed at Daryl. He hated to see Kara color her hair if they could find another way. He was still debating whether to say anything when Kara rose and spread her hands.

"Whatever we must. Lead the way, Lexi."

He followed Kara and Lexi to the Turners' house and folded his arms over his chest as Lexi made the preparations. Emma came to stand beside him and seemed to sense his ambivalence. She rubbed his back then linked her arm in his. Warmth filled Daryl's chest. He never got tired of the family's unqualified support of him and his endeavors.

"Emma," he said in a low tone as Lexi tied a plastic cape around Kara's shoulders. "If Lexi didn't use the hair dye at Halloween, what did she do for her costume?"

She glanced at him and shrugged as if the answer were obvious. "A wig."

Daryl felt slapped between the eyes for having missed such an obvious solution. His only excuse was he'd never had anything to do with women's beauty routines or hairstyling.

"Stop!" he cried louder than he intended, making Kara and Lexi both flinch.

"What the heck?" Lexi said, frowning.

He marched forward and hauled Kara into his arms, sighing his relief. "Don't dye your hair."

"But I thought—"

Shaking his head, he framed her face with his hands and whispered, "I can't stand the idea of you doing anything to change it. Your hair is beautiful as it is. It's…"

He stroked a hand over the silky tresses, and his voice faltered. "It would just be such a shame to cover such a beautiful color. It's such a part of who you are. Your heritage and—"

She blinked and smiled, then framed his face in her own hands. "That's so sweet of you. But what about my disguise?"

"I think he's leaning toward a wig now, if I'm right?" Emma said.

Lexi twisted her mouth in thought. "It'd have to be a good one that fits well to fool anybody. The one I wore at Halloween last year was cheap and showed a gap at the hair line."

"So we get a better one. Or she wears a hat with it. Or...something." Daryl grew self-conscious of the intimate touching between himself and Kara while his family looked on. He dropped his hands to his sides, but before she stepped back, Kara leaned in to give his cheek a kiss. "Thank you."

"Okay. So no hair color." Lexi started packing up the supplies. "But we can still get some baggy clothes and sunglasses. And we can sneak you into town to buy a good wig."

"No." Daryl gave his niece a stern look. "If I'm charged with protecting her, then my first rule is, she doesn't go out in public unless absolutely necessary. We'll send someone out for any part of a disguise we don't have here at Cameron Glen."

He faced Kara. "All right?"

She nodded. "All right. I trust your judgment. That's why I'm here. I knew you'd keep me safe."

Daryl gritted his back teeth, and his gut flip-flopped.

His every instinct was to protect those he loved and anyone he deemed at risk. But knowing he, without any real training as a bodyguard or law enforcement of any kind, was the invisible wall between Kara and wealthy men who meant her harm gave him pause. Was he up to the challenge? How in the world was he going to translate his promise of safety into reality?

He released a slow, tense breath as he gazed into Kara's mesmerizing green eyes. He might not know how, but he knew he was already deeply invested in protecting her. He had been from the moment he chose to chase down her kidnapper's car that rainy night last spring. Maybe from the moment he took her hand to calm her fear of flying.

Deeply invested. And probably too much so. A British movie star had no place in her life for a computer geek from a tiny mountain town in North Carolina. The sooner he came to terms with that truth, the better off he'd be in the long term.

Chapter 12

Kara spent the next two weeks ensconced at Cameron Glen, getting to know Daryl's big, loving family. When Daryl had made arrangements with his office to take unpaid personal leave for no more than two months, Kara had repeated her offer to pay him for his protective services. He had refused her money, but Kara was determined to find a way to repay him and his family for their assistance.

As her stay progressed, the reason Daryl was so kind and protective became clearer daily. Every member of her host family, young and old, had the same welcoming, compassionate, good-humored traits. In addition, the beauty of the property, from the quiet ponds to the Christmas tree–lined hills, provided a tranquil setting where she could gather her thoughts, as if the property itself were an extension of the Camerons' gracious hospitality.

Busy little chipmunks scurried up and down the hills, gathering and hiding food, rabbits chased each other through the newly planted fir trees—future Christmas trees—and wild turkeys strutted through the cabin lawns without a care in the world. Daryl had been right. His family's property was a little slice of heaven.

But as in Eden, a serpent arrived one day to ruin her

restful idyll. A delivery driver brought a package to the older Camerons' front porch while she, Daryl and his parents were enjoying a cup of coffee in the rocking chairs of their front porch. Habitually chatty, Daryl's mother, Grace, struck up friendly banter with the delivery man as he snapped a photo of the package on their doorstep as proof he'd done his job. He shifted his gaze to the four adults rocking and sipping steaming mugs, and he flashed a polite grin. "How're y'all doing?"

"Just fine. We sure appreciate you making the trek way out here to bring us our goodies. Can I offer you a snack or some water? It's gonna be another scorcher later today," Grace replied.

For her part, Kara tried to keep her face averted, her gaze down or her drink up hiding most of her face. She cut a side look to Daryl, who was studying the delivery man with obvious concern.

"Oh, no, ma'am. Thank you anyhow. I'm...all set."

When she heard his words falter, the hesitation, Kara raised her eyes but not her head. She'd learned those hesitations were the moment a person was mentally connecting the dots, recognizing her or making a spontaneous decision. Her pulse tripped as she watched the delivery driver do something suspect with his phone at his side. When he smiled again and nodded as he turned to return to his truck, his attention was locked on her. He even cast a last look to her as he shifted his truck's gears to depart.

Daryl grunted as the vehicle pulled away. "Damn."

"What is it, dear?" Grace asked.

"I think he recognized her," Daryl said, confirming her suspicion.

"Why do you say that?"

"More important," his father said, "if he did, what do you want to do about it?"

Kara squeezed the mug in her hands more tightly and heaved a sigh of regret. "Unfortunately, I think that's our signal it's time to change location. Moving about had always been the plan, but I'd hoped I could stay here in this blissful setting a little longer."

"You're welcome to stay as long as you want," Daryl's mother said.

Kara reached for the older woman's hand on the armrest of the chair next to hers. "I appreciate that more than you could know. But I think the prudent thing would be to change locations." She angled her head toward Daryl. "Agreed?"

He lifted his cell phone and woke the screen. "I'll call Fenn now and see if we can crash there for a while."

Not only was Daryl's niece, who was two years older than he was, willing to have them camp out at her apartment near Durham, but Fenn said she would be thrilled to have Kara, an actress whose career Fenn had enjoyed following, staying in her home. The trick would be getting Kara into Fenn's flat, where the residents trended toward social media savvy college students and a more international, soccer-centric population, without being recognized.

Thus, for the final walk from Daryl's rental car, across the busy car park and through the often crowded lobby of Fenn's building, Kara wore a dark brown wig and a baseball cap, hid her eyes behind large sunglasses and kept her gaze down, her pace brisk without calling attention to her hurry.

Just before they reached the lobby door, a stiff wind

blew her cap off, taking the wig with it, and her hair tumbled down past her shoulders.

She bent to snatch the hat from the ground, but without breaking stride, Daryl hustled her through the fortunately empty lobby and onto the lift. Once Daryl was in the carriage with her, she slipped off her sunglasses in order to read the buttons on the panel. "Fifth floor, you said?"

"Yeah."

She poked the appropriate button, and the doors started to slide closed.

"Hold the door!" a voice called, and an arm reached through the closing doors, triggering the auto stop. A woman with a large package tucked under one arm trundled into the carriage with them, chirping, "Thanks! This thing is so slow. I hate waiting on it!"

As the lift doors closed, Kara ducked her chin and angled her body away from the woman. Should she put her sunglasses back on? Or would doing so when already inside merely call more attention to herself and her attempts to hide her face?

They rode in silence for several seconds until the woman blurted, "You look familiar. Have we met?"

Kara's heart tripped, but she didn't dare look up or meet the other woman's eyes.

"I don't believe so. I'm just visiting my sister."

"Not you, sugar," the chatty woman said, laughing. "I was talking to her."

Kara balled her hands, praying the lift would move faster. It *was* as painfully slow as the woman had said.

"Although," the lady said, "you do look familiar, too." She gasped, and an excitement filled her tone as she gushed, "You're the guy in the picture with Kara O'Quinn! The one all over Facebook and Insta."

Without turning, Kara sensed when the woman's attention shifted back to her. A tingling dread crawled down her back and left a cold puddle in her stomach.

"Wait," the woman said in an awed, breathy tone. "You're her! Kara O'Quinn! The whole world is looking for you, wondering why you disappeared. Oh, my God!"

"No," Daryl said, and Kara heard the forced incredulity. "We're not whoever that is you're talking about. She's my sister's roommate, Imogen. They've been best friends since high school outside of Asheville. You've got the wrong person."

The woman snorted. "Of course you'd say that. We'll just see what the internet has to say about—"

"Hey! Put that away!" Daryl growled, and Kara heard a tussling. "Don't—"

The tone of his voice brought Kara's head up, her eyes toward the scuffle. The woman's phone was pointed right at Kara, and the gloating grin the woman wore told Kara she'd gotten the pictures she wanted.

The lift dinged as it lurched to a stop, and the doors slid open. With a hand at Kara's back, Daryl pushed past the intrusive woman and rushed Kara to the door marked 509. He knocked, then tested the knob, but it was locked. "Fenn! Open up!"

From the edges of her vision, Kara saw that the woman had followed them off the lift and stood just steps away, still snapping pictures with her phone.

Daryl placed his body between Kara and the wannabe paparazzi. "I said stop taking pictures!"

"It's a free country," the woman replied.

"It's an invasion of privacy!" he retorted, his voice vibrating with rage.

"But she's a public figure, and the public has an interest—hey!"

Kara angled her gaze in time to see Daryl toss the woman's phone down the hall. As the woman scrambled after the mobile phone, the apartment door opened.

Daryl pushed Kara through the open portal, following on her heels. Kara stumbled into the living room, almost tripping over a black cat that cut across her path to dart down the hall and out of sight.

Daryl turned and closed the door with a slam.

"What in the world?" the brunette by the door said.

"Your neighbor recognized Kara and took pictures," Daryl said. He appeared at Kara's side and put a hand on each of her arms. "Are you all right?"

"Physically, yes, but… Bloody hell. I haven't been here five minutes, and my cover is blown!"

The brunette stepped over and offered her hand. "Hi, Kara. I'm Fenn. And the nosy neighbor was Nancy Banks. She's well-known in the building for minding everyone else's business. I'm sorry you encountered her. I should have thought to be on the lookout for her, but—"

Kara shook her head. "Not your fault. I'm the one imposing on you, and, well—"

"And, well…" Fenn repeated with an apologetic twist to her mouth. Her expression shifted to one of awe, and she shook her head. "I'm sorry. I'm really trying not to fangirl right now, but… I love your movies. I really think you should have won the BAFTA for *Brutal Love*. You were magnificent!"

"You're kind." Kara forced herself to brighten and shake Fenn's hand. "And thank you for letting us come here. It's a pleasure to meet you. Daryl has nothing but raves to say about you."

Fenn's eyebrows lifted. "Oh, really? Do tell."

"C'mon, Fenn," Daryl said, giving her shoulder a nudge with his fist. "You know I got nothin' but respect for you."

"Aw, likewise, D," Fenn returned with a grin and her own shoulder bump to Daryl.

Kara tried to smile at the family antics, but she couldn't get the woman from the hall out of her mind. After all their careful planning, was her location going to be plastered across social media again so soon?

"Hey," Daryl said, giving the base of Kara's neck a massage. "Try not to worry about that lady."

"But if she shares those pictures..."

"Maybe she won't," Fenn said. "She's a busybody, but she might not be the most tech savvy. Maybe the pictures will go no further than her phone."

Kara wanted to believe that. So much.

"And maybe Fenn could talk with Nancy and explain why it's important the pictures don't get out." Daryl gave Fenn a meaningful look.

His niece shrugged. "I can try. First, let's get you guys settled. Follow me, Kara. I'll show you to your room. D, you're on the couch, I'm afraid. But it's actually pretty comfy. I nap there all the time."

After Fenn had given her the full tour of the apartment and they'd all settled in the living room to unwind, Kara finally felt her muscles relax a bit. She was safe... for now. And most important, she had Daryl with her. She wasn't alone, didn't have to fear facing Holt by herself, even if the football club's henchman did catch up to her. That was something.

Chapter 13

Any illusion that Nancy's recognition of Kara would be harmless evaporated early the next morning with a ruckus out in the apartment building's parking lot. Woken by loud voices and slamming car doors, Daryl went to Fenn's window and looked out. A swarm of vehicles and people with cameras of all sizes milled about the building's small lawn and residents' cars. He spotted several people, likely residents, confronting the newly arrived crowd that blocked parked cars as the owners tried to leave for work or school.

"Damn," he muttered under his breath.

"Meow."

He looked down to find Fenn's black cat winding around his legs. "Hello, Sadie. You know anything about all this?" he asked, hitching his head toward the window.

Sadie flopped over on her side, and he squatted to scratch her proffered stomach. Loud rumbling purrs erupted from the cat as she started making air biscuits.

"She's such a pushover for belly rubs."

He glanced over his shoulder to Fenn, who chuckled and shook her head at her cat's behavior. "They found her. The parking lot is full of photographers."

Fenn sighed. "Nosy Nancy strikes again." Tightening

the belt on her bathrobe, Fenn strolled to the kitchen and took a can of cat food from the cabinet.

Sadie sprang up when Fenn popped the can's top and ran to the dish on the floor.

"Clearly breakfast trumps belly rubs," he said, chortling.

"So what do we do about the cameras?"

"Not sure what we can do. Keep Kara inside, out of sight until they lose interest and go away?" he said. "Your neighbors are none too pleased with the news vans and paparazzi blocking traffic."

"We could call the police to have them cleared out," Fenn suggested.

"They have a right to be on public property. If the apartment management wants to file a complaint about them trespassing on private property, that's a different matter."

"Do I want to know what you're discussing?"

Daryl pivoted to face Kara, whose hair was rumpled and sexy. He was struck again by gratitude she hadn't dyed it and ruined her beautiful auburn coloring. "I'd say take a look outside, but it's probably better you stay away from the window. A lot of those cameras have telephoto lenses. If they know which apartment you're in, they could—"

As if confirming his speculation, a loud knock sounded on Fenn's door.

Kara's eyes widened, and her cheeks drained of color. Putting a finger to his lips to quiet her, Daryl marched across the room to guide Kara down the hall to the back rooms, whispering to Fenn, "Get rid of them. Call if you need me for backup."

When they reached the back bedroom, Kara dropped on the edge of the bed with a dispirited sigh. They sat in strained silence while listening to Fenn at the front door, her tone firm as she dismissed whomever had knocked.

Finally Fenn appeared in the bedroom door, her hand on her hip. "Other residents, complaining about the hubbub. They're gone now. I insisted that, while you had been seen here yesterday, you left again last night, and I didn't know where you'd gone."

"You admitted she was here?" Daryl asked, aghast.

"I figured that horse was out of the barn, and denying it, when there were pictures to prove Nancy's claim, would only cast doubt on any other denials I made. If we want to be believed that she's left, I had to establish some credibility."

"She's right," Kara said, rubbing her arms while a frown dented her brow. "Damn. Why did I think things would be any different here than anywhere else I've been pursued by the media? Hounded, really."

"I can't imagine how it must be, unable to leave your home without being chased by cameras and knowing photographers with high-power lenses could be shooting you without your knowledge in your most private moments."

Kara lifted a shoulder. "It wasn't really so bad before this business with Ian. I had moderate fame, and only got recognized by a few people now and again. I knew as a public figure I'd lose a certain amount of privacy, and I could live with that. But the way this situation, the lies from Ian's people have exploded in the media and online…"

Fenn grunted. "The public loves a scandal, loves to revel in other peoples' misery."

"Schadenfreude," Daryl said. "That's the German word for it."

"And isn't it sad that enjoying someone else's misery is common enough for the Germans to have a word for it?" Fenn added. With a huff, she let her hands fall to her sides. "Well, I'll go make sure the blinds are closed and get started making breakfast. Is there anything special you'd like to eat, either of you?"

"Tea and maybe toast?" Kara asked. "I don't want to be an imposition."

Daryl gave Kara's shoulder a rub of encouragement before he stood. "How about pancakes and bacon? I'll make them if you point me toward the ingredients in your pantry, Fenn."

Kara's stomach rumbled, and that was all the confirmation he needed.

"Pancakes, it is," he said, clapping his hands together and heading into the kitchen.

"Let me get you that tea while D cooks. Sugar?"

"No. Just milk."

Fenn lifted her eyebrow and grinned. "Oh, right. That's how y'all do it across the pond." She cocked her head to the side. "Has D taught you to drink sweet iced tea yet? Sweet tea is called the house wine of the South."

"Ice in your tea. Oh, right. That's how *you* do it on *this* side of the pond." Kara grinned. "I promise to try it iced later, but for now, just hot with milk, please."

Fenn returned with a steaming mug of tea a few moments later and set it on the small café table in her dining nook. Kara sipped the tea. "Perfect. Thank you."

"Kara?" Fenn said, an odd hesitation in her voice.

"Yes?" Her reply held a similar vacillation.

"Would you allow a friend of mine to interview you? I was thinking that if she wrote a feature article about you, telling your side of the story—"

"No." Cradling the mug between her hands, Kara shook her head. "I decided a long time ago that I wouldn't get drawn into a tit-for-tat media war with the paparazzi."

"But—"

"The public will believe what it wants to believe, and I can't change that. All I can do is hold on to my truth."

Fenn sat across from her and used her finger to trace the wood grain pattern in the table. "This is a little more than the paparazzi spreading rumors that you've gotten collagen injections or slept with your director." Daryl's niece glanced up at her, her gaze bright with passion. "The lies being spread about you are vicious and cruel and have put your life in danger."

Kara nodded acknowledgment. "I still don't like looking desperate. As if I'm clamoring for attention or justification. I shouldn't have to plead my case in the media."

"You're right. You shouldn't *have to* justify or defend yourself. But here we are." Fenn sighed and stared at the table again as she began tracing the wood grain again. "Maybe instead of thinking of it as justifying yourself, you could think of it as fighting back?" Fenn angled a hesitant look at Kara. "Sticking up for yourself and the truth?"

Fenn's characterization needled Kara uncomfortably. She leaned back in her chair, her pulse stuttering. "Do you think I'm…cowering?"

Eyes widening, Fenn jerked a look of dismay toward her. "Gosh, no! I didn't mean to imply that! I just…wonder where the line between taking the high road and not responding to bad press crosses over to the need to stand up for what is right, what is fair and honest."

"I see your point. I do." Kara took another comforting sip of her tea, but a disquiet buzzed inside her.

Should she respond to the horrid allegations or would that just feed the frenzy? An indirect response, allowing Fenn's friend to write an article about all that had transpired in the last year might be the best way to approach the issue. But just the suggestion of exposing so much of her private life to public scrutiny sent a sick feeling to her core.

She was roused from her internal debate by a light tapping on her arm. She glanced down to find Sadie standing on her back legs, one front paw on the edge of Kara's chair and her other paw padding lightly. Wide green eyes gazed up at her, clearly asking for attention.

"Hello, kitty." Kara reached for Sadie's head, but the cat shrank away from her pat. "No?"

Fenn laughed. "Sadie is the queen of contradiction. She wants your attention, but also not. I find scratches on her cheek and chin are generally your best bet."

Kara complied, smiling as Sadie's rumbling purr greeted the tickle under the feline's chin.

When Daryl brought in a plate with the first pancakes and a pile of bacon, Sadie scuttled off.

"Go ahead and eat while these are hot. I've got another batch almost ready." He slid the plate onto the table and plunked down a bottle of maple syrup and a plastic tub with butter.

The question of whether to respond to the media was temporarily forgotten as Kara and Fenn served themselves pancakes. Kara savored her first bite, dripping with sweet maple. Divine!

When Daryl returned with another plate laden with hotcakes, he joined them at the table. "How are they?"

"Wonderful. And both thicker and fluffier than what I've had before. The maple syrup is inspired. I'm used to strawberry jam or lemon curd on my hotcakes."

"I'll make a Southern gal of you yet," he said with a wink.

The loud, sustained blast of a car horn sounded outside, interrupting her enjoyment of her breakfast. The harsh honking reminded her she wasn't on an American holiday. She had both a mob of paparazzi and a violent hit man tracking her. Before she'd have peace in her life or even a shred of normalcy, she had to deal with both menaces.

By staying inside, out of view of the cameramen and busybodies cluttering the car park and sidewalks outside Fenn's flat, Kara and Daryl passed a relatively quiet couple of days as Fenn's guests. While Fenn was at work, Daryl taught Kara card games, they watched American game shows on the telly and she spent the evening hours sipping wine with Fenn and Daryl and getting to know more about their childhood and life at Cameron Glen. The lull, after the hubbub of her arrival, was welcome, even though the crowd of paparazzi wasn't thinning outside.

On the first Saturday of her stay, after sleeping in and lingering over their coffee and tea, Fenn suggested they make deli-style sandwiches for lunch.

"D, will you get out all the condiments from the fridge? And, Kara, can you slice that tomato?" Fenn asked, rallying the troops.

"Of course," Kara said, moving to the sink where a bright red tomato sat on the windowsill. She washed the fruit, careful to keep her finger splint dry, then started peeling the tomato with small cuts that lifted the thin skin. As she worked, the tomato grew increasingly slippery, especially since the splint on her broken finger made her grasp awkward at best. When she made her first slicing motion, the fruit shot from her grip, and the knife swiped straight into the palm of her hand. She gave a panicked cry, although the sharp knife had made a clean cut she barely felt…at first.

"Kara?" Daryl asked, turning from the table where he set out bottles and jars of condiments. "What happened?"

"The tomato slipped. I—" The sting and seep of blood kicked in then, and she winced. "Oh, dear. I've cut my hand. Rather badly it seems." She tried to keep her tone calm and even. No need to panic. It was just a cut. With a sigh, she stuck the injured hand into the stream of water from the sink and hissed in pain.

"Let me see," Daryl said, drawing her hand from the water and dabbing at it with a paper towel. Blood flowed faster now. "Fenn, grab a clean towel. This sucker's bleeding pretty hard."

As Fenn stepped closer and pressed the clean dish towel to Kara's hand, she examined it. "I'm no doctor, but I know when one is needed. That's a serious cut. You're gonna need stitches at a minimum. That sucker's deep."

"Do you know a doctor who can come to us?" Kara asked, then watched the cousins exchange a knowing look. Her stomach sank. They were going to have to venture out to the emergency department again. This time in a different city without the benefit of Daryl's sister-in-law sneaking them in a back door and helping to keep her presence a secret.

Fenn shook her head, her scowl confirming Kara's suspicions. "We're going to have to get you to the ER as quick as we can. We'll do our best to shield you, but…" Fenn motioned to the towel on Kara's hand, which was already soaked with blood. "You need to go now."

Kara dropped her gaze to the red stain growing on the towel, and her stomach swam. "I… Okay."

Fenn hustled to collect a hooded jacket for Kara, her own sunglasses and car keys. "I'll take you, but let's minimize speculation about you, Daryl. We'll go now, and you follow in a few minutes. No need letting the cameras see the two of you together and blood. That's just grist for the mill."

Daryl changed her towel for a new one and gave her forehead a quick kiss. "She's probably right. But I'll be right behind you."

Kara swallowed hard, not willing to tell her hosts how much she dreaded this necessary excursion. Already her head felt faint at the sight of her bleeding and throbbing hand, and her stomach bunched with anxiety.

She let Fenn slide the sunglasses on her and struggled to get her splinted fingers and towel-wrapped hand through the sleeve of the jacket. Daryl flipped the hood up and gave her an encouraging smile. "You'll be all right."

Fenn checked the hall and whispered, "Come on. Coast is clear."

Knees wobbling, Kara gave Daryl a weak smile and hurried out behind Fenn. They made it down the elevator and out of the lobby without incident, but the minute they stepped out of the building into the parking lot, Kara was recognized. A swarm of paparazzi surged toward her, cameras shoved in her face and questions shouted at her. Fenn did her best to block the more aggressive reporters, towing Kara forward with her grip on Kara's good arm and pushing bodies out of her way as she plowed forward. "Move please! No comments! Step aside."

The bloody towel on Kara's hand slipped as she was struggling to get past a woman who grabbed at her jacket sleeve, trying to get Kara to turn around for a picture of her face. When the towel fell to the ground, the woman gasped and shouted, "She's bleeding! Her wrist is bleeding!"

Chapter 14

Fenn finally reached her car and keyed open the passenger side. She yanked open the door and tried to block cameras as Kara pushed her way through the throng to the front seat.

The pushy woman had grabbed the towel from the ground and waved it for all to see. "She's bleeding! She was trying to hide it, but here's the proof!"

"She wasn't hiding anything!" Fenn shouted as she shoved bodies out of the way to close the passenger door. "Please move before I call the police!"

Kara locked the car door quickly, preventing the groping hands trying to open the door again for a picture. She drew her bleeding hand inside the sleeve of the jacket, hoping to hide it from more pictures. She noticed it had begun to seep again without the pressure from the towel. Fenn unlocked the car again and hopped into the driver's seat quickly before relocking the doors.

"Vultures!" Fenn grumbled. She cranked the engine, casting a side glance to Kara. "Did they hurt you? How's your hand?"

"No and bleeding again. On your jacket, I'm afraid." Kara kept her face down and angled away from the window as Fenn honked her horn and pulled slowly through the mob blocking their path.

"Find something else, as clean as possible, to press on it. Pressure on the wound is important."

Kara pulled a wad of facial tissues from a box on the center console and shoved them against her hand.

After finally navigating the crowd of paparazzi and other media filling the driveway, Fenn made it to the hospital emergency room in good time. They hustled out of the car and inside the ER lobby before the cars that had followed them could arrive.

"My friend has cut her hand and needs stitches, and while I understand that's lower in the triage list of importance, if you don't want a media frenzy and chaos in the waiting room, you'll get her back and out of sight ASAP."

The clerk at the check-in window gave Fenn a haughty look. "Excuse me?"

"The paparazzi is right behind us," Kara said, sliding off the sunglasses. "I don't mean to use my celebrity for faster care, but whether you recognize me or not, there's a horde of cameramen about to descend on your lobby. There will be chaos if you don't find an exam room for me."

"You're some kind of celebrity?" The man in scrubs gave her a skeptical glance. "Who are you?"

"Doesn't matter," Fenn said. "But if you don't let her come back now, your waiting room is about to become a zoo. Is that what you want? Is that what these sick people need?" She waved a hand to the other patients waiting to be seen.

"I'm not asking to be seen out of turn, just to not be out

here where the press will swarm us. I'll wait in a closet if I must, but—"

The sliding door to the outside opened, and a cluster of photographers bustled in. "There she is!"

Kara groaned and ducked her head.

"Hey!" the admitting clerk shouted past her. In a matter of seconds, he'd come through a side door and blocked the men with cameras from approaching Kara. "This is a hospital, not a free-for-all!" He hustled Kara and Fenn through the side door and gave a final shout as the door closed behind them. "Clear outta here, or I'll call security!"

"Thank you," Kara said, as she followed the man to a set of chairs in the back hallway.

Three hours later, her hand stitched and given an injection for pain, Kara was released from the ER. A nurse helped her leave through a less conspicuous side door, wearing scrubs and an operating theater mask. Getting back inside Fenn's apartment was more difficult, since a number of paparazzi had returned and camped out waiting for her.

Daryl ran interference, and Fenn held up a jacket to shield Kara from most of the lenses.

Once safely inside Fenn's apartment, Kara dropped onto the couch and gave a low groan. "I know what's coming. Every sighting of me means another flurry of lies and rumors in the British media and influencer blogs. Seeing as I've been spotted in the place we just finished batting down rumors, I can imagine they will find a way to villainize me all the more."

Daryl settled close to her and draped an arm around her shoulders. "Does it matter what the tabloids say? We know it's not the truth. Surely your family knows not to believe what the rag sheets print."

"I know it shouldn't matter, but… Well, how would you feel if lies were being spread to the public about you? Your reputation ruined, your career sullied? Every aspect of your private life scrutinized and misinterpreted?"

"Horrible. Just as I'm sure you do. I don't mean to minimize your feelings." He stroked her nape, and she laid her head on his shoulder. "These are unchartered waters for me. I'm not sure how to navigate."

"Can you counter what you know is coming?" Fenn asked. "Release a statement explaining that you cut your hand, before they turn your trip to the hospital into plastic surgery or a secret pregnancy."

"Or a drug overdose?" Kara said and shook her head. "They've certainly set me up for *that* lie." She exhaled and said firmly, "No, if the royal family makes it a policy never to comment on tabloid stories, that's good enough for me. Even though every lie makes me cringe and gnash my teeth, why feed the fire? Why say anything that can be construed the wrong way or picked apart? I've always thought responding to lies was just wallowing in the gutter with the trashy people who spread the slander."

"Not even to defend yourself?" Daryl asked.

She tipped her head back to look into his eyes. His expression reflected the same frustration that gnawed at her, as well as a compassion for her situation. "But doesn't defending myself imply there's some truth to what's said? That I have to tell my side? And why would I want them to know they've gotten under my skin?"

His brow furrowed, but he said nothing.

"Daryl? What?" she asked, angling her body to study his face.

He shook his head. "It's not my place to judge. Your choices are yours to make."

"But you'd do things differently. Is that what you mean?" A kernel of doubt planted at her core. She respected his opinion and wanted to make the right decision about how to handle the mess she was in.

"Look," he said, his touch gentle and his tone warm and sweet. "My priority is keeping you safe. That's why you came looking for me and drafted me into duty. So my opinion is colored by that. You, naturally, have to consider all aspects of this business, so you have a different perspective."

The stroke of his hand on her cheek, her neck, her hair mesmerized her. She took a moment to savor his touch before mustering her thoughts to respond. "Well, not really that different. I definitely want to stay safe."

She leaned into him more fully, letting the sedative effects of the painkiller from the hospital and the hum of pleasure from his nearness seep into her core.

"But?" he prompted as if he'd read her mind.

"But it's bloody hard to have rumors spread about you that aren't true. Having the good opinion of the public is quite important in my line of work. A movie can flop or be a blockbuster based solely on a media scandal or a star's popularity and likeability with fans."

"I get that, more than you might think." Daryl eased back, deeper into the cushions of Fenn's couch, tugging Kara with him to recline against his chest. "I'm no stranger to lies and hurtful rumors."

She perked up and twisted to gaze into his face. "You? Mr. Nicest Guy Ever?"

"Yeah. Me. When you're the Black adopted son of a white family in a predominantly white high school, you're bound to be the focus of some harsh rumors about your parentage. Then throw in questions surrounding the circumstances that got me on the varsity football team without having played junior varsity..."

Kara raised one eyebrow, curious and already offended on Daryl's behalf without even having heard the story. "What happened? What did they say?"

He tried to wave off her questions, dismissing the hurtful things that he'd endured.

Kara nestled close to him again, pulling his arms around her. "You don't have to tell me, of course, but... I do want to get to know you better. Your past is more than just the golden memories and holidays with your family and friends. I want to share your hurts and disappointments, as well. I want to know how you put the bad things said about you behind you and became the generous and respectful man I know."

Daryl covered her arms with his, being careful of her well-bandaged hand with splinted fingers. Resting his chin on the top of her head, he sighed. "Okay. Well, the first thing said about me was when I entered kindergarten. I knew I was a different race. I wasn't blind, you know? I just never thought about it, because my family never made a big deal about it. I don't remember my birth mother, but Mom and Dad—that is Grace and Neil Cameron—didn't hide my birth mother from me. They made sure I knew who she was, and that I had pictures of her. They told me stories about Grace's friendship with her. How they met and became close. How Grace promised to look after me when my birth mother was diagnosed with inoperable cancer. It was my birth mother's wishes that I be raised by the Camerons because she loved Grace like a sister."

Kara smiled and hugged his arms closer. "That's a lovely story. And bittersweet, knowing your mother died." She chewed the inside of her cheek. "So what happened in kindergarten? Dare I ask?"

"Easy enough to guess. I was teased for not having 'real parents,' told the Camerons only took me in because they felt sorry for me. In elementary school, I heard racist terms for the first time and had to ask the Camerons what the words meant."

"How awful!" Kara said, her chest squeezing with sympathetic hurt and anger on his behalf.

"Kids will be kids and repeat what they hear at home. The gist of the teasing stayed much the same, although the language and mythology of the rumors changed as I got older. One story was that Neil had had an affair with my birth mother, and I was the product. That that's why they adopted me, and why my skin is lighter than some Blacks." He waved a dismissive hand. "And so on, until I tried out for football as a freshman, having had a growth spurt over the summer." He stopped and twisted his mouth as he reflected. "I killed it in tryouts. I lifted more weight, ran faster, blocked better and caught more balls than guys older than me. Coach put me on the varsity team, and I got comments about my race being the reason. Clichés about Black athletes were used to taunt me."

"But he shut the naysayers up," Fenn said, "when he helped lead our school team to a district championship two years straight." Fenn's smile reflected pride and satisfaction. "And we almost won state his senior year. Once people got to know Daryl, the teasing stopped or became more good-spirited. He was voted 'Friendliest' along with Shelly Camp for his senior yearbook."

"Yeah, says the girl who was voted 'Most Likely to Succeed' the year before," Daryl returned, and Kara didn't have to see his face to know he was smiling. She could hear the grin in the mellow tone of his voice.

"Wow! Bravo!" Kara said. "I take it you were a good student then, Fenn?"

Fenn shrugged modestly, and Daryl chuckled. "She made straight A's, but the extracurricular service projects and help she gave her parents to establish a nonprofit organization to fight human trafficking were the clinchers."

Fenn blushed, then volleyed back with, "Daryl was also voted 'Best Looking,' but no one can have more than one title in the yearbook, so he had to choose which one he wanted. He went with 'Friendliest.'"

Kara felt Daryl squirm, and she angled her head to grin at him. "No part of that surprises me. You are the handsomest, and also the most modest about it, such that you'd choose personality over superficial beauty."

They'd clearly embarrassed him, and he snorted and shook his head as he pushed off the sofa and headed into the kitchen. "I'm getting a snack. I'm famished. What can I bring you ladies?"

Just you, Kara thought, missing the strength and warmth of his body to snuggle against.

Fenn popped up from her seat. "I'm starving, too. Let me finish getting those sandwiches we started earlier and abandoned for our little emergency." She gave Kara a playful wink. "I'll pass on the bloody tomatoes, though."

"I will, too," Kara said. "Can I help with—"

"No!" Daryl and Fenn said at the same time, then laughed.

Heat flushed Kara's face. "I'm not usually so clumsy, but... I suppose I should sit this one out. Aye?"

Daryl's nose wrinkled as he said, "Yeah."

Spying Sadie asleep on a chair across the room, Kara moved to kneel by the chair and stroke the cat's soft fur.

"We had two cats when I was growing up," she called into the kitchen, not sure why she felt compelled to share that tidbit. The memory stirred a pang of homesickness. She missed her family, longed to hear her mother's voice, have one of her father's hugs. An accompanying scrape of resentment gnawed at her that Ian's behavior, his employer's lies, the paparazzi's hounding had forced her to maintain radio silence with her parents and siblings in order to protect their privacy and safety throughout her ordeal. She never wanted them to suffer because of her life choices or the dark side of her fame.

"Oh? And now? Do you have any pets?" Daryl asked.

She shook her head, then realizing the kitchen crew couldn't hear a head shake said, "Not at the moment. When I was working, I traveled too much to have a pet, and in the last year or so...well, before I came to the States to get away from the Ian business and the tabloids, I just felt too unsettled. I guess I sensed that my life was about to be upended and—"

Sadie stretched and rolled to her back, offering her stomach for rubs. When Kara obliged, the feline rumbled with bliss, her paws kneading the air, and Kara enjoyed the calming effects of the cat's purr. She forced aside the worrisome and plaguing thoughts of Holt and the haranguing media to savor the feline and her memories. "Our cats lived primarily in the barn. Working animals, my dad called them. They kept the rodent population down in the cows' grain and hay. I always wanted to bring them inside in the winter and on rainy days. Da said no, but he knew I snuck them into my bedroom and didn't call me out on it."

Fenn appeared at the door to the kitchen and was grinning broadly.

"What?" Kara asked.

"Do you know what you just did?"

Kara furrowed her brow in question. "What did I do?"

"When you started talking about your family and your childhood, your Irish brogue was thick as honey."

She blinked, laughed. "Was it? My acting coaches will be disappointed. They've worked hard to rid me of it so I can do British films, play English characters."

Fenn smiled. "I love it. I think it's charming."

Daryl emerged from the kitchen carrying a plate laden with sandwiches. He set the food on the table and arched an eyebrow at Fenn. "You sure it's not insulting to call her native accent *charming*?"

"Charming is a good thing!" Fenn defended, then glanced to Kara. "At least that's how I intended it. Were you insulted?"

Kara shook her head. "Charming is fine."

Daryl shrugged. "Okay. I just know that from the time I left North Carolina to go to West Point, people have commented on and reacted to my Southern accent in ways that set my teeth on edge. They hear me talk and think I'm uneducated because of my accent."

"I've run into that stigma when I've spoken at conferences promoting the work of STOP."

"I can't imagine anyone would think you were uneducated," Kara said. "Anyone who gets to know you can see you're brilliant."

"Brilliant is British for nerd," Fenn teased, and Daryl swatted playfully at her.

"There are Irish stereotypes that bother me, but I'll take charming all the day long." Kara selected a sandwich and took a big bite.

"It worked for Prince Charming," Fenn said.

"Touché," Daryl said with a tip of his head.

After lunch, Kara walked back to the guest room where she'd slept and dropped wearily on the bed. Between the good meal and the chaos of the trip to the hospital, she was knackered. Or maybe it was just the post adrenaline fatigue of feeling safe after days of tension and hiding. She could still hear the buzz of activity outside, the occasional honk or raised voice, but tucked away in the cozy apartment with Daryl and Fenn for company, she could more easily block out the outside world. She'd been lonely, she acknowledged. The summer months, by herself at the coastal rental, had been more stark than she'd let herself admit. Confessing that truth felt like saying Ian and his bosses had won. She wanted desperately to emerge from this ordeal with her head held high and a sense that she and her integrity had prevailed.

Where's the dignity and victory in hiding like a mouse? a sneaky voice whispered to her, piercing her good mood.

Daryl knocked on the door and stuck his head in the room. "Can I come in?"

"Please do."

He frowned at her. "You okay? You look…mad."

Her eyes widened in offence. "Sorry?"

"You look angry about something. Or maybe hurt?"

She laughed mildly. "Oh. The language thing again. I thought you were saying I looked crazy."

He grinned. "No. I wouldn't do that."

She faced him and draped her arms around his shoulders. "Of course you wouldn't, because you are the best man I think I've ever met. The kindest, gentlest bloke I know." She leaned in and kissed his cheek, enjoying the scent of soap on his skin, the light scrape of his unshaven chin.

As she withdrew, Daryl caught the back of her head and pulled her close again. He pressed a kiss to her lips, and her pulse scampered. Her breath stilled inside her. As he ended the kiss and lowered his gaze to the floor, she blinked at him, a bit dumbstruck. Now she knew how he must have felt when she'd stunned him with a kiss at the Atlanta airport last spring when they parted. Greater than her surprise was the wonder and warmth that curled in her core.

He dropped his hand from her nape and sighed. "Sorry. I shouldn't have—"

She cut off his apology, cupping his face with her good hand and resting her bandaged one on his shoulder. She caught his mouth with hers and returned his kiss with one that drew greedily on his lips. The sweet and mellow pool in her center spread its heat through her veins, and she angled her mouth to more fully capture his. Her fingers curled against his scalp, and Daryl made a happy sound deep in his throat that spun tingles over her skin.

He slid his arms around her, holding her closer and combing his fingers through her hair until his palm settled at her nape. Pleasant as the lingering kisses were,

Kara became restless for...more. More contact of his body against hers. More ways to show him how deeply her feelings ran. More of his touch, his kiss, his heat.

She tugged at his shoulders, lying back on the bed and bringing him with her. Her boldness broke the spell. He shifted his weight away from her and shoved to his feet. He rubbed a hand over his mouth and stared at her with a furrow in his brow.

"Don't overthink it, Daryl," she said. She scooted higher on the mattress and rested her head on the pillows. Patting the space beside her, she beckoned him with a smile. "Keep me company?"

He moved slowly toward the side of the bed, his hands flexing and balling at his sides. Despite her request, he was clearly analyzing the situation ten ways to Tuesday— as most of the computer geeks and engineers she knew tended to do.

Finally he kicked off his shoes and stretched out beside her. A honeyed sweetness flowed through her as she tucked herself against his muscular frame. She draped her injured arm across his chest and stroked her toes along his calf. Tipping her head to peek up at him, she asked, "Did anyone ever tell you you're an excellent kisser, Daryl Cameron?"

A red flush stained his chestnut cheeks. "Not in so many words, but... I've never had complaints, either." After a short pause, he twisted his mouth and grunted. "Although now that I've answered, I realize that was probably a rhetorical question. So I should have said thank you."

She propped on her elbow to lean over him and chuckled. "You're so adorably geeky." She dipped her head to kiss his lips, then sidled on top of him. "Kiss me some more."

With his hands framing her face, Daryl did as she bid. His mouth was tender at first, but as their passion built, his kisses deepened and his tongue dueled with hers. He nipped at her bottom lip, and she moaned her delight. As she cleared her mind of everything but this dear man she was with, it occurred to her that she'd never felt as truly free and secure with anyone the way she did with Daryl. The feeling went beyond her physical safety. The feeling swelled from her soul, from her very core being. Daryl liberated something inside her that she'd never wanted to share with anyone else. Never trusted anyone else to reach so deeply into her heart. *This man,* a small voice whispered from her soul. *You can be your truest self with this man.*

Believing that voice took no effort. She recognized the truth of her instinct about Daryl, the nudging that had directed her back to him when danger had arrived at her door. She wanted Daryl in her life because he spoke to her soul.

Sitting up, still astride his hips, she drew her shirt up and off, tossing it aside. With full confidence in her request, she said, "Make love to me, Daryl."

Chapter 15

Daryl stilled, though his pulse was hammering triple time. His mouth dried as he drank in the creamy complexion of Kara's midriff and the pink lace of her bra. The juxtaposition of her body straddling his was making it hard to think rationally, and he was nothing if not rational. He wanted her. That was painfully obvious and had never been in dispute, but somewhere in his muddled thoughts he heard a clanging warning. He wanted to silence the niggling doubt and roll Kara over and love her until she couldn't remember anything, anyone but him.

But...

She bent over him, kissing his face, his neck. Her loose auburn hair tickled his cheeks and surrounded him in a cloud of her floral scent. He couldn't concentrate with her heady, arousing distraction. Bracing his hands on her shoulders, he pushed her away.

"Daryl?"

He cleared his throat and squeezed his eyes shut, gathering the wispy edges of his sensibilities. "I, um..."

He inhaled a slow breath, grasping for that vague sense of imbalance or caution that nagged him. In order to hear that voice, he had to battle past desire and ego and impulsiveness. *You want her, and she's willing. Go for it!*

He bodily moved her off of him so he could sit up. He swung his legs off the bed and pinched the bridge of his nose.

Kara scuttled up behind him and wrapped her arms around his neck, hugging him from behind. "It's all right, Daryl. I trust you."

Perhaps it was her wording—*I trust you*—that made things click into place for him. Making love to her shouldn't be based on the fact that she trusted him. Such an important and intimate act, for him, should be about love and commitment. About a bond between two people that involved deepest emotions and—

He laughed a short, frustrated chuff as he broke the clasp of her arms around his neck and stood.

She was a British celebrity, on the run because of a private scandal. They had nothing in common.

She'd come to him, *hired him* to protect her, because she was scared and alone. He could not take advantage of that vulnerability.

Her heart had been broken by a selfish man who thought only of himself and his career. Daryl did not want to be her rebound relationship.

He faced her, regret and heartache swirling inside him, a bitter medicine to swallow. "No."

Her forehead crinkled in confusion, and she dragged her shirt back over her head. Color stained her cheeks as she muttered, "Can I ask why?"

How did he voice the cocktail of doubts and matters of his conscious without sounding…pedantic? Hurtful?

Yet as he fumbled to give her some explanation, he heard himself ineloquently say, "We're…not in love."

He saw the sting of his words on her face before she

sobered and regarded him with a pleasant smile. A fine show of her acting skills.

He opened his mouth to call her back as she scrambled off the bed and straightened her clothes. "I understand. It's fine. You're right, of course."

"Kara, wait. I—"

She wouldn't look at him. Damn it, he hadn't meant to hurt her, but…his bumbling ineptness was a perfect example of why she deserved more than an awkward computer geek from Nowhereville, North Carolina.

"It's fine," she repeated in a voice that quavered and told him it was anything but "fine."

He exhaled his frustration, making his lips buzz as she marched out of the bedroom and closed the door behind her.

Without hesitating, he followed her, knowing he had fences to mend.

Fenn gave the two of them a smirking grin when they emerged from the back hall. Clearly she thought they'd been doing…what they'd almost done, had he not had an attack of conscience. His side glance to Kara, to see if she'd noticed Fenn's knowing look, told him why Fenn's assumption was so easy to make. Kara's thick hair was rumpled, her cheeks flushed, and the fair Irish skin on her neck and jaw were marked with beard burn. When was the last time he'd shaved? He rubbed a hand over his chin and grimaced at the scrape of stubble.

Kara tugged at the collar of her shirt and fanned one hand ineffectually. "You'd think I'd be used to the heat here in the States by now. I spent a whole summer at the Carolina coast. Can we crack a window or something?"

"Not sure a window will help," Fenn said as she swiped

a condensation dampened glass across her brow. "What you're experiencing, my fair Irish lass, is what I like to refer to as bonus summer, an inevitable fact of life in the southern states. Quite often we have temperatures in September that rival peak summer weather. The weatherman predicted ninety degrees today and lots of sun. I will, however, turn on the air conditioning. I'm hot myself." Then she added with an impish wink, "although not *hot* the way you might be..."

The red in Kara's face deepened as she dodged the quip, saying, "Air conditioning. Yes. A blessing I grew very fond of in July and August."

"Besides, an open window would just let in the noise of the crowd outside," Daryl muttered as he nudged the curtain aside. Through the gap, he studied the assembly below and the giant lenses, tripods and satellite dishes on the roofs of vans. "And give the parabolic microphones out there, better access to our conversations."

Kara shot him a stricken look. "Microphones? You've seen microphones?"

"There's something that looks a lot like one I saw once at West Point." With a sigh, he moved to the couch and dropped onto the cushions.

"Could this get any worse?" Kara groaned.

"Oh, friend," Fenn said with a grimace, "I learned a long time ago not to ask that question. It only invites worse to happen." She waggled the cell phone in her hand. "And, well... I've been monitoring social media since we got back from the hospital and...some nasty rumors are already circulating about your trip to the ER."

Now Kara staggered to the sofa and flopped beside

Daryl with an exaggerated moan. "Nooo. Now what are they saying?"

"They think you attempted suicide."

"What!" Kara gasped.

"They claim the blood they saw on your arm is proof of it. They've assumed you'd tried to hurt yourself," Fenn said, her own voice dejected.

"You've said they'd already tried to paint you as mentally unstable and drug addicted," Daryl said. "I'm afraid it won't be much of a stretch for gullible readers to buy into a self-harm theory."

Kara grunted. "Lovely. So I can run, but I can't hide from the constant stream of lies and rumors meant to damage my reputation."

"I'm sorry. I hate this for you," Fenn said gently. "Because of this new rumor, I'm afraid the crowd of cameras outside is bigger than ever."

Daryl felt Kara flinch, saw the tightening of the muscles in her jaw. "So…she doesn't go out again for a while—" he started.

"I have to move again," she interrupted, shoving to her feet and stalking restlessly around the couch to pace. "I'll relocate."

When Fenn's cat trotted toward her food bowl, Kara stooped to lift Sadie into her arms. The feline only tolerated this for a moment before jumping from Kara's arm to the back of the sofa.

"We could go back to Cameron Glen, at least temporarily," Daryl suggested, even as he searched his brain for a better idea.

Fenn's skeptical frown echoed the doubts he had.

Kara shook her head firmly. "Not Cameron Glen. I

won't risk disturbing the peace at that sweet haven your family has created. It's not fair to them. Besides, I still don't know how much danger I could be in. I don't believe for a second that Holt or the Knights organization has magically lost interest in me."

"Then where?" he asked, as much of himself as the room. He dragged a hand over his face and analyzed the situation. "The first step, it seems to me, is getting you out of the apartment building without being seen. Disguises won't be enough, I'm afraid."

Kara bit down on a fingernail, her brow furrowed in thought. "I did a movie once where the main character snuck into the laundry cart at a hotel to escape the bad guys. Covered herself with the sheets and towels. Can we do something like that?"

"No laundry service here," Fenn said, her shoulders drooping. "But I like your thinking."

Kara wrinkled her nose and said, "The rubbish bin? I hate the idea of getting cozy with your neighbors' trash, but it worked for me last time."

"Hmm." Daryl frowned. He didn't want Kara grubbing around in filth if she didn't have to. "Let's stick a pin in that idea. We can come back to it if we need to, but…"

"Fenn," Kara started, her tone holding a hint of hope. "What's the largest piece of luggage you own? Do you have one of those really big rolling kind?"

"The set I bought a couple years ago included a thirty incher." Fenn sat straighter as Kara came around the end of the couch and perched on the edge. "You're not thinking—"

Daryl saw where this was going and shook his head. "Naw. We can't stuff you in a suitcase like—" All he could think of to finish the sentence was a murder he read about where the body of the deceased was hidden in a suitcase. He shuddered with revulsion.

"I'm small. I could fit. We could at least try it." Kara swiveled to face him. "It's more appealing to me than hiding in rubbish."

He twisted his mouth, wary but willing to hear her out. "And then?"

"Load the suitcase in the trunk of my car," Fenn suggested. "Drive a short distance, until you're far from prying eyes and it's safe to let you move to the front seat."

"They know your car." Kara waved that idea off. "We need a different vehicle."

"Hire a rideshare?" Daryl asked.

Kara wrinkled her nose. "Last time we had someone outside our circle involved, he snapped a picture that gave me away. I'd rather not if we can do this any other way."

"I can ask a friend about borrowing their car without telling them the real reason," Fenn said.

"Or we have Mom or Dad or a sibling drive over and bring one of the several our family has at Cameron Glen." Daryl pulled his cell phone from his pocket and waved it. "They could be here in as little as two hours."

"And go where?" Kara flopped back on the couch, nibbling at a hangnail. "We still need to figure that out. Of course, we can check into a random hotel…"

"Anya's parents are in Charlotte," Daryl said.

"As are Eric's mom and stepdad," Fenn added.

"Are we really going to drag more of your extended family into my mess? I feel bad enough bringing this chaos to your door," Kara said, motioning toward the window where the hubbub of media was clearly audible.

Fenn chuckled. "Kara, if anyone could understand and be of service in a time of crisis, it's our family. We've got lots of experience and firsthand knowledge of why secrecy and the assistance of others is important. We've all got reasons to pay it forward and memories of getting help in times of need and emergency. You couldn't have asked a better family to help you out."

Daryl felt a stir of warmth in his chest, reflecting on the many ways his family had helped not only him, but dozens of other people in need, whether family or not. "She's right. Let me call Gage and Jessica, my sister Cait's kinda sorta in-laws."

"In-laws? Well, more like step—no, ex—" Fenn barked a laugh. "It's complicated. They're Eric's mom and stepdad. Did you meet Eric?"

"Dr. Eric Harkney, at the Valley Haven hospital," Daryl clarified. "He was at the big lunch a couple weeks ago."

Kara nodded. "I remember him. I liked him. He had a great bedside manner and got my finger splinted without the whole hospital knowing I was there." She divided a gaze between them. "So that's the plan. A borrowed car and a suitcase."

"And hiding with various family or random hotels until we come up with a better idea," Fenn added.

Daryl gritted his teeth, unsettled with the way the plan had shaped up, but unsure what else to do. "Okay, then. If you're settled on this, let's get moving."

Two hours later, Dr. Eric Harkney's mother, Jessica, texted to let them know she'd parked her car in the parking garage of a building next door to Fenn's apartment. Jessica had gone to a coffee shop down the street to wait a reasonable time before meeting her husband with their second vehicle in the same garage. Her sedan's keys were hidden on top of the back tire. She and her husband would meet Kara and Daryl later that afternoon at Jessica's home near Charlotte.

Kara gave Fenn a giant hug, more remiss to be leaving her new friend than worried about folding herself into the cramped space of the hard-shell suitcase.

After profuse thank-yous and promises to stay in touch, Kara nodded to Daryl. "Leave a small gap in the zips so I can breathe."

"Way ahead of you." He leaned in to kiss her forehead and whisper, "If you change your mind or need out immediately for some reason, poke a finger through the gap. I'll get you out of there pronto. Okay?"

"I'll be fine." She framed his face and gave him a lingering kiss.

His arms circled her waist and drew her close, deepening the connection.

We're not in love.

A fresh wave of pain sliced through Kara at the memory of his dismissive words. While she couldn't say categorically that she was in love with Daryl, his denial stung. Clearly his feelings for her were not the same as hers for him. After all, she was the one who sought him out. He was only with her now because she'd *hired* him.

Yet he kissed her as if he cared. She'd thought she'd seen a deep emotion in his mahogany gaze. Apparently she was seeing the things she wanted to see instead of the truth.

Her heart aching with this knowledge, she stepped back from him and climbed into the suitcase. Lying on her side, she curled in the tightest ball she could. Daryl closed the suitcase, and when he stood the case on its wheels, Kara fought an unexpected wash of claustrophobia. Squeezing her eyes shut, she forced herself to breathe slowly and deeply and think of pleasant things. The greens of an Irish spring. Sadie's purr. Daryl's warm smile.

"You okay?" he called.

"Yes." She refused to chicken out.

The suitcase bumped and jostled as he rolled it out of Fenn's apartment. As the sound of the wheels changed pitch and the suitcase stopped and started, Kara could guess where they were. The hallway outside Fenn's place. The elevator. The basement. The back door. The driveway—complete with uneven bumps and holes. *Ouch.* And finally a smoother roll, the garage.

She waited while he found the keys, unlocked the boot and unzipped the suitcase. She prepared to climb quickly into the open boot. When the suitcase opened, she took a deep breath of car exhaust-tinged air and lifted her gaze to smile at Daryl.

She'd barely registered the relief on his face when a figure surged forward from behind the next vehicle. *Reggie Holt.*

The man's arm was raised, a bar of some kind in his hand.

Kara gasped, feeling the blood drain from her face. "Daryl, look out!"

Chapter 16

The thud of the bar connecting with Daryl's head reverberated sickly in Kara's core. "No!" she cried as his eyes rolled back, and he crumpled to the concrete. "You animal! Leave him alone!"

Wanting to protect Daryl, Kara lunged toward Holt, who caught her wrist in a vise grip.

"I believe you were headed for the boot?" Holt growled and pushed her toward the open boot. "Get in."

"No!" She tugged on her arm and tried to get away from him. Her gaze fell to Daryl, who hadn't moved yet. Her chest squeezed with regret and fear. If anything happened to Daryl... With a painful twist of her heart, she amended, if anything *worse* happened to Daryl, because clearly she'd already been the cause of his current injury. Guilt tripped through her as she struggled to reach for him.

"You bloody bastard! Let me help him!" she shouted. "He hasn't done anything wrong. Why did you have to hurt him, you beast?"

Dropping the metal bar, Holt jerked her closer, holding her tight against his chest and slapping his newly freed hand over her mouth. "Pipe down, before you draw unwanted attention. You wouldn't want any other innocent bystanders to get hurt, would you?" He wrapped an arm around her waist and lifted her feet from the ground. Walking forward, he dropped her in the boot of the borrowed car and shoved her down. "As for your friend, he was an obstacle that had to be dealt with."

When he released her, freeing her mouth, she drew a deep breath, prepared to scream as loud as she could for help. As if sensing her plan, Holt reached inside his jacket and pulled a gun from a holster near his armpit. He aimed the gun at Daryl's prone form, snarling, "Do it and your friend gets a bullet. I'll kill him if I have to. The choice is yours."

Kara choked on the scream as she swallowed it. She couldn't know if Holt would really murder Daryl in cold blood, but she couldn't risk it. As long as they were both alive, they had a chance to get free, to rectify the situation, to salvage something from this mess. "Don't hurt him," she grated, her voice trembling with rage and terror. "Don't you dare hurt him any more."

"Then be a good girl and lie down in there, while I get him loaded up."

"Loaded up?"

"Can't leave him here to wake up and alert the coppers. Besides the fact he's blocking the way for backing the car out." Holt collected the metal rod from the ground then aimed the gun at Daryl again. "Your choice. Cooperate or your chum gets a plug in his skull."

Tears puddled in Kara's eyes. She hated to capitulate. Hated her weakness, her lack of resources or ideas. She cast a nervous glance around the parking garage. There was a security camera recording what was happening, but without someone monitoring said camera, it did her little good in the moment. No one else was around. She heard no voices, no footsteps, and saw nobody headed their way. *Bloody hell!*

Her stomach roiling in disgust and self-loathing, she settled into the car's boot. For Daryl's sake. At that moment, with adrenaline and panic pouring through her, she couldn't think of another option.

She heard Holt grunt as he hoisted Daryl's flaccid body, draping him over the end of the car, half in the boot. When he unceremoniously shoved Daryl's legs inside, Daryl rolled limply onto his side, crowding her to the far back of the cramped space. He patted Daryl down and extracted his phone from his back pocket.

"Now," Holt said, his hand outstretched. "Give me your mobile."

"I don't have it." That much was true, and now she wished she'd not stashed it away. Even a simple call to Fenn could have helped them.

Holt glanced to the backpack Daryl had dropped when he fell. He rummaged through it until he found her phone, then stuffed Daryl's in with it.

"Where are you—"

Holt slammed the lid of the boot closed before she could finish her question. Not that he was likely to tell her where they were going. The tears that had hovered in her eyes spilled freely onto her cheeks now. She fumbled blindly to find Daryl's arms, his head, his face. She stroked his cheeks tenderly and scooted as close to him as she could. "Daryl? Daryl, love, wake up."

She needed some grunt, some movement, some sign he wasn't dead. How hard had Holt hit him? The thump noise had been ominous. She felt his head, groping blindly until her fingers found a damp, sticky spot. With a swooping sensation under her ribs, she realized he was bleeding.

She heard the engine start, felt the car move. She cradled Daryl's head as best she could and closed her eyes to pray. "Please let him wake up. Please let him be all right. If you save him, I'll do anything!"

She realized that was true, not just a grandiose promise made in desperation. He was in this untenable situation because of her, and she owed it to him to get him out. But more than the staggering guilt she felt for having involved him in her mess, she cared deeply for Daryl. For that reason alone, she would do whatever it took to extricate him.

We're not in love.

But wasn't she? She shoved that matter aside for the time being. What mattered now was what would happen to them, hostages of Holt and trapped in the boot of a car. Would she have to give her own life to save Daryl?

A chill raced through her. She would if it came to that. She scoffed with ill humor at the irony. She'd sought out Daryl because she had been scared and alone. Now she had Daryl and his large family in her corner, but she was still frightened and in danger. Only she'd put the Camerons in danger, as well.

To repay the tremendous debt she owed, to protect the family who'd sheltered her and shielded her, could she give her life? Her pulse raced, and she swallowed hard. Her life…or her reputation, which seemed to be what Holt really wanted. In light of her current situation, Daryl's injury and the harsh tactics Holt seemed willing to take on behalf of the Knights owner and Ian's money-making potential, perhaps the solution was as simple as sacrificing herself. Giving in. Resigning her good name and career and making the unsavory deal with the devil.

A rancid taste filled her mouth at the notion of letting Ian and his loathsome management win. But at that moment, Daryl stirred, groaned. And she knew it was a deal she'd make for the man she loved.

He was suffocating. Hot, achy all over. His head hurt like fire. None of that made sense to him. He tried to roll over. To stretch out. Couldn't. The hard bed he was on jostled and vibrated like the military transports he'd taken... Was that where he was? A training maneuver with the Army? A transfer?

"Daryl? Can you hear me?"

The female voice sounded panicked. And she hadn't used his rank when addressing him. A grunt probably. Needed to practice staying cool under fire.

An especially large jolt had his head bouncing on the hard surface like a rubber ball. He groaned as lightning streaked through his skull. He managed to work an arm up to press his palm against the top of his head where the sharpest pain was.

"I know. You have to be hurting so much. I'm so sorry!" The female voice again. "I think the bleeding has stopped. I can feel a lump there, which is actually a good thing, I hear. Better than having the swelling under your skull and pressing on the brain."

"What—where—" A flash of memory stopped him. A scream that had rung in his ears. A car trunk. An explosive pain in his head.

Kara.

He stiffened as his circumstances came into focus.

"Kara!" His voice croaked.

"I'm here." Her hands found his face, stroked his cheek. The simple touch filled him with relief, with a strange pleasure wholly at odds with their situation.

"Holt knocked you out. Hit you so hard. You were bleeding and—oh, Daryl! I'm so sorry!"

He wiggled until he freed the arm trapped beneath him, then covered her hand with his. "Not your fault. Are you all right?"

"As much as a person trapped in a car boot can be. I'm better, knowing you're awake now."

"But you aren't hurt?" he asked, groaning as the car bumped over another pothole. He'd swear the driver was hitting them on purpose to make them suffer.

"No." She curled her body around his more tightly, despite the searing heat inside the trunk. "Just scared."

"Yeah," he said, "understandable." He was rather freaked out about their dilemma himself, though he'd not say as much aloud. He didn't want to give Kara any more reason to worry. The guy who'd hit him clearly wasn't playing around, and Daryl wasn't in a good position at the moment to do much to defend Kara if it came to it. "Did the guy who clobbered me say where he was taking us?"

"No."

He grunted an acknowledgment of her response. "How long was I unconscious?" If he could calculate how long they'd been driving, he might have a better idea where they were when they stopped. Every morsel of information would be useful.

"About five minutes maybe? It felt like hours. I was so worried."

He squirmed again, unable to straighten his legs, and felt his pocket for his phone. "My phone is gone."

"Holt took it, along with mine."

Daryl sighed. "Of course he did. Damn it. Holt, huh? You know him?"

"Reginald Holt. He works for the owner of the Knights. He's the man who crushed my hand and has been after me since I fled the beach house."

Where did that leave them? Could they escape the trunk somehow? Not that they could bail out while the car was going interstate speed, which, based on the tire sounds and vibrations of the car, was where he guessed they were currently driving. He tried to recall what Fenn may have told him about escaping from a vehicle trunk. He felt sure the STOP organization taught basic worst-case escape scenarios to the women they spoke to. Why had he never paid attention? In his macho comfort with being a large adult male, he'd never given the need for rescue a second thought. That was a woman's problem. He grimaced at the hubris, the sense of personal safety he'd taken for granted.

"Daryl," Kara said, and her voice cracked with emotion. "If you get the chance to save yourself, I w-want you to take it. Leave me. I should never have involved you. Save yourse—"

"Are you kidding me? I could never abandon you," he said with more heat than he'd intended. He twisted his body, shifting as far as he could, trying to face her, even if he couldn't see more than a dim outline in the dark. "What kind of man...no, what kind of *person*, male or female, could do that? Ditch someone to save their own hide? I'd never—"

"You have to! I couldn't live with myself knowing anything else happened to you because of me. I'm sorry I dragged you into—"

Daryl caught her behind the head and hauled her closer, his nose smashing hers as he captured her mouth with his. Angling his head, he deepened the kiss, despite the awkward angle of his neck. Beneath his hands, he felt her sweat-dampened hair, felt the tremor that raced through her. He tasted salty moisture as he savored her lips, though whether it was perspiration or tears, he couldn't be sure. Her face was as drenched with sweat as his.

Damn, but this trunk was hot. As he eased back, both of them sucking in deep breaths, he whispered, "*No.* You're stuck with me until the end. No more discussion."

He felt her grip on his shirt tighten. "You really are the best of souls. The dearest of men, Daryl. I… I could fall in love with you."

Something sweet and terrifying squeezed his chest. *Don't say that*, he wanted to tell her. He didn't want to foster any false dreams that he knew could never be. His heart might be telling him he could fall for her, as well, but his practical side, the louder, blunter part of his brain, told him when this crisis was over and her movie career was back on track, Kara would return to her life of glamour and privilege. Who was he, an ordinary computer geek from small-town North Carolina, to think he could make Kara happy long-term? He was hardly in the same league as the millionaire soccer star she'd been dating.

She sighed heavily. "Well, your lack of reply tells me all I should know. I don't know why I said such a rash thing. I know you said—"

"You just surprised me, is all." He fumbled for the

right words to answer her with. A reply that let her down gently, that told her how much she meant to him without misleading her about any future they might have.

"But if we—" A loud noise cut her off, startling a yelp from her. The car lurched left and then right, accompanied by a telltale *thwap thwap thwap* noise as the car slowed and shimmied.

"Well, this is an interesting development," Daryl muttered.

"What happened?"

"I believe we've blown a tire." He made mental calculations. What could he do with this hiccup? Could this be their opportunity to escape?

"You mean we're stranded? Stuck out here? *With Holt?*" Kara asked, and he could hear a note of desperation in her voice.

"This could actually be a good thing." Even as he said this, the car bumped to a stop. "He'll have to open the trunk to access the spare. If we're ready and act as a team, maybe we can overpower him."

He felt more than saw her nod her head. "How? Daryl, he has a gun. I don't know if we should risk—"

He heard the driver's door open, the crunch of footsteps on gravel, and the grumbling curses of their kidnapper.

"Shh," he warned softly.

"Kara!" Holt said without opening the trunk. "I have to get something from the boot to fix this bloody puncture. Don't be a plank and try anything you'll regret. You or your chum. Do you hear me?"

Kara said nothing, her breathing fast and shallow in his ear.

"Do you hear me?" Holt shouted.

Kara gasped and said, "Yes."

Daryl reached blindly for her hand, found her thigh instead, but still gave a quick squeeze of encouragement.

Speed would be his best chance to catch Holt off guard and gain the upper hand, Daryl reasoned in the precious split second he had to prepare. He'd have to disarm him and—

Keys rattled, and the lock on the trunk popped. When the trunk lid opened, the sunlight that poured into their dark prison blinded him. Still, he shoved up and toward Holt as fast as he could. The change of position and sudden movement shot lightning streaking under his skull. Ignoring the pain, he seized Holt around the shoulders and let his own weight and momentum send them both tumbling backward.

Chapter 17

Daryl's legs were dragged from the trunk as he and Holt landed with a collective "oof" on the shoulder of the highway. Holt, who had both the advantage of no splitting headache and clear vision, seized Daryl with a wrestler's hold around the neck and rolled them both away from the road.

"Daryl!" Kara cried.

As he fought back, shoving aside the screaming ache in his head, he put his advantages to work—his strength and his military training. As he grappled with Holt and tangled their limbs, he worked at gaining a dominant position. He soon became aware that Kara was above them, kicking and swinging whenever she could to strike at Holt.

Just as Daryl tumbled the knot that was his and Holt's bodies so that he was above the man and better able to pin him down, Holt reached for something at his ankle.

Adrenaline spiked in Daryl as he caught the flash of metal and felt the press of a blade against his throat.

"I warned you not to be a prick," Holt wheezed. "Get off me now, or I *will* cut you."

Daryl knew a small flick of the man's wrist could sever his carotid artery and he'd bleed out in minutes. The tone of his voice and the steely glare he drilled into Daryl were enough to convince him the man meant his threat. This man had surely been hired because he was perfectly willing and able to carry out his lethal potential.

Much as he hated to give in, he was no use to Kara if he was dead or bleeding from a sliced throat. *Damn it!*

Daryl released Holt and climbed unsteadily to his feet. A wave of nausea from the excruciating head pain hit him, and he bent to wretch in the grass. When he straightened, Holt had the knife at Kara's throat. And what about the gun Kara claimed Holt had? Where was it?

"Now," Holt rasped as his breath sawed heavily from him. "Get the spare out and change the tire. If you pull another stunt like that, the pretty thing loses an eye or an ear."

Daryl held up both hands, trying not to meet the terrified expression in Kara's green eyes. He might do something stupid like try again to beat the man to a pulp if he let her fear pierce his thin control on his anger.

And if Holt did have a gun somewhere on his person or stashed in the car, his fists were no match for a bullet. "Stand down. I'll change the tire. Take the knife away from her throat. I won't make any false moves."

Holt shot a quick glance to a car that whizzed past on the highway and dragged Kara behind their parked car. He pushed her down so that the vehicle blocked any passerby's view. Easing toward the passenger door, Holt retrieved something from the front seat, then sat with Kara against him. He'd traded the knife for a pistol, and Holt held the gun at a menacing angle under her chin. "Get busy, chum. And you better hope nobody stops to help, because I don't mind wasting anyone who interferes."

When sweat stung his eyes, Daryl wiped his brow with the hem of his shirt. Keeping a wary glare on Holt, he moved to the trunk of the borrowed car and rummaged about until he found the hidden compartment where the spare tire was stored. After hauling out the smaller and far less durable spare, he crouched beside the spot where Holt had hunkered down with Kara.

She met his gaze, and he gave her a weak smile and tiny nod of encouragement. She responded with the same. As he set to work, wrenching the lug nuts loose on the shredded tire, he monitored Kara. Her face grew redder and her eyes less focused as the minutes ticked by. "Can't you put her in the car with the air conditioning on? She's overheating."

"And you think I'm not?" Holt shot back. "Number one, sitting inside with the engine running in this heat will make the car overheat. Number two, climbing in while the car's on that jack could make it fall and cause more damage."

Daryl gritted his back teeth. "I'm well aware of both of your points, but her health is more important than the engine or the rims."

Holt's eyes narrowed. "Not to me. Hurry up and get done."

He studied Kara another moment, realizing she wasn't perspiring any more. His chest clenched realizing the serious risks of heatstroke. His best option was to finish with the tire change quickly, then convince Holt to put Kara inside the car with the AC as they continued to their destination.

Speaking of their destination...

He turned the donut spare in his hands and frowned. "How much farther are we going?"

Holt's only answer was an arched eyebrow that dripped disdain.

"I only ask because this thing—" he tapped the replacement tire "—is in terrible shape. It's starting to dry rot, and we aren't going to make it far on it."

Holt scowled darkly at him as if he suspected Daryl of pulling a trick and leaned in to examine the donut himself.

"Bloody hell!" Holt snarled.

"I can't see it holding up more than twenty or thirty miles," Daryl said. "We need to find a tire shop for a replacement—"

"So you can sneak the mechanic an SOS?" The older man chuckled dryly. "I'll deal with this my own way."

Daryl had rather hoped the questionable spare would offer a solution, an opportunity to flag someone or make a decisive move toward freeing Kara from this goon.

Instead, he heard Holt get on his cell phone. "I've been delayed. I have both her and the Black man she was seen with here with me, but we had a puncture and the emergency tire is no good."

Holt was meeting someone?

"On the byway between cities. Last mile post I saw was 177. I can't go to a shop without them causing a ruckus."

Daryl continued to work but kept his ears perked to the conversation Holt was having.

"I've got her friend changing the tire now. Maybe thirty miles at most." Silence, then, "Right. I'll get back with you."

Heart sinking, he tightened the bolts holding the spare in place. He cut a glance toward Holt as he finished.

The man strode closer. "Are you done?"

"Yeah."

Before Daryl could gather the scraps of the ruined tire he'd removed, Holt grabbed it and flung it into a ditch at the side of the road. Daryl glowered as he watched the old, damaged rubber bounce and roll away, polluting the otherwise pristine and scenic stretch of highway.

"That's not the best way to dispose of a tire in this country," Daryl groused.

Holt shrugged. "It's not the best way to dispose of a tire anywhere, but once you and the girl get back in the boot—"

Daryl stiffened at this news.

"There'll hardly be room for rubbish, as well, now, will there?" Holt stood and poked Kara with the gun, motioning for her to get up. "Let's go, O'Quinn."

Kara didn't move. She had her head leaning back against the side of the car. She'd shut her eyes, and her breathing was too fast and shallow.

"I said let's go!" Holt shoved her with his foot. "Get up. Get back in the boot."

Daryl took a long step toward Holt, his shoulders squared, his jaw rigid. "Do *not* touch her again." His volume was low, but his tone hummed with menace and resolve. "She's clearly overheated. She's not used to these temperatures, and she's likely suffering heatstroke."

Holt puffed his chest out and stepped close to Daryl. The man put his nose close to Daryl's in a manner clearly intended to intimidate. "I'm not used to these insufferable temperatures, either, but you don't see me wilting like a flower. Now get her up and in the boot!"

Daryl could have laughed at the man's attempt to cow him. He'd survived basic training at West Point and served under some of the toughest and meanest officers the US Army had to offer. He didn't flinch now, not when Kara's life was at risk. Only the man's weapon kept him from returning any further threats to Holt. What they needed was to cool tempers as much as their overheated bodies. "She needs the air conditioning and any water you have inside the car." He worked to keep his tone even and reasonable. "If you put her back in that trunk now, she could die."

"Seems to me that would solve all of my boss's problems. If she's gone, they can spin it any way they want. Ian's cleared to keep making them rich." Holt's smug grin hit Daryl like a fist to his gut. His hands balled at his sides and itched to pound the son of a—

With every bit of restraint he had, he checked the violent impulse. If he lit into Holt with his fists now, he felt sure he'd get shot in retaliation. He checked his fury and modulated the tone of his reply without losing any of the meaning. "Let me tell you what will happen on this side of the pond if she dies. You will be charged with a minimum of negligent manslaughter for allowing her to die. I will testify against you, and you will go to prison for a very long time."

Holt lifted his pistol again and touched it to Daryl's throat. "You can't testify if you're dead. Now get her into the boot. We're in a hurry."

Daryl blinked. "A hurry? Why? Who were you talking to? Where are we going?"

Holt pressed harder with the gun, and his voice dipped

to a growl. "You don't get to ask questions. You are unwanted baggage, mister, and at the soonest convenience you will be discarded."

He suspected the hateful man was just trying to manage and manipulate him—would Holt really risk shooting him here on the side of a public road?—but Holt's comments stuck a nerve. For too much of his life he'd felt like he might be a burden, an encumbrance. The Camerons had put on a good face, but adopting a Black kid when they were already in their fifties and already had four nearly grown kids had never been in their life plan.

Now, the suggestion that he'd be discarded at the soonest convenience cut close to the bone. Especially when he thought of his relationship with Kara. Once she was safe, she'd have no use for him. He didn't fit into her London film star lifestyle. Why would she want a nerdy American hanging around?

He took a slow breath, forcing down the twist of pain in his chest. His feelings of not fitting in, of not hitting the high mark, of never quite being what he was expected to be would have to wait.

Holt pointed at Kara. "Now get her in the boot and climb in with her, or I'll start slicing on her. That pretty face of hers will be first."

Daryl's pulse stuttered at the thought of Holt hurting Kara in any way. As much as he wanted to reengage Holt, wrap a chokehold around the man's neck or punch him so hard he'd not wake up until tomorrow, the saying about taking a knife to a gun fight rolled through his head. Or in this case, going unarmed to a gun fight.

His jaw clenched, he squatted next to Kara and patted her cheeks lightly. "Kara, honey, can you stand? We have to go."

Her cheeks were dry, a concerning sign that she'd stopped sweating. He glanced up at Holt. "Give me some water for her, and I'll move her to the trunk. But if you let her die, I swear I will see you hang for it."

With a scowl of disgust, Holt opened the passenger-side door and took out a nearly full bottle of water, still cool from being in the air-conditioned car. Daryl held the bottle to Kara's lips and helped her drink. "Just sips right now, or you'll throw it up."

He also worked her shirt up and off of her, giving her body a better chance to breathe. Using the shirt as a towel, he poured some of the bottled water onto the T-shirt and swabbed her face, her neck, her wrists.

Holt snatched the rest of the bottle back from him and grabbed Kara by the arm. "Enough of that. Get in the boot. Now. Hurry up!"

Daryl wedged himself between Holt and Kara. "Let go of her. I'll help her."

With a steely glare, Holt stepped back, but the way he wielded the pistol at his side left no question what he was prepared to do if either he or Kara resisted. A curse filtered through Daryl's mind along with a sense of futility and failure. He'd told Kara he was no bodyguard. He wasn't trained for this sort of situation. His instinct to keep her safe overrode any impulse to take a risk that could backfire. Someone trained for this work might try again to overpower Holt. If it were just his own life on the line, he might try that approach, but Daryl couldn't justify the risk that Holt would hurt Kara the way he'd threatened. Damn it, he hated being out of his league, knowing he was likely letting Kara down. But at this moment his best plan was just staying close to her, weighing the situation moment to moment.

Scooping her into his arms, Daryl helped Kara get into the trunk of the borrowed sedan. When they didn't show up as scheduled at Jessica's house, how long would it take before someone in his family alerted the police? That time was still a few hours away, he estimated. They weren't even due at Jessica's home for a couple more hours.

With a glower for Holt, Daryl joined Kara in the trunk and positioned himself so that his arm pillowed her head from the hard floor of the compartment. The hood thudded closed, and soon they were back on the road.

Daryl wasn't sure whether to hope the spare held or for it to blow out, as well. Neither scenario seemed promising as long as Holt could threaten them with that pistol.

"Kara, how are you holding up?" he asked as they rumbled down the road.

"I'm...okay," she said, sounding anything but.

"I've failed you. I was supposed to protect you from this very scenario, and I—"

"Don't." Her voice was stronger now. Almost angry.

"But I—"

"Don't blame...yourself." She was winded, her speech labored. Further signs of her heatstroke. "My fault. All of it."

He snorted his disagreement, using the back of his free arm to swipe the sweat from his eyes. "We'll agree to disagree on that point. Right now, conserve your energy. I'll work on a plan, some contingencies based on different circumstances we might land in."

"Such as?"

"If the spare blows. If it doesn't. If we make it to a new location where there might be a telephone." He sighed. "If I can find a way to get that damn gun away from him without either of us getting shot in the process."

She was silent, too silent.

"Kara? Stay with me."

"I—Daryl, I don't—was a mistake…get involved…you."

She believed it was a mistake to get involved with him? His heart crashed to his toes. Yet…hadn't he expected as much? Maybe so, but knowing she'd realized they had no future together stung.

He swallowed the sigh that swelled in his chest. If he were the gentleman his parents had raised him to be, he'd make it easier on her and step aside voluntarily. Take the initiative, so she could walk away with no regrets or compunction. He just wished doing the right thing didn't have to hurt so damn much.

"I understand," he said quietly, as his heart broke. For several minutes, neither spoke. He dug deep for the words to ease their parting, to assume the weight of the choice and free her from any burden. "I mean, I never saw us having anything long-term. We're so different. In so many ways. I have a life in California, roots in North Carolina. You have a career in London. After all, that's what this whole mess is about, right? Salvaging your reputation and protecting your career? Of course we'll both go back to our regular lives when this is over."

Kara made an unintelligible noise that he took for agreement.

"I don't want you to feel bad about any of it, either. I was never cut out to be an actress's boyfriend. You deserve someone with the kind of charisma that can hold up in the spotlight. I'm a geek, not an actor or sports star or business titan. I'd be…a drag on you. So… I freely step aside, and you need not give me a second thought."

Kara sighed, and he tried to decide if the tone of it was dejection or relief. They hit another pothole, jarring him back to their situation. Rather than dwell on their eventual parting, he needed to focus on getting them both out of this trunk and back to safety in one piece.

Several minutes later, the car slowed, turned, and the sound from the tires changed. They bumped over uneven terrain. Some sort of pothole-pocked driveway or parking lot? Finally, the vehicle stopped, and the engine quieted.

Daryl held his breath, and his heart hammered. He needed to be ready for anything.

Except he wasn't. The instant Holt opened the trunk, he swung something hard at Daryl's temple. And Daryl's vision grew black.

Chapter 18

Kara would have cried if she'd not been so terribly dehydrated already. As it was, she was barely conscious. But her heart still ached from the sting of Daryl's words and the shock of Holt's brutally knocking Daryl out again.

Holt dragged Daryl out first, apparently knowing she was in no shape to climb out of the boot, much less run away or fight back. When Holt returned from wherever he'd taken Daryl, he leaned in and seized her wrists.

Blinking against the bright sunlight, she tried to determine what Holt was doing to her arms. A thin tie of some sort. He used the soft strips to bind her wrists together before clasping her under her arms to haul her out of the vehicle. He carried her over his shoulder into the shade of a building of some sort. A stable or barn, she decided, smelling hay and petrol.

Holt put her down on the straw-littered ground next to Daryl, who was propped against a metal gate of some sort with his hands tied to a crossbar. His head lolled forward, and a new goose egg was forming on his brow.

"Daryl…" she rasped.

Holt used more of the binding—strips of cloth?—to tie her arms firmly to the gate next to Daryl's.

"No," she said weakly, too limp and dizzy to do anything to back up her protest. "I'm the one… Knight wants." She used all her breath to plead for Daryl. "Please, just…let Daryl go. This trouble…has nothing to do with him."

"And let him go straight to the bobbies?" Holt scoffed. "No chance."

"Then…what do you plan…to do with him?" Her heart was thumping so hard, so fast, she could barely hear herself think. Spots swam in her vision.

"That's still to be decided." Holt gave a firm tug on the bindings around her arms. Her bandaged hand already throbbed, and having her wrist tied so tightly didn't help. When she narrowed her eyes, bringing the ties into focus, she recognized the fabric as her shirt. The one Daryl had removed to help cool her down earlier. Holt had obviously torn it into strips to shackle them.

She should feel something, knowing she was sitting there in her bra, but couldn't muster the energy to be embarrassed or modest. But she was angry. Holt's treatment of Daryl continued to enrage her.

And her chest ached with grief over the heart-wrenching things Daryl had said just moments earlier. She wished she could blame her heatstroke for her understanding of his statements, but he'd been too clear. Twice. He didn't love her. He didn't want a relationship with her, didn't see a path forward for them. Wasn't interested in trying to make a future possible.

Had she really expected him to drop everything to build a relationship with her? She'd already caused far too much disruption, inserted herself in the life of a man who'd simply been a compassionate seatmate on a turbulent airline flight. She wouldn't make a scene. She'd let him go, if that was what he wanted. Even if her heart shattered in the process.

"There. That should hold you." Holt stood as he finished tightening the knots on the strips that pinched her wrists.

While she was still miserably hot, at least they were in the shade now. She even felt a small breeze stirring now and then.

"Now what?" she asked, raising a glare to Holt.

"Now we wait."

"Wait? For what?"

"You'll see." Holt stomped off and climbed into the sedan, where he cranked the engine again, presumably to run the air conditioning, since he didn't drive away.

Kara turned her attention to Daryl, her throat tightening with despair. "Daryl?" She tried to nudge him with her shoulder. "Wake up. Please!"

For several heartbreaking moments, he didn't respond, but she didn't stop bumping him with her shoulder or knee and calling to him, until she heard a soft groan. "Daryl!"

He winced and tugged against the arm restraints. Another low moan rolled from his throat before he lifted a bleary gaze to her. "What…happened?"

She didn't like the unfocused glaze to his eyes. But what did she expect after he'd been knocked on the head twice in the span of a couple hours? "Holt's tied us up in some kind of barn."

He squeezed his eyes closed, then blinked rapidly as he stared down at their bound hands. He mumbled something in a dark tone that sounded like, "Great."

"I'm sorry, Daryl. This—"

"Stop it," he said with a surprising sting and volume behind it.

Startled by his vehemence, she fell silent and studied him with her heart in her throat.

"Stop—" he paused to catch his breath "—apologizing for what that creep Holt is doing," Daryl said slowly. He angled his head up, his gaze firm but kind. "You've done nothing to deserve any of this. I hate hearing you blame yourself. Let's focus our energy on getting out of here, instead. Agreed?"

When moisture prickled her eyes, she fought the tears back. She hadn't forgotten the finality and grim tone of Daryl's last words before they arrived at the barn. He'd pushed her away with his words, begun the process of separating himself from her and her horrid, messy life. But for his sake, she gathered herself.

She let her tangled emotions—gratitude toward Daryl, anger toward Holt, fear and guilt for their situation—fuel her determination. She'd played strong women in her movies. She'd even believed herself to be one of those same capable and motivated women in real life. She'd only become this frightened and doubting kitten when she'd fled London and found herself alone and trying to hide. She'd believed she was protecting her family and closest friends by cutting off all communication so Ian, the Knights and scum-for-hire like Holt couldn't harass them.

But she wasn't alone. Daryl was by her side—for now. In fact, hadn't the whole large Cameron family stood ready to help, offering friendship and loyalty and protection?

A warmth she hadn't known in many years washed through her, and the tears that bloomed in her eyes now were not weakness, but joy. Love. She had to find a way to show Daryl that his family's efforts and his own sacrifice hadn't been in vain. Step one was to rally herself, to use her wits, to give as much back to Daryl as he'd unconditionally offered her. She sat taller, feeling buoyed by this new confidence and courage. "Agreed."

"Good. So first things first," Daryl said. "Where's Holt?"

She nodded her head toward the open barn door. "Staying cool in the jammer."

"Hmm?"

"The motor." She paused. "The *car*. I swear. How can two countries—" she paused, trying to swallow and wet her aching throat "—speak the same language so differently? He said we were waiting on something, but wouldn't tell me what."

Daryl furrowed his brow. "Well, language differences aside, not having Holt hovering gives us a chance to talk. To plan to figure out a way out of these bindings." He gave a nod toward their wrists. Then, slanting a tender look toward her, he said, "You seem to be doing better. Did he give you water?"

She smacked her dry mouth, yearning for even a sip of something wet. "No, but…this shade has helped. I'm still lightheaded, but I feel a good bit better than before."

His grunt sounded skeptical. Daryl turned his attention to tugging on the rolled strips of her T-shirt wrapped around his wrists. "We both need water and soon. You were dangerously overheated earlier."

"We *need* to get word out to someone about what's happened to us and where we are," she countered.

"Well, yeah. That, too." He let his lips buzz as he

exhaled his frustration. "But how? Telepathy? Smoke signals?"

Kara heard a loud squawking and flutter of wings. She glanced up to find a pair of sparrows flapping around the rafters before settling in. She chuffed a dry laugh. "Maybe we could tie a message to their legs like homing pigeons. Rescue sparrows. Here, birdies! Fly a message to Fenn please."

Their teasing fell silent as the crunch of tires on the gravel-littered dirt drive alerted them to a new arrival.

"Oh, please, let that be the farmer who owns this barn investigating the trespassers," Kara whispered.

Daryl leaned as far as his tied arms would allow, trying to see out the open barn door. "It's a dark SUV."

"Do farmers in this country drive SUVs?"

"Possibly, but unlikely. This one's a Cadillac Escalade." He glanced at her and added, "Pricey."

Her shoulders drooped. "Then who could it be?"

"He was on the phone with someone earlier. Maybe he—"

When she heard car doors slam and male voices, she cut him off with, "Shh."

Closing her eyes, she perked her ears to the low rumble of conversation outside. She only caught a word or two here and there. *Puncture. Delay. Inside.* A particular voice, not an overheard word, stopped her pulse.

"Oh, my God," she rasped.

"What?" Daryl whispered back, urgency in his tone.

She opened her eyes just as the men strolled into the barn from outside. Holt entered first, carrying an attaché case that he set on the ground by his feet. Then behind him…

Her ears hadn't tricked her. "Ian! What—why are you here?"

Beside her Daryl stiffened, sitting as erect as he could.

"I didn't want to come," Ian said, his tone and frown both petulant. "But Mr. Knight insisted. He thought I might have some sway with you. Be able to convince you to cooperate."

Seeing her opportunity, she beseeched him with her eyes. "Ian, you can stop all this. Tell them to let us go. How is kidnapping and violence the answer to anything?"

Ian's mouth tightened. "Don't put this on me. You brought all this on yourself." When she made a squawking noise of protest, he aimed a finger at her, and his eyes grew hard. "You betrayed me! You violated my trust and could have ruined my career!"

Her heart sank, and acid pooled in her stomach at the idea of relitigating the same argument they'd had a dozen times before they split. Before the team management got involved and threw her under the proverbial bus.

She shook her head and gritted her teeth. "I didn't. I was not the leak. And I only ever said anything to the team doctors to help you. I cared about you and wanted—"

"That's enough." A man in suit trousers and golf shirt, dampened by sweat stains, stepped forward and put a hand on Ian's shoulder. "Get back in the motor. If we need you, we'll call you back."

Ian's jaw tightened, a muscle jumping as he clenched his teeth. As he turned to leave, Kara called, "Ian, wait!"

He glanced back to glare at her. "What?"

"Daryl and I have heat exhaustion. We need water at the very least. And given your hit man is armed, we're not likely to try to run. Are the wrist restraints really necessary?"

Ian turned to Holt and Henry Knight, the football club owner. "You heard her. They need water. And I never signed off on kidnapping or holding her hostage."

Knight's returned gaze was nonplussed. "Because you don't have a say in how we extract her cooperation. I pay you to play football and win games, not meddle in my business affairs. Now, go back to the motor."

Ian cast another look to Kara before marching out of the barn. Her disappointment in Ian, his willingness to comply with the tyrannical team owner gnawed at her. Had Ian been this selfish and uncaring when they met? Had she been blinded to his true character by his good looks and flashy lifestyle? She hated to think she could have been caught up in such shallow qualities. By contrast, she'd seen Daryl's core goodness from the start. He radiated a kindness and integrity from his pores.

We're so different. In so many ways.

Her chest squeezed. Did that mean he didn't see the same kindness and character in her? Was she deluding herself about her own redeemable qualities? More than anything she wanted to be someone worthy of Daryl's love.

She had no time to analyze what this realization meant. Knight advanced on them and stood over her and Daryl with a menacing scowl. "I'm out of patience with you, Miss O'Quinn. Either we come to an agreement about your culpability in this smear campaign you've launched against Ian, or—"

"Against Ian?" Daryl said, his timbre churlish. "You've done everything you could to ruin Kara. Her reputation and career, her privacy, not to mention sending your goon after her to break her fingers and threaten her life!"

Kara sent Daryl a side glance, afraid of what would happen to him if he aggravated Knight.

"No one's talking to you, chum," Knight snarled.

"Break her fingers?"

Kara snapped her attention back to the door of the barn. Ian had returned, a bottle of water in each hand. Hope swelled in her chest that maybe some seed of decency or compassion was still alive in her ex's soul.

"I told you to wait in the motor!" Knight said, his volume rising.

"And Kara needs water. You can look at her and tell she's about to keel over. How is it helpful to us if she passes out?" Ian strode forward, elbowing past Knight as he knelt to extend a bottle of water toward her. She frowned and nodded her head to her bound hands.

Setting one bottle on the ground, he opened the other and held it to her mouth for her to drink. It took every morsel of her restraint not to gulp the whole thing, but as Daryl had warned her earlier, too much too fast would make her sick.

Ian shifted his gaze to her splinted and bandaged hand. "Did Holt do that to you?"

"He broke one of my fingers, yes. The cut on my palm was an accident. My fault."

Ian whipped an angry scowl toward Holt. "What the hell? Was physical force necessary? This whole business—" he angrily waved a hand toward her bound wrists "—is brutish. I won't stand by and let you hurt her like this. Untie her!"

Holt only folded his arms across his chest and returned

a level, impassive stare, but Kara's mood improved, if only a micron, to hear Ian defending her and disagreeing over her treatment.

When Ian glanced to Knight with an expectant gaze, the team owner lifted his chin and narrowed his eyes on Ian. "Again..." he intoned, his voice taut. "You are my employee." Knight reached in his chest pocket without breaking eye contact with Ian and pulled out a pack of cigarettes. He tapped one out and returned the pack to his pocket. "I will do as I see fit to protect my assets and investments. Now return to the motor before I have Holt *escort* you there."

Knight held the cigarette between his lips as he found his lighter in his trousers pocket and held the flame to the tip. Puffed. And returned the lighter to his pocket.

Kara tensed. Growing up on her family farm, though her father and brother had been smokers, her *da* had had a cardinal rule that no one smoked in the stables or barn. She could hear her father warning her brother, "Would you bring water into a salt mine?"

Ian continued to glower at Knight, then turned to help Kara take another sip of water. She hitched her head toward Daryl. "He needs water, too."

Ian and Daryl exchanged dark looks, as if two combatants sizing each other up. After a brief hesitation, Ian tipped the bottle up for Daryl to drink, allowing the liquid to slosh and dribble down Daryl's chin.

"Thank you," she whispered as Ian rose to his feet and turned to leave. She watched him stalk past Holt and Knight to the sunny exit from the barn. There, he paused and dug something out of his pocket, his back to the barn. The small bottle he extracted rattled as he pried off the top and shook some of the contents into his mouth before re-capping the bottle and jamming it back in his pocket.

Kara's spirits sank again. She knew what that bottle likely held, knew that Knight was likely helping supply Ian's habit in order to maintain further control over his star player.

"Now," Knight said, exhaling a stream of smoke. "Let's talk about how we resolve this standoff."

Her stomach churning, Kara shifted her attention to the team owner, her body quivering with rage and anxiety.

"Holt says you refused to sign the papers with our first offer. You could have taken responsibility for your actions and saved us all of this trouble. I'll be generous and give you one last chance to change your mind." Knight cut a look to Holt. "You have a pen, yes?"

Holt drew a pen from his breast pocket.

Kara glanced at Daryl's stony countenance, then back to Knight. "I won't negotiate anything until you release Daryl. Unharmed. He has nothing to do with our business and shouldn't pay for—"

"Then you shouldn't have involved him. He's an accessory to your crimes now," Knight said, his expression dark and unsympathetic.

"Kara," Daryl said quietly, "Don't worry about me. You do what you have to in order to save yourself. I'll be fine."

She frowned at him, but before she could reply to Daryl, Knight's surly voice cut in.

"I'll take that as a 'no' on the original terms, then." He waved his cigarette toward Holt. "Tear up the first offer, and we'll move on to plan B."

Holt took a document from the briefcase at his feet and made a show of shredding pages.

Kara's heart thumped harder. She tried to match Knight's stare without showing weakness. Could he see her trembling? She balled her good hand, noting her fingers were growing numb from the tight cloth strips around her wrists.

"Plan B?" she asked, trying to sound haughty and unmoved, but hearing the warble in her voice.

"Yes. I'm afraid our second offer is less favorable to you. But you come out with even less auspicious terms the longer you hold out, so…" He took a drag on his cig and blew out a smelly cloud. "Think carefully before you turn it down."

"Do you really think you can get away with blackmailing her?" Daryl asked, his body vibrating with hostility. "Anything she signs under duress can be overturned in an American court, and she's got family and friends who'll vouch for her side of—"

Holt's foot was swift and hard as it connected with Daryl's ribs. He wheezed hollowly, as if the kick knocked the wind from his lungs.

"Stop that! I swear to you, I'll not give you *anything* if you don't stop abusing Daryl!" she cried, fury finding a foothold and strengthening her voice.

Knight flicked his cigarette, and ashes dropped to the floor. "Reggie, read her the new terms and let's get out of this bloody heat."

Holt flicked open a different document from the briefcase and began reading a list of demands. Kara listened in horror as the terms were laid out. They were, indeed, grimmer than the first paper she'd refused to sign. Not only did they expect her to claim she'd lied about Ian's drug use and had falsely blamed him to cover her own addictions, Knight expected her to commit herself at a mental health hospital. Knight's contacts at the mental health facility would allow word to spread that she was emotionally unstable, violent and being held for her own safety and that of the public.

"The footage we've accessed of you leaving earlier this week for the hospital with bloody hands supports the violent and unstable angle. It would be a simple matter to convince the public you were deranged, addicted and dangerous."

"I do not need a mental health hospital! You do, if you think I'll cave to your demands!" she shouted.

He wagged a finger at her, his tone condescending as he said, "Uh-uh-uh. Be careful what you say. Option C involves the two of you found dead in a suicide pact… or—" he drew again on his cig, lifting his eyebrows as if he'd had a bright idea "—better yet a murder-suicide. Then your friend here can be known as a killer. Holt can arrange it for your deaths to appear the result any scenario we wish."

"You son of a bitch," Daryl growled, his arms tugging against their restraints.

Kara was mildly appreciative that the binding kept Daryl from assaulting Holt or Knight in anger. That sort of retaliation surely wouldn't end well for Daryl. Above all else, she had to get Daryl out of this horrid situation safely. He'd so selflessly helped her when—

Her breath stuck in her lungs. Daryl had been selfless. He'd had numerous opportunities to walk away but had stayed with her. She didn't let herself pretend his actions were based in a love for her. He'd already said they had no future together, that he saw them as too different.

But she could be like him in one vital way. She could return his sacrifice and kindness with her own. Her problem with Ian and his ruthless employer was hers to resolve. If that meant sacrificing her reputation, allowing lies to be broadcast to the world, ruining her acting career, so be it. The notion shot a deep ache to her bones. Her father, who'd valued his good name above all else, save his family and his God, would be devastated. When she'd left Ireland to build her career in London, her father's only request of her had been, "Remember who you are." An oft-repeated mantra throughout her youth meant to keep her honest, honorable and humble.

"Well?" Knight groused. "I won't stand around in this bloody heat all day waiting. Sign the papers or move on to option C?"

"Maybe, if—" The words choked her as the image of her heartbroken father flashed in her mind.

"Kara, no!" Daryl whispered, his brown eyes flashing with dismay. "You can't negotiate with terrorists."

"What choice do I have?" Her voice broke, and her eyes pleaded with him to understand. She was letting him down with her capitulation, as well. Damn it! Why couldn't she get this right? How did she negotiate this seemingly dead end labyrinth and get Daryl out unharmed?

Daryl jerked his head up, meeting Knight's malevolent stare boldly. "You want out of the heat? Go. Leave us here if you must. Clearly we're not going anywhere." He rattled the metal gate with his bound wrists to demonstrate their plight.

Kara angled a confused look toward Daryl but said nothing. She wasn't sure what Daryl had in mind, but she trusted him implicitly. Knight's wary, narrowed glower said the opposite.

The team owner was silent, his mouth twitching slightly as if mulling his options, looking for the trick he hadn't expected. Finally he took a handkerchief from his trouser pocket and wiped his sweaty brow, muttering a curse. "All right. Stay out here and swelter a while longer then. Maybe a few hours of baking in this infernal heat will help you see reason." He turned and stormed toward the barn door, hitching his head to signal Holt to follow. Just before stepping back out in the sun, he paused and barked over his shoulder. "Just know that when we return, the terms will not have changed, and the clock will have expired."

With that, he flicked his cigarette butt on the ground behind him and stalked away. Holt snatched the bottle of water Ian had set before Daryl and took it with him as he left. Kara wanted to weep for the man's pettiness. Not that they'd have been able to open and drink the water while their hands were tied, but...

She heard a brief exchange of words outside, motor doors, engines roaring to life and the rumble of tires as the men left. She closed her eyes and exhaled her relief that they had at least a brief reprieve. Daryl hadn't moved, hadn't said anything, and suddenly his silence clanged inside her like a warning. "Daryl? Wh-what are you thinking? Say something. Please. I... I only wanted to find a way out of this for you. If I have to sign their—"

"I'm thinking," he said, and he tipped his head back to look up and scan the barn's structure, their immediate surroundings. "We have to get out of here somehow before they come back."

She blinked, trying to make the mental shift to an escape plan, but her head felt heavy and it was hard to focus. The water Ian had given her revived her briefly, but she realized she was still suffering heat exhaustion. "How... how long do you think they'll be gone?"

Daryl grunted. "If they find an air-conditioned bar or hotel where they can hole up and be comfortable, I can't imagine they'll be in a hurry to come back out here."

"So what is your plan?" she asked, allowing her head to loll weakly back on the hard bars of the stall gate.

"Working on it. We'll never get these knots untied. We need something sharp, so we can try to saw through the cloth strips."

Kara turned her head, glancing from one side of the nearly empty barn to the other. All she found were piles of old hay, a crumpled crisps wrapper and oil stains where some manner of leaky, motorized farm equipment had clearly been parked. "Some kind of machinery has been in here. See that oil?" She sent Daryl a hopeful look. "Do you think the farmer will return with his tractor or whatnot shortly?"

"We can hope."

She drew a deep breath of frustration, the air soiled with the stink of Knight's ciggie smoke. "Hope..."

With no better idea in mind, Kara bent her head to the strips of her T-shirt that pinched her wrists and gnawed at them like a mouse. Her injured hand throbbed while her uninjured hand had gone numb.

Her injured hand. Kara stilled. Raised her head to stare at the bandages wrapped around her hand...and the aluminum splint taped to her broken finger. "Can we use my splint somehow? It doesn't have a sharp edge, but it is metal."

Daryl whipped his head around, his eyes brighter than she'd seen them in hours. "Certainly worth a shot." He leaned in and smacked a kiss on her brow. "Kara, you're a genius!"

A gooey sweetness flowed through her. She might not agree with his assessment, but having his approval, his admiration buoyed her spirits. "Help me get this tape off."

Within the restricted mobility of her secured hands, she began picking at the first aid tape that held her splint in place. Her hurried fingers fumbled and floundered.

"Kara."

She glanced up at Daryl. His expression was calm.

"Do they have the saying 'Haste makes waste' in the UK or Ireland?" His fingers flexed to brush against hers. "Take a breath. Take your time."

She inhaled as he'd instructed and was disconcerted when the breath seemed even more tainted by Knight's cigarette smoke than before. She coughed, a tickle irritating her parched throat.

With slow and intentional movements, she picked at the tape around her fingers until a corner lifted and she could start pulling the adhesive.

With constrained, awkward movements, Daryl helped her unwind the tape and free the aluminum splint. "If we bend it and try to break it here—" he pointed to one of the evenly spaced ventilation holes at the centerline of the splint "—perhaps we can create a sort of serrated effect."

Holding the aluminum brace between his restricted hands, Daryl placed his thumbs diagonally and parallel to each other. He began folding the aluminum, working it back and forth, creating a weakened fold line.

Kara tried to be patient, knowing that if the splint broke in the wrong place or lost its structural integrity, their best plan would be foiled. As she waited through Daryl's careful flexing of the splint, slowly back and forth, she shifted her attention toward the barn door. The glance had only been a restless move, a subconscious check that their captors weren't returning, but she realized how hazy the space by the door seemed and paused.

A fog seemed to pollute the area near the barn door, and with her heart thumping anxiously, she searched for the source of the haze. From a spot in the middle of the hay-strewn floor, a small thread of smoke spiraled up and dispersed, clouding the air.

She gasped, and dread pooled in her. "Daryl, look! The cigarette butt Knight threw down as he left. It's causing the hay to smolder. It could fully ignite any time. A breeze could fan it or—"

Her throat closed as she took in the old wooden barn, the straw, the oil stains. If the smoldering cigarette caused the hay to flame up, the barn would burn like the kindling it was. She faced him, alarm bells clanging in her head.

He blinked, refocusing his eyes from the close-up work he'd been doing to the growing stream of smoke billowing up not twenty feet from them. His Adam's apple bobbed as he swallowed, and his eyes filled with the same concern and urgency that rang discordantly inside her. He took a breath, coughed, repeated quietly, as if to himself, "Haste makes waste."

Yet it seemed to her he was flexing the aluminum strip with more vigor now. When the metal finally gave, leaving them with two angled strips of soft metal with ragged edges, he audibly sighed.

He passed one piece to her, and she took it in her right hand. Following his lead, she slipped the homemade knife under the strips of cloth and began sawing. Her hand shook as adrenaline poured through her. She tried to strike a delicate balance between hard enough to cut through the cotton fabric without being so vigorous as to warp her tool into uselessness. At one point, her numb fingers fumbled and dropped the makeshift blade, and as small cry of despair and frustration slipped from her.

Daryl paused in his ministrations, hacking at his own bindings. "It's all right. We can do this."

She glanced up at him, grateful for the encouraging smile that tugged his cheek. His eyes reflected his own worry, his fatigue, his sense of urgency, yet beyond all this, his expression clearly sought to give her strength.

"Here. Take mine. I think I can reach yours." Daryl passed his blade to her, and she resumed sawing. He contorted his body to inch his bound hands along the gate and stretch his fingers toward the fallen metal strip. After a couple minutes of fumbling, he managed to nudge the aluminum piece close enough to pinch between two fingertips and wiggle into his grip.

He exhaled loudly, clearly chuffed with himself. "Ta-da!"

Despite their dire circumstances, Kara couldn't help a wry chuckle for his attempt at levity. She knew he was trying to keep her calm, using what little was available to him to put her needs first, to take care of her, to support her. And she loved him for it.

Love? Her pulse stumbled over the concept, but she didn't have the energy or time now to consider her feelings.

Her muted laugh morphed into a cough. The cloud of smoke continued to thicken and sting Kara's eyes. She paused only long enough to squeeze her eyes closed against the bite of stringent grit. Few tears formed thanks to her dehydration, and her eyelids scratched like sandpaper. Straightening her shoulders, she set to work again. Finally, a few fibers of the shirt frayed. Then more.

Daryl seemed to be making progress, as well. She glanced at the spot he sawed and watched a whole band of fabric pop and the ends drop loose.

She gave a gleeful yip. "You did it!"

"It's a start," he said, his head still lowered as he continued.

Encouraged by his success, Kara returned to her tedious, limited cutting motions. When she sliced through a strip and it fell away, she thought she might cry for joy. If she'd had any tears available...

But her happiness was short-lived. When she cut a side glance toward the smoldering hay, monitoring that situation, she tensed. A few blades of hay had ignited, and a dancing flame consumed them.

"Daryl! Fire!"

They were out of lead time. In a precious few moments, the whole barn would be ablaze.

Chapter 19

Daryl didn't waste time with swear words, although they were totally called for at the moment. Instead, he shifted fully into emergency mode. He'd learned a bit about channeling his thoughts and energy into performing under pressure while at West Point. He'd even had to manage crises in the years following as he helped navigate touchy IT situations and prevent data breaches for the Army.

Right now, the goal was simple if not easy. Get free of the wrist restraints and get himself and Kara out of that burning barn. He continued sawing on the thin cotton fabric. Slow and steady was still the best game plan, even if adrenaline and the creep of flames was pressuring him to panic. Another strand of the taut shirt strips fell away from his wrist, and he moved to the next one. He spared a glance first to Kara, to check her progress, then to the fire.

Kara, though clearly frightened, her breathing rapid and her face pinched, was doing admirably using one hand to slice at the fraying fabric bands that bound her.

Meanwhile, the flames moved like falling dominoes, consuming one strand of hay until it reached another. The fire snaked in all directions, growing hotter, spreading faster, consuming everything in its path. Sparks filled the air and ignited new piles of hay. Smoke billowed and stung his eyes. The conflagration was inching closer, while also heading toward the far wall. More concerning, their path to the open barn door would soon be completely blocked by fire.

Daryl used his feet to shove what hay littered the floor around them as far away as possible. Seeing his efforts, Kara did likewise, clearing a space in each direction. A minor effort he hoped would create even a small fire break around them.

Putting his head down, Daryl sent up a silent prayer as he cut into the next strip of cloth. When the last carved strip fell away, he didn't hesitate to move his efforts to helping Kara.

Another check on the inferno's progress sent fresh waves of alarm through him. The oil stains had caught fire, flashing hot and shooting larger flames dancing across the barn floor. More concerning were the flames crawling up the support posts and walls of dry wood surrounding them. The barn was going up like a tinderbox.

The heat was intense, and the ever-thicker smoke made it hard to breathe. Kara whimpered and shot him a look that spoke of her fear. Finally, he cut her last strip loose, and she surged closer to him.

He wrapped his arms around her and surveyed the roaring fire. The door, the most obvious exit, was blocked by burning beams and flaming bales of hay that had already fallen from a loft overhead. But fire had spread to their left, their right, and was inching behind them. Not that there was a door behind them.

"We're trapped!" Kara cried, reaching the same conclusion he had. "It's all around us!"

Cleared floor or not, the danger was getting closer. Daryl tipped his head back, surveying the loft. And had an inspiration. "Up."

"What?" Kara asked over the crackle of the fire.

"We'll go up. Look! The loft on this side isn't involved yet. The pattern of sunlight through the smoke indicates there's a window or some other opening up there."

She bent her neck to gaze above them. "How do we…" She coughed and used her arm to cover her mouth and nose. "…get up there?"

Daryl whipped off his shirt and tore it at a side seam. He handed half to her. "Cover your face with this. It's not much, but it will help."

He tied the torn shirt around his head like a bandit, creating a poor excuse for a mask. It would have to do. As he bent his head back to study his options for climbing to the loft overhead, his temples pounded and his head swam. The two earlier hard blows to the head were not making it easier to concentrate. While he might have a concussion, he couldn't let that stop him from doing everything to get them out of this mess alive. He gritted his teeth against the pain and started climbing. "Follow me."

He held the nearest support post and used the bars of the gate they'd been tied to as ladder rungs. Even when he stood on the top bar of the gate, steadying himself with the center post, he was a couple feet shy of reaching the edge of the hayloft. He wobbled as a dizzy spell washed through him, and he clutched the weight-bearing post more firmly.

"Daryl! Be careful!" Kara cried. "If you can't get up that way, don't hurt yourself by—"

He spared a glance toward her, flashing a smile to encourage her. "I haven't given up. Don't you quit on me."

He sized up the old wooden post he had his arm wrapped around. Not exactly the steel poles or nylon ropes he'd climbed in basic training, but...he could make it work. He hoped.

He rubbed the sweat from his palms onto his jeans, wishing he were wearing something more suited to these gymnastics, and began his ascent. The rough wood, which had dried and cracked over the years, scraped his hands. Splinters and bent nail heads bit his skin as he shimmied up the last few feet to the edge of the loft.

As he swung a leg up to wiggle onto the floor of the loft, a loud *boom* rattled through the barn.

Kara yelped. Daryl jolted, slipped. He clutched the jagged floorboards of the loft, and his foot scrabbled again to gain purchase. Arms and legs shaking from heat exhaustion and adrenaline, he heaved himself up and rolled onto his back. Daryl allowed himself only two seconds to catch his breath before turning on his belly to lean over the edge of the loft. "What was that?"

Before Kara could answer, another *boom* and ball of fire shook the burning barn. He looked toward the source of the sound, and his gut swooped. Stored fuel cans and various bottles of what could be anything from insecticide to spray paint—all obviously flammable—were exploding and feeding the fire. And releasing toxic fumes. "Hurry, Kara! Climb up like I did."

She stared at him over the top of her shirt-mask, her eyes wide and terrified. She held up her injured hand, no longer wrapped or protected, and seemed to be considering how to manage the climb with the injury. Without her saying so, he could tell she was dubious of whether, in her dehydrated state, she had the strength to do more than stand. As she hesitated, she was gripped by a wracking cough.

"Sweetheart, you have to try," he said.

She blinked rapidly as if against the sting of smoke and nodded. "I know. I—"

"If you can get to the top of the gate—" he had to stop and choke down a bout of coughing "—holding on to the post, I'll reach down and pull you up. Okay?"

He watched her climb, struggling weakly one-handed with every rung of the gate-ladder. He could see her arms shaking as she pulled herself up and clung to the post for support. His heart swelled for her courage, her determination as she battled the debilitating effects of heatstroke and fear.

"That's it. You've got it," he said over and again, maintaining a litany of encouragement as she tottered and strained. He cast an eye to the encroaching flames, and a thread of anxiety curled through him. She had to go faster.

He stretched as far as he could, extending his arms, his hands ready to grab hers. "Can you reach me? Give me your good hand."

"But that's the one I'm holding on with!" she said.

"Sweetie, we're out of time. The fire—" he stopped to cough.

She glanced behind her at the chaotic flames, and a note of terror cracked from her throat. Shifting her weight, she wrapped the arm of her injured hand around the splintered post and held her good hand up to him. He seized her wrist, and she clasped his. He tugged her up a bit, her toes walking up the post as she released her grip. The first time he grabbed for her other arm, he missed, but he managed to snag her wrist the second time, even as he hoisted her with all his strength.

When she was finally high enough to swing a leg up, he released her injured arm to hook his hand around her thigh. He scrunched backward, then rolled to his back, hauling her with him. They tumbled together onto the wood plank floor of the loft and panted. Gasped. Coughed.

Heat rose in searing waves through cracks in the floor of the loft as the fire moved under them and licked at the walls. He turned toward the source of the sunlight he'd seen below and found a few planks of the barn wall had rotted or been eaten by termites and fallen. The broken boards had left a narrow hole in the outside wall.

Saving his breath, he motioned with his arm for Kara to come with him to the gap and stand aside as he attempted to make the opening large enough for two adults to climb through. With a step back, he lifted his foot and kicked at the wood. The rotting planks near the hole cracked easily. A couple more kicks knocked the neighboring wood away. He eased forward, testing the strength of the loft floor.

He could feel the heat of the fire below on his feet, even through his shoes. Edging closer to the opening, he peered through the clouds of smoke to estimate the distance to the ground below and look for hazards they'd need to avoid.

"Do you—" Kara coughed "—mean for us to jump?" Above the scrap of shirt over her mouth and nose, her eyes were wide, bright and turning red from the smoke.

"Better than staying in here to cook." He braced his legs as he leaned his head out the hole. It wasn't *too* far down—

the same eight to ten feet they'd just climbed up inside—and the ground was clear of debris or farm equipment.

"What if—"

Whatever counter she was prepared to make was lost in the crack and crash as a large section of roof on the other side of the barn caved in. An urgency flared inside him. "No time to debate, Kara. Come on!"

He waved her forward, and she edged up to him.

"Look, every instinct…is gonna want to brace yourself…when you land." He cleared his throat and took the deepest breath he could. "But don't. That's how… injuries happen." His voice sounded more strangled and hoarse every time he spoke. "Land on your feet—" cough "—not your butt or back. Soft knees, then flop to the side—" cough "—and roll. Arms by your head—" he demonstrated with his arms bent by each ear "—to protect your noggin. Don't brace your arms!" He gripped her shoulder and drew her closer to the open gap. "Go!"

She grabbed his arm with her good hand and stood on her toes to kiss him soundly on the lips. Then with a nod, she turned, and without hesitating, Kara leaped.

The impact as she landed rattled through her bones. Feet, flop, roll. Arms up. She lay motionless for a second or two, assessing. She'd done as he said. The landing hadn't felt good, but—her limbs appeared to be intact.

She tugged down the makeshift mask of Daryl's shirt and gasped for air. When Daryl dropped beside her, he only hesitated a few seconds before scrambling back to his feet. He caught her under her arm, wheezing, "Get away…from the building. Could fall…"

He didn't have to tell her twice. The heat from the fire

was still unbearable. Mustering what little adrenaline-fueled strength she had, Kara clambered to her feet. She followed as Daryl headed across the weedy barnyard toward a pair of scraggly pine trees. Part of an old real estate sign leaned against the trunk of one pine, and some knotted barbed wire had been abandoned in the scrub brush beneath the other. Rotting wood planks had been piled between the trees, and a screen of kudzu vines grew thickly over the rubbish and up the pine trunks.

Daryl crumpled at the base of the closest pine tree, flopping on his back and gasping for air. A moment later, he rolled to his hands and knees to facilitate the coughs that racked him. "Are you...all right?"

Kara's injured hand hurt. She could barely get a breath. Her skin stung as if burned by the searing heat. She was exhausted from dehydration, and she had a splitting headache. But she was alive. They'd gotten free of Holt's restraints.

And Daryl was with her. Whole. Breathing. And that was all she needed in that moment.

"I'm...bloody great," she said, meaning it. Kara chuckled hoarsely then coughed. "Really wonderful."

Daryl flashed a grin and coughed hard. "Good."

They'd barely gathered their composure and begun taking stock of their situation when, across the wide pasture behind the barn, a dark vehicle approached on the motorway. A sinking feeling weighted her stomach as she aimed a trembling finger toward the road. "They're coming back."

Daryl groaned and cast a quick glance around. "Behind the trees. Stay low. The kudzu should hide us."

Alternately coughing and sucking in deep lungfuls of

clean air, Kara staggered another several meters away from the inferno, around to the far side of the pines and collapsed. Daryl dropped beside her, sputtering and spitting out the soot singed phlegm that choked him. Her eyes watered slightly, as much from relief as smoke irritation. When she raised her fists to rub her eyes, Daryl caught her arm above her wrists.

"I know your eyes are gritty," he said, his voice rasping. He coughed again before wheezing another breath. "But resist the urge to rub. Until you can flush them with water, you'll…just make the grit scratch deeper. It'll hurt even more. Blink. Force as many tears as you can."

So she blinked. And coughed. And tried to discreetly spit out the ash and phlegm that strangled her. Her exposed skin stung like she had a terrible sunburn. She supposed that she did have essentially that. Mild burns from the intense heat of the fire. One Irish lass, lightly toasted.

"I know it probably goes without saying," Daryl rasped, "but…when they get here, try…to stay quiet. Hold your…breath if you have to. Don't cough."

Cradling her injured hand against her chest, she nodded her agreement and understanding. A paroxysm seized her chest again, and she nearly choked as she coughed and gagged.

The vehicle kicked up dust as they sped to the barnyard.

From behind the screen of kudzu, Kara and Daryl huddled low and peered through tiny gaps in the leafy greenery to watch.

The vehicle hadn't come to a full stop before Ian lurched from the back door of the SUV. He stumbled as he charged toward the burning barn. "Kara!"

Kara caught her breath, hearing the real terror and dismay in Ian's cry.

Did he still have real feelings for her after all?

"No! Karaaa!" Ian fell to his knees and covered his face with his hands.

Holt climbed out and stared at the burning farm building with narrowed eyes and one hand shielding his gaze from the sun. After shaking his head, he marched up behind Ian and shoved him with his toe. "Get up. There's nothing we can do for her now. We have to go."

"Call 999 or…whatever they use here in the States!" Ian said. "There may be a chance to get her out!"

"Are you daft?" Holt pointed at the blaze. "No one could survive *that*." He flailed a hand toward the all-encompassing blaze. "She's gone, and now *we* have to be gone before someone calls it in and the coppers show up."

Ian wailed some more and shouted a few colorful obscenities. Rounding on Holt, he screamed, "Look what you've done! I told you I was not on board with violence, and look what you've done!"

"We didn't do this. Now did we? We were far from here when this fire started. Besides, this works to our advantage. She's gone and won't be a hindrance to your career any further."

Holt's cold assessment of the possibility that Kara had burned to death in the fire struck her with a stupefying force. She managed a grunt of disgust, but Daryl touched a finger to her lips to quiet her.

For his part, Ian recoiled, his face contorting as he gaped at Holt, but when the henchman yanked on Ian's arm, her ex stumbled to his feet.

"We have to go now," Holt said grimly, brooking no

argument as he dragged Ian toward the waiting vehicles. "We can't be anywhere near here when the firemen and bobbies come."

Ian held his face as he staggered behind Holt and slumped into the back of the SUV. The vehicle departed almost as quickly as it arrived.

"You know what this means?" Daryl said quietly, covering another cough.

She glanced at Daryl. "That maybe my ex has a heart after all, but Holt doesn't?"

He flinched, his brow furrowing briefly. But what had she said that displeased him? Did he not agree that Holt's actions and attitude were heartless? Or was it upsetting to him to think that Ian wasn't as cold as she'd believed?

"I meant…" He paused to clear his throat. "That if Holt and his boss believe you are dead, they won't be looking for you. You're safe."

She pondered that truth for a moment, her spirits rising. They seemed to realize the next logical part of that assumption at the same time. "But only until—"

"Until you're seen in public, and word spreads you are alive and where you are again," he finished for her.

It wasn't over, after all.

Chapter 20

"Damn." Daryl's gut tightened as he completed the thought. He rubbed a hand down his face then winced and shook out his fingers.

"Burns?" she asked and leaned in to study his palms.

"Well, they're tender, yeah, but I have splinters, too. Nothing life-threatening." He stood and stretched his aching muscles. "At least we have a short reprieve to get somewhere safe. Surely someone will see the smoke and call the fire department eventually. We'll just wait here and hope the rescue team can be trusted not to talk."

She nodded. "Surely if we tell the law enforcement that shows up what we've been through and have them looking for Holt and Mr. Knight—"

"Mr. Knight?" Daryl cocked his head and arched an eyebrow. His skin stung and moving hurt, but they were alive so he wouldn't complain. "The owner's name is Knight? Like the team?"

She nodded. "When he bought the team, he gave the organization his name."

"Vanity or just extremely uncreative?" Daryl asked.

Kara scoffed, which started another round of coughing. "Both, I'd say."

She pressed her good hand to her chest as she wheezed in a breath.

Moving closer to her, he carefully took her injured hand in his. "How does it feel?"

"Sore. But considering we used my splint to get free, I count it a blessing in disguise."

"That it is." With the gentlest of fingers, he tucked wisps of her hair behind her ear. Following the direction of her gaze, he turned back to watch the rest of the barn's roof as it collapsed in a profusion of flying embers and billowing smoke.

Emergency vehicles didn't show up for another ten minutes. By then, the barn was rubble and ash. Daryl revealed his presence to the rescue team, signaling for Kara to stay hidden until he explained the situation to whomever was in charge. From behind the same veil of kudzu they'd hidden behind earlier, she watched Daryl talk to the bobby. The officer stood with his hands on his hips, his head canted slightly as he listened to Daryl. The man's face was skeptical. Or was he squinting because he didn't have sunglasses in this bright, unrelenting sun?

Kara smacked her dry lips, imagining the sweet water they would have in just a little while. Surely the rescue teams would have something they could drink. It didn't even have to be cold, if it was just wet.

Finally, Daryl turned back toward her hiding place and led the officer across the dusty yard to her.

The bobby stood over her, such that his shadow fell over her, and she could look up without being blinded by the sun. However, backlit this way, she could tell little about the man's expression. "Ma'am, this fella says you two have had a bit of trouble today."

She chortled a wry laugh then fell into a fit of coughing. "He called it 'a bit of trouble'?"

"Well, no. But I'd like to hear your side of things. Privately."

She nodded and continued to bark like a seal. Daryl moved to sit beside her, resting a hand lightly on her back.

"But first let's get you seen by the EMT. Okay?" The officer turned and gave a loud shrill whistle that startled Kara and sent a shimmy down her already frayed nerves.

"Do you have…any water?" she asked.

The man gave his head a tight jerk. "In my squad car. Can you walk over to the ambulance? It'll be a lot cooler in their air conditioning."

Kara tried to stand and found that without adrenaline fueling her, her knees buckled and her muscles felt flaccid. Daryl positioned himself under one arm, and the officer supported her other side as they crossed to the arriving ambulance.

Over the course of the next couple of hours, Kara and Daryl were transported to the closest hospital, where they received IVs to rehydrate, oxygen for their struggling lungs and both painkillers and a cooling balm for their burns. Kara's finger was re-splinted and her cut hand treated and wrapped in fresh bandages.

Once they'd received adequate medical attention, they gave separate statements to deputies from the sheriff's department. Kara was promised no one from the sheriff's department would identify her when speaking to the media about the fire. Daryl assured her an American law called HIPAA would protect her privacy in the hospital where they were both admitted for continued oxygen therapy and observation. Daryl was able to borrow a phone to call Fenn and explain what had happened and where they were.

"Thank heavens! When Jessica said you hadn't arrived, and neither of you answered your phones, I was frantic!"

Fenn promised to share the news they were safe with the rest of the family phone tree, and sure enough, members of the Cameron family began arriving at the rural hospital by dinnertime.

Later that evening, a sheriff's deputy arrived, bringing news that the car they'd borrowed from Jessica had been found abandoned on the roadside where the spare had apparently given out. Kara's backpack had been on the back seat, and both her phone and Daryl's were still inside the pack.

"Well, wonders never cease," Daryl's oldest sister, Emma, said.

Emma and Lexi had arrived with Fenn in the first group of Camerons to descend on the hospital. Daryl's parents were in their son's room with him, and Lexi floated back and forth between rooms delivering messages, cafeteria coffee and vending machine snacks as needed.

While most of the family rented rooms at a nearby hotel, Fenn slept on the guest cot in Kara's hospital room overnight. Daryl's mother did the same for her son, despite his arguments to the contrary.

Exhaustion and a painkiller dragged Kara into a deep sleep, but the next morning she still felt drained. Emotionally and physically.

We're not in love.

We're too different.

Of course we'll both go back to our regular lives when this is over.

Now that the crisis had passed, Daryl's words returned to haunt her. She was ruminating on his harsh assessment when Fenn's voice broke into her morose musing.

"Mind if I put the news on? I'm curious what if anything is being said about the barn fire. The media was out in force in the hospital lobby looking for information about the fire victims, and while I don't think anyone on the medical team leaked info about you, you never know what might get whispered to a reporter by janitorial or cafeteria staff."

Kara squeezed the sheet with her good hand, dreading the thought of her anonymity being busted again. She gave a nod, and Fenn turned on the television with the sound muted.

"How is Daryl this morning? Have you checked on him?" Kara asked, her voice still raspy. Her doctor had told her it would take several days for her throat to heal, and the best thing she could do for it was rest her voice.

"I haven't heard, but I'll poke my head in his room now if you want," Fenn said.

Kara bobbed her head. "Please. And tell him if I can get all these tubes to cooperate—" she motioned to the web of IV lines, monitor wires and oxygen cannula tubing she was connected to "—I'll come see him later today."

"Will do." Fenn set the television remote on the bed within Kara's reach. "Here. Your TV. You're in charge."

Kara picked up the remote and hugged it, giving Fenn a playfully shocked look. "Me? Control of the remote? I thought just men got that power."

Fenn laughed and gave her a wink. "Not in our family. Equal remote rights for all!"

Kara found herself grinning as Fenn stepped out of the room. On the heels of the moment of amusement came a bittersweet pang. *Our family.*

Kara was hit with a longing to see her own family. She'd kept her distance and silence with them for good reasons, but those reasons were chafing more every day. Her resentment toward Ian and his employers sat like acid in her belly.

And what of the Cameron family, who'd been turned upside down and inconvenienced by her ordeal? She owed it to them to get out of their hair and let them return to their quiet, ordered lives. She would miss them. Especially Fenn, who'd become a close friend. And, of course, Daryl.

Her heart ached terribly when she thought of walking away from Daryl, but he had been clear about his feelings…or lack thereof. His bluntness told her he might have sensed her growing feelings for him and wanted a clean cut to spare her heartache. That sort of kindness and consideration was exactly the Daryl she'd come to know. He would—

Kara blinked, jolted out of her dreary musings when she realized what was on the television screen. A smoldering barn. The text scroll at the bottom read, "Foul play suspected in Moore County fire."

She grabbed the remote again and turned the volume up. The reporter's voiceover was saying, "Two unidentified individuals were injured in the fire and have been interviewed by the police. No charges have been filed, but contacts within the sheriff's office report authorities are looking for three men in association with the blaze. No further details have been released."

The screenshot returned to the news studio, and a sharply dressed man at the news desk announced, "In other local news, the apple festival—"

Kara muted the sound but stared blankly at the screen as the man continued his report. She mentally replayed what she'd just learned, thankful that, for now, she and Daryl were still anonymous. If she could—

The image on the screen changed again, and the new picture immediately snagged her attention. *Ian.*

The caption stole her breath. *English soccer star found dead in North Carolina hotel room.*

Chapter 21

Hand shaking, she unmuted the report. The roar of blood in her ears made it hard to hear. The dump of adrenaline made it hard to focus. But she caught the critical words as the report played out. *Apparent drug overdose. Found this morning by hotel housekeeping. Team management unavailable for comment.*

Fenn rushed into the room and cast a glance at the television and then to Kara. "Oh, honey. I'm so sorry!" Fenn hurried to her bedside and took her hand. "Daryl was watching the same station in his room, and I came as soon as I—" She sighed and shook her head. "Can I... do anything?"

Kara's heart was thumping wildly. She searched for her voice but couldn't speak. A cold settled into her bones, and she shivered.

"Kara!"

Hearing Daryl's voice, she shifted her gaze to the door. He wore a hospital gown as she did, and he pushed an IV pole with tubes trailing. Whatever oxygen he'd been receiving or monitors he'd been attached to, he'd apparently detached for himself. He crossed the floor, and Fenn moved so he could sit on the edge of Kara's bed and take her hand. "I just saw...about Ian. I—I'm sorry. I—"

She forced a few drops of spit down her throat and rasped, "I tried...to tell them. They...wouldn't listen. Wouldn't get him help..." Then another thought occurred to her and nausea swamped her. "This...is my fault!"

"What?" Fenn cried sharply. "No way!"

Daryl shook his head. "No."

"He saw the barn...yesterday. He thought we died. If he was upset over... If he felt guilty or grieved...did he do it on purpose? Or...was he reckless because he was hurting?" All the possibilities tumbled in her brain, jumbled, confusing, overwhelming. When her chest tightened, making it hard to breathe, she knew this airlessness had nothing to do with the smoke damage to her lungs and everything to do with the numbing shock of Ian's death.

Ian. Dead. Overdose.

Her heart thundered. Her head spun. The fist on her lungs squeezed harder, and she gasped for air.

"Kara? Are you okay?" Fenn's voice sounded as if it came from the bottom of a well.

A monitor beeped. Daryl squeezed her hand. "Kara?"

"I'll get the nurse," Fenn said, fleeing the room.

Can't. Breathe.

Ian. Dead. Her fault.

She gasped. Shook her head. Croaked, "Tried...to... warn...them."

Daryl grasped her arms and shook her gently. "Kara, look at me," he said. The gravelly sound of his voice penetrated the fog. "I think you're having a panic attack. Look at me. Focus on me. Count to ten. Then focus on what you smell. Breakfast is coming. I smell coffee. Then what you hear. My voice."

A nurse bustled in, followed by Fenn, who was saying, "She had some shocking news and started gasping for breath. When her heart rate monitor went off, well..."

Daryl moved out of the way for the nurse, asking, "Panic attack?"

"Likely," the nurse replied as she moved in closer. "Ms. O'Quinn, can you hear me?"

Kara nodded. She closed her eyes and tried to calm her mind. Her chest loosened, and she dragged in a shallow breath.

"That's it, honey," the nurse said. "Nice and slow. You're safe. Slow, deep breath."

When Kara's cell phone rang, her pulse spiked again. She reached for it, but Fenn got to it first. "Ignore it. You don't have to talk to anyone."

"Who?" she rasped, pointing to the phone.

Fenn scowled but showed her the screen. Kara didn't recognize the number and waved the phone away.

The nurse tapped a few things on the monitor screen, and the warning beep quieted. "There. Now we can hear ourselves think, huh?" She tipped her head and studied Kara's face. "Better now? Can I get you anything? Some juice? Or water? Fruit juice will probably sting for a while. Maybe a Popsicle?"

"Like when I had my tonsils out," Fenn said with a smile that didn't hide the worry in her eyes.

Kara's attention shifted back to Daryl, who was being silent and watchful. His brow was creased with a deep V, and his brown eyes shone with compassion. The panic eased another degree, and she drew in a stuttering gulp of oxygen. Her heart swelled.

Her rock. Her comforter. Her protector.

Even as those thoughts tripped through her, a prick of

uneasiness dogged her. Their relationship had been so one-sided. He was only here today, in this mess, because of her longing for his steadying presence and her craving for companionship ever since arriving in the States. The needling guilt poked harder, and her shoulders drooped.

Daryl sat down on the edge of her bed and covered her hand with his. His gaze pierced hers as he said firmly, "Not your fault."

She opened her mouth to reply, and with a lift of his eyebrows, he repeated, "Not your fault. None of this."

He seemed to have read her mind again. Or was her face that transparent? A director had once complimented her on how well she evoked emotion and conveyed meaning with her facial cues and subtle body language. Maybe it was second nature. Or a tell she should work to better control.

The nurse angled the monitor screen and gave a satisfied hum. "Your heart rate is coming down. That's good. You feeling better now? Did you decide you wanted that Popsicle?"

She gave her head a shake, and, maintaining eye contact with Daryl, she said, "I have all I need."

His cheek twitched with the hint of a grin, telling her he caught her meaning.

With a reminder for Kara to buzz her on the call button if she needed anything, the nurse headed out, pausing long enough to direct a glance to Daryl and say, "Don't stay too long. You still need your rest and oxygen, Mr. Cameron. And the doctor will be making rounds soon."

"I'm on it," Fenn said, checking her phone. "Five minutes, D, and then back to bed. Grandma is supposed to be back from breakfast in time to hear what the doctor says, and you don't want your mom to find you out of your room and off your oxygen. She'll flip out…and blame me for not supervising you properly."

Daryl aimed a withering glance at Fenn, then turned back to Kara. "I hate to say it, but she's right. I'd better get back to my room." He pressed a hand to his chest as he dragged in a breath. "I'm kinda missing that oxygen feed."

She nodded and managed a weak smile to reassure him.

When he disappeared into the hall again, she released a stuttering sigh and sank deeper into her pillows.

"May I offer some unsolicited advice…you know, in light of your panic attack and all that you've got to cope with at the moment? Or maybe I could just tell you a little about how I dealt with the stuff that happened to me?" Fenn asked, her countenance hesitant. "Maybe something I learned could be of use to you."

Kara tipped her head, her mind still muddled. "Something happened to you? Because of me?"

Fenn shook her head vigorously. "No, no. I mean my kidnapping and so forth when I was a teenager. Daryl didn't tell you about that? It's the reason we founded STOP." She waved a hand as if dismissing the need for Kara to answer. "Of course he didn't give the details. He's too mindful of respecting other people's privacy." Fenn settled back in her chair and cracked the knuckles on her left hand as her expression grew introspective.

"So…when I was sixteen, I ran away from home. Long story about why, but I blamed myself for some things that weren't my fault and…" Fenn let the comment trail off, giving another flip of her hand. "Story for another time. The thing is, after I ran away, I was targeted by sex traffickers, who kidnapped me and sold me to a guy in Florida."

Lurching upright, Kara stared at Fenn, her heart in her throat.

"What!" Her voice was stronger than it had been since yesterday.

Fenn pressed her lips in a thin line and nodded, her eyes confirming the truth. "All's well that ends well, as far as my experience goes, but that's not my point."

Kara flopped back on the pillows again, still goggling. "Ooo-kay. Um, go on."

"I had a lot to deal with when I got home. Guilt. Fear. Bad memories that haunted me. But I talked to a counselor and had tremendous support and love surrounding me from my family. Both were essential parts of my healing process. But something stuck with me and helped more than anything else, something my counselor said after I'd been seeing her for a few months."

"What's that?"

"She said that I needed to take ownership of my life, take control back. That one of the things that had shaken me and frightened me most was the loss of power and control over my life when I'd been kidnapped and sold like a commodity. When I got back home, I had the power to decide how I would move forward. I had control over my thoughts and my attitude. Her favorite phrase was, 'Always strive for an attitude of gratitude.'"

"Gratitude?" Kara rasped. "For being kidnapped and traumatized?"

Fenn rocked her head side to side, her nose wrinkled. "Not specifically. More for the results. The outcome. My parents gained a needed fresh start on their marriage, and I was rescued and returned without any lasting harm done." She lowered her voice to whisper, "And still a virgin."

Kara clapped a hand to her chest, exhaling a breath of relief.

"You see, you always have the choice in life to focus on the positive or to dwell on the negative." Fenn paused and smiled. "I didn't want to spend my life in fear or continue letting the bad memories control me. And while there are no miracle cures, and everyone needs time to heal at their own pace, time does heal, if you let it."

Kara lowered her gaze to her lap, digesting Fenn's advice.

"My counselor helped me shift my thought patterns," her new friend continued, "so I could move forward instead of getting bogged down, kicking myself for mistakes. To be thankful for my family, who gave me the strength to keep going. Since then, I've been using my experience to help save others from the same trauma. To educate and protect young people and support families of runaways."

Kara felt tears prick her eyes. "Fenn, that's…incredible. I had no idea how much you'd gone through. I mean… Daryl mentioned that the Camerons have had several difficult years and brushes with danger but… Bloody hell."

Fenn flashed a crooked smile. "Bloody right." Sobering, Fenn added, "What I'm saying is, don't try to stuff your emotions down or go it alone in the coming months. I'm not a professional, and a professional counselor is who I recommend, but I am available to talk whenever you want someone you can trust as a sounding board."

The sob came from nowhere. Kara was so overwhelmed by the offer of friendship and continued support from Fenn that tears gushed up. She didn't "stuff" them, either, as Fenn had warned. Her shoulders shook, her chest heaved and her eyes streamed. Her tears were cleansing and releasing, if somewhat embarrassing for the intensity of her outpouring.

Fenn flew to her and wrapped her in a hug. Kara clung and wept, until the crying became laughter. "Look at me blubbing all over you. A fine way to treat a friend."

Fenn levered back and dried Kara's cheeks. "This is exactly what a friend is for." When Fenn's cell phone rang, she checked the screen and frowned. "Sorry. It's from STOP. I should take it."

While Fenn answered the call, Kara closed her eyes, wiped her face and searched for calm. She needed some clarity about the twists her life had taken in recent days.

"He what!"

She didn't mean to eavesdrop, but the alarm in Fenn's voice penetrated her weariness.

"Was anyone hurt?... No, you did the right thing. I... gosh. I can be there in about half an hour. Just say 'no comment' until further notice. Have you called my mother and the rest of the board?... Yes. Do that... Right. I'm on my way."

Kara sent Fenn a worried look. "What's happened?"

Fenn raised a palm to calm her. "An incident at the STOP office. I need to go and..." She paused as she gathered her purse and hiked the strap onto her shoulder. "Ironically...talk to the media." Her new friend hesitated at the door. "Will you be okay if I go? Should I send my grandmother down to sit with you?"

"I'm fine. I actually would prefer some time alone. To

nap. And...think." When Fenn's brow dipped, Kara shook her head. "Not dwelling. Just...making some decisions. I'll be fine."

Fenn gave a finger wave as she scuttled out.

In the still room, Kara listened to the hiss of the oxygen feed, the muted sounds from the corridor, the low clicks and beeps of the medical equipment by her bed. A silent review of recent events paraded through her head, and she suppressed a shudder. Heatstroke. Fire. Men with guns.

She let Fenn's story, her encouragement settle in. She pondered the sense of peace she said Fenn had gotten since her traumatic days being kidnapped and having her life in jeopardy.

No miracle cures. Time does heal. Talk to someone who can help you sort through your feelings and release them. An attitude of gratitude.

Gratitude.

Maybe instead of dwelling on the anger and fear, she should be thanking a higher power that she was alive. Thanking Daryl for *keeping* her alive. Rejoicing that she had a second chance at life. Another chance to get things right.

But how did she get things right? How did she make up for the toxic relationship with Ian? The cowardly way she'd dodged the media? The selfish way she'd depended on Daryl?

She dialed Imogen's private number, and her assistant answered with a hesitant, "H'lo?"

"Im, it's me."

"Kara!" Then in a quieter voice, "Hold on. Let me get somewhere private so I can talk." A few seconds later,

Imogen whispered, "Are you safe? Where are you? Oh, my god, have you seen the news? Did you hear about—"

"I heard. That is, if you mean Ian's death. Has something else happened?"

"I meant Ian." Imogen's tone was equal parts sorrow and shock. "It's so… I mean, it's tragic and sad, but…it changes everything for you."

A shiver chased through her. *Change*. Lord, she hated change. She'd had enough upheaval in her life recently. "Wh-what do you mean?"

"Oh, come on. Surely you've realized what this means for you?" Imogen said. "You can come home! All the threats the team made against you were designed to protect Ian and his ability to play for the Knights. They had to change the conversation and offer the public and doping agencies an alternate reality to protect their investment in him."

A dull buzzing filled her ears and left her body numb, cold. She hadn't played the repercussions of Ian's overdose out. She listened in stunned silence as Imogen continued.

"Without their star player to protect, especially with the circumstances of his death that have already leaked to the media, the team has no reason to go after you anymore."

Kara stared at the opposite wall, not really seeing anything as she processed this truth. A bubble of relief swelled in her, but it stuck in her throat behind a knot of guilt and grief. She wanted to be free from the harassment and danger the brutal men connected to the football team had posed. She wanted to be free to go back to London, return to work, put the trauma of the past year behind her.

But not at the cost of Ian's life. She wasn't heartless.

She couldn't celebrate her change in fortune when the price had been a talented athlete's life. She gritted her back teeth as a fresh swell of frustration and anger that the team had not taken her requests for intervention on Ian's behalf seriously. That they'd turned a blind eye since the PE drugs had benefitted the team with wins on the field and with advertisers. The greed of the team's owner had killed a man she'd once cared for.

"...get you on the next flight back to Heathrow. What airport would you be leaving from?" Imogen was saying when Kara yanked herself from her somber musing.

"Hmm?"

"I can get you on a flight home tonight. I'll be so glad to have you back here! By the by, you have messages from three different producers here, and your agent has called no fewer than a hundred times in the last few months. I know she'll be so glad once you're back in the country."

She could go home. Still staring blankly at the dry-erase board on the far wall, Kara sat with the knowledge she could return to London and let it settle. Permeate.

"Kara? You there?"

"I—yeah."

"Which airport do you want to leave from? Is Charlotte closest? Atlanta? I really don't know American geography like I should."

Leaving the US meant leaving Daryl. That was the thought that fixed itself front and center.

"Well, I can Google it, eh? So where are you now?" Imogen asked. "You never said."

Kara squeezed a handful of the bedsheet before rasping, "Charlotte airport."

"All right, then. I'm on it. I'll let you know when your flight is as soon as it's arranged."

When she disconnected with Imogen, Kara sat with the decision she'd made. She was going back to London. Tonight, if Imogen could manage it, and Imogen had a way of performing magic when it came to making arrangements work out. Kara was ready, so ready to get back to her flat, to be in her own bed, to get her life back on track.

She wanted to have baked beans and black pudding for breakfast, to look out her window and see Big Ben, to hear the King's English spoken without American accents. She wanted to talk to her family, reassure them she was all right. She'd been homesick for months and too scared of returning to England to admit it. But now, at last, she was going *home*.

Chapter 22

"When can I go home?" Daryl asked the doctor as he made his rounds.

The doctor looked up from the chart he was reviewing and flipped the file closed. "I'm satisfied that you're making good progress. You still need another dose of preventive antibiotic for your lungs. That's an IV, so you'll be here another couple hours, but I think by late morning or early afternoon you could get your walking papers."

"Oh, thank goodness!" his mother said, a wide smile of relief lighting her face.

"And Kara? My friend who I came in with?" Daryl asked.

The doctor pushed his glasses up his nose and tucked the file under his arm. "She'll have to be the one to tell you anything concerning her medical treatment. Privacy laws, you know?"

Daryl sighed. "Right. Of course." He motioned to the monitors and tubes he was hooked up to. "Can some of this be removed? I'd kill for a shower."

Even though the nurses had sponged most of the soot off him, he still reeked of smoke and felt gritty.

He received permission to bathe, with a recommendation to keep the water as cold as he could stand it.

"Anything else will sting for a few more days as your skin heals." The doctor moved to the door. "I'll tell the nurses' station, and they'll come unhook things in a moment."

His mother beamed at him from the guest chair. "In case you need it spelled out, you're coming home with me to Cameron Glen until you are completely well. I've had enough scares about gunmen and kidnappings and barn fires. I want you where I can take care of you myself."

"The same offer applies to Kara, I hope." He gave his mother an all-business look. "Because I'm not going anywhere without her. I have to make sure she gets well, too."

"Certainly." Grace Cameron linked her hands in her lap. "You know we've never turned away anyone in need of protection or TLC. But…" His mother frowned. "Do you think she's still in danger? The death of this soccer player who she was dating…" His mother motioned vaguely toward the television where they'd seen the horrid news a couple hours ago. "Does that change everything? Or will the men who were hunting her still be a threat?"

Daryl ground his back teeth hard. He'd pondered similar questions and not gotten far. "Logic says they have no reason to harass her or try to hurt her anymore. But I don't think I'll rest easy until I know they've been arrested for what they did to us." He paused and rubbed his throat. His voice was still scratchy, but he could talk without as much discomfort this morning. He took a sip of the ice water by his bed.

"Or barring that," he continued, "Mr. Knight and his man have to prove that they'll leave her alone. A retraction of the things they said about Kara would be great, but I'm not holding my breath." Daryl angled his head to stare at the ceiling as he sighed. "Little chance that the press and the paparazzi will back off now. Ian's death will just stir the pot. They'll want comments from her about it and—" He buzzed his lips in frustration. "I wish they'd just leave her alone."

His mother's mouth firmed, and her brow knitted in concern. "You know…" She chewed her lip as if debating what to say. "If you pursue a relationship with this young lady, the paparazzi will be a fact of life for you, as well. Have you considered that?"

A knot twisted in his chest, but not from the notion of being hounded by photographers. Instead, he thought about how shocked, how upset Kara had become when she'd learned of Ian's death. To Daryl, it had been obvious she still had feelings for the soccer star. So what did that say about his relationship with Kara? Had he just been a bodyguard? Someone who made her feel safe? Had he mistaken her gratitude for romantic feelings? Had her feelings been real or just rebound emotions after her split from Ian? And now that Ian was dead, what did that do to the equation? Not just for Kara's safety, but for her emotional confusion. He didn't want any part of competing with a dead man for her affection.

"I know that look," his mother said.

"Hmm?" He blinked as he refocused his attention on her.

"You're deep in your analytical mind. You do this every time you have a decision to make. It's your beautifully overactive left brain at work."

Don't overthink. Hadn't Kara told him that just a day or two ago? Before they'd kissed and tangled in each other's limbs and almost made love. But he'd stopped them.

He'd overthought after all, deciding sex was more than the relationship was ready for. Or had he had a premonition that Kara wasn't in love with him the way he was in love with—

A shot of adrenaline raced through him. Love? Was he in love with her?

His mother chuckled. "You're still doing it. Is there anything you want to talk to me about, darling? Maybe I can help."

"I, um…don't—"

A nurse bustled in with a cheery smile. "Feeling up to a shower, huh? That's great. I'll get you unhooked from your tethers and show you where the shower room is. This IV port has to stay. Your doctor ordered a last round of antibiotics when you get back to your room."

Daryl met his mother's gaze. "Would you check on Kara while I clean up? With Fenn off with her emergency, Kara's by herself."

"Of course," his mother said. "But don't think we're through with this conversation. You're obviously troubled by something, and I want to help."

When Daryl got back to his room, he felt immensely better just being clean. His mother wasn't in his room, so before the nurse came to reconnect his IV line, he padded down to Kara's room.

When he arrived, Kara was standing next to her bed, dressed in her dirty clothes from the day before, signing paperwork on a clipboard that a nurse held for her.

"Kara? What's going on? Have you been discharged?" He divided a look between Kara and his mother.

"I'm discharging myself," she replied.

"Against medical advice," his mother added, "but she convinced her doctor to let her take her last course of antibiotic in pill form."

He turned back to Kara. "Why are you leaving? Where are you going?"

She finished inking her name on the forms and handed the clipboard back to the nurse, who tore off the top sheet and handed her a copy.

"I'm going home. Imogen has gotten me on a flight that leaves in a few hours. I've called for a rideshare already, and they'll be here in a few minutes."

Daryl goggled at her. "Just like that? Were you even going to say goodbye?"

She sat back down on the edge of her bed and curled the fingers of her uninjured hand in the sheet. "Of course I was. And to tell you thank you again."

Daryl's hand tapped restlessly against his leg. "So that's it? You're just...leaving?"

His mother sent him a look of distress, but moved to the door. "I'll give you some privacy to talk." As she stepped past him, her mother touched his arm and mouthed, *Tell her how you feel*.

Daryl's gut clenched. Tell Kara he'd fallen in love with her, just in time for her to give him a pitying look and walk out of his life? No, thank you.

When he turned back to Kara, her gaze was downcast, and she heaved a ragged sigh. "I don't like long goodbyes. Not in the movies or in real life."

He gave a muted hum of acknowledgment, the best he could manage as his throat clogged with emotion. Anger and grief and shock tangled in his chest, and if he opened his mouth, he wasn't sure if he'd yell at her or cry or howl with frustration.

"Imogen pointed out that with Ian's death, the motive behind Mr. Knight's campaign against me is gone. In theory, my life is my own again, and I can go home. I realized how homesick I was."

He grunted again, his jaw aching as he clenched his teeth and bit back retorts full of pain.

"And I knew it was time—past time, really—that I get out of your way and stop inserting myself into your life. You and your family have done so much for me, and I will be eternally grateful. But I've imposed long enough. I need to go. Let you get back to California and your job and…your life."

"I see," he said tightly.

A thousand thoughts were pinging in his brain, but somehow the thing that made it to his tongue was, "What about Holt and Knight? Are you sure you're safe from them? They still have reason to keep you quiet."

He saw the shiver that passed through her, making her petite body quiver. "I suppose that's true." She squared her shoulders. "I'm working on a plan. It's not fully formed, but by the time my plane lands at Heathrow, it will be."

Her phone pinged, and she checked the screen. "That's my Uber. I have to go." As she passed him, she rose on her toes and kissed his cheek. "Goodbye, Daryl. I'm sorry to leave so abruptly, but I need to—there's something I need to do, to put things right. You'll understand soon."

He puckered his brow, but before he could ask her what she meant by that, Kara had slipped out of the room and was gone.

He stood motionless, stunned, silent. When his mother

came back in the room, she opened her mouth as if to ask a question, but clamped it shut again and folded him into her arms for a tight hug.

"No matter what, darling, your family is here for you. We love you."

Squeezing her back, he closed his eyes and muttered, "I know. Love you back."

Three days later

Kara woke slowly, blinking into focus the familiar room that felt oddly strange. She was in her own bed as she'd longed to be for months, yet her bed felt lonely. No one waited in the kitchen to have coffee with her. Or tea. Now that she was back in London, she supposed she should drink tea again. She could have beans and black pudding for breakfast if she wanted, yet what she craved was American biscuits and sausage gravy.

She sighed, knowing she'd been stalling on the task ahead of her, but when she'd arrived in London two days ago, she'd been so tired. So…heartsick. Physically exhausted and emotionally bereft, she'd crawled into the king-size bed in her flat and rarely left it since, except to scrounge for food in her empty kitchen or to open the door for Imogen. Her assistant and friend had been by to visit each day, so that they could consult on needed arrangements for the event scheduled later today.

Kara's stomach pitched considering what lay ahead that afternoon. As much as she dreaded what she'd planned, she knew she owed it to herself. And especially to Daryl. She'd dig deep and draw on every technique she'd ever learned to quash stage fright to muddle through today.

She took her phone from the nightstand where it had been charging and checked for messages from Imogen. She also wished she'd have some communication from Daryl. She had neither this morning. Unusual for Imogen, but not for Daryl. She'd heard nothing from him, even though she'd texted him and Fenn to say she'd arrived home safely. Fenn had returned a short acknowledgment, but the person she'd most wanted to hear from had been as mute as a rock.

He'd been stony and unresponsive when she left the hospital, as well, his eyes uncharacteristically flat and his countenance cold. Had this been his way of showing he'd been serious when he'd said they had no future, were too different and he wanted no relationship with her? She'd wanted to explain her intentions, her feelings, but her Uber driver's early arrival and Daryl's stark demeanor had foiled that intention. Later she'd decided to let her actions be her explanation. At the moment, reflecting on his lack of reply and their awkward parting, she was second-guessing her approach. Could she ever get things right with him? Why was she so bad at relationships?

Her phone pinged with a notification from the local news.

Footballer buried in his hometown yesterday, read the headline. She'd known about Ian's funeral but stayed silent and out of the spotlight out of respect for Ian's family as they mourned. Today, she had a tightrope to walk, but she'd rehearsed her script with Imogen, trying to manage a respectful balance.

An hour later, Kara sat on her couch with her legs crossed, listening to Imogen update her on messages she'd received from industry personnel and interview requests from the press. "And Helen called," Imogen said, referring to Kara's agent. "She wanted to know if you'd look at a script for another period drama. She said you need to do something soon, because the longer you stay gone, the more offers dry up."

Kara sighed. She didn't want to deal with her agent or interviews or anything else until she'd gotten through today and seen how her truth was received, how the world reacted. And what happened with Daryl when he heard about it.

When her grandfather clock finally chimed 3:00 p.m.—10:00 a.m. in North Carolina—she smoothed her hair and straightened her clothes as she followed Imogen to the lift of her apartment building. It was showtime, and she had a lobby full of cameras and reporters waiting for her.

Chapter 23

Daryl's phone pinged as he hunched over a bowl of soggy cereal at his parents' kitchen table. He glanced at his phone, expecting his boss questioning when he'd be back to work, or his company softball team captain asking if he'd be playing in an upcoming game, or one of his siblings doing a wellness check. Instead, it was Fenn. Her text merely read, Watch this! and included a link to click.

Curious, he tapped the URL in her text and was taken to a livestream of what appeared to be a news conference of some sort. When he expanded the screen and turned up the volume, he realized what he was seeing, hearing.

Kara stood at a podium, surrounded by lights and cameras and journalists with microphones. His muscles tensed, instinctively wanting to rescue her from the clamoring mob of paparazzi. But as he listened and watched, it became clear that she was not trying to avoid the journalists. She was giving a statement.

He increased the volume on his phone and started the feed from the beginning to hear the entirety of what she had to say. He held his breath as the video started with Kara and another young woman arriving together to the flash of cameras and the din of questions shouted at her.

Kara looked beautiful. Her hair was slicked into what

he'd heard his sisters call a chignon. She wore a dark green pantsuit and tiny earrings that winked on her lobes in the bright media lights. But what struck him most was her composure. She held her head high, her shoulders square, her back straight. When she reached the podium, she gave a brief smile that only hinted at her nerves. Most people likely wouldn't have noticed the tremor in her cheeks, but Daryl had learned to read Kara's subtle cues over the past weeks.

Or had he known her at all? He'd certainly not expected her to flee the hospital before the doctor advised and rush off to London with only a perfunctory goodbye and cryptic comment about a plan. His pulse throbbed. Was this her mysterious plan? A press conference? What—

His spinning thoughts stilled as she spoke, and he focused on what she had to say.

"Good afternoon, and thank you all for coming. I want to start today by offering my deepest condolences to the family, friends and teammates of Ian Stafford. His death is tragic, painful and something I will grieve for the rest of my life."

Daryl's chest squeezed. Here was more evidence that Kara was still in love with her ex, and he'd misinterpreted everything that had happened between them.

Acid puddled in his gut, and he shoved his soggy breakfast away. Had Kara played him? Used him? She was an actress, after all. Perhaps she'd been playing the part of a damsel in distress to earn his sympathy, pretended to care for him to win his favor and assistance in her time of need. While that needle pricked him, another voice whispered that the Kara he'd gotten to know wouldn't have been that manipulative. Yet how could he be sure he'd gotten to know the real Kara O'Quinn at all?

He shook off the morose thoughts and focused again on what Kara was telling her audience.

"I asked you all to be here today so that I could set the record straight. I've been silent for months, while lies and rumors and innuendo have spread about me. I kept quiet for a few reasons. First, I believed, perhaps wrongly, that addressing the falsehoods was undignified and counterproductive. After all, the royal family has for years stood by its policy not to respond to rumors, and I saw validity in such an approach.

"Second, defending myself would have required a more expansive explanation of circumstances in my relationship with Ian Stafford than I was prepared to give. Explaining the truth meant breaking trust with people I cared about, causing pain and embarrassment to someone I had hoped to help. I refused to cast blame or point fingers when what was needed was assistance and support. I refused to add fuel to a firestorm I'd hoped would blow itself out if left unfed.

"And finally, the source of the lies and smear campaign has infinitely more resources and influence than I, and I felt powerless. In fact, as public opinion was turned against me, I felt quite alone and without hope. I found myself being accosted in the streets, and I grew frightened for my safety."

Daryl's father strolled into the kitchen, casting a side glance at Daryl as he made his way to the coffeepot. "Goodness. What's got you so thoroughly absorbed this morning?"

"Kara's giving a press conference," he said.

"Oh." His father sounded as surprised as Daryl had been. "Wow." He carried his filled mug over to sit beside Daryl at the table and leaned in to watch the feed on his son's phone.

"I left London to take refuge in the United States, believing that if I kept my head down, the storm would blow over, and I could return to my work and my private life once the stories died down. But this didn't happen. Instead, the people behind the smear campaign upped their game and followed me to the US. They threatened my life in an attempt to pressure me into issuing a statement owning the lies and confirming false rumors in order to salvage their own monetary interests. The harassment continued until, in a final desperate move, I was kidnapped and put in the boot of a car, tied up and abandoned in an isolated barn, where the carelessness of one of my assailants with his cigarette caused the barn to catch fire. I barely escaped the conflagration with my life. The redness and peeling you can still see—" she pushed up her sleeve to show her arm "—are remnants of the injuries I sustained in that fire."

Neil Cameron grunted and folded his arms over his chest. "She makes it sound like she did all of this alone? What about you? What about the danger you were in, or the sacrifices you made to save her life? Protect her from those thugs?"

Daryl wondered the same, but pressed a finger to his lips, hushing his father so he could hear what Kara was saying.

"I've stayed silent about the full extent of recent events and the people who have waged this slanderous and violent campaign against me for too long. The people who have hurt me and discredited me and terrorized me don't deserve my silence."

Daryl shifted in his chair, his heart slamming against his ribs.

"The truth I want you to know today is that I *did not* leak stories about Ian Stafford's drug use to the media. As Ian's regrettable and tragic death from overdose confirms, he was abusing a number of dangerous drugs. When I learned the truth, I begged him to get help for his addiction. He refused, denying he had a problem. And so, purely out of concern for a man I cared about, whom I saw traveling down a perilous path, I spoke to the Knights' team doctor and the management team, hoping they'd intervene. Someone else, I know not whom, leaked this information to the press. But I was blamed. The owner of the Knights, Henry Knight himself, was behind the false narrative pushed to the press, and a man in Henry Knight's employ, Reginald Holt, was tasked with tracking me down, threatening me and taking all manner of extreme measures to extract my compliance to this false narrative, which I refused to do. I—"

"Kara!" The interrupting voice came from the assembled media.

Kara raised a hand toward her audience, saying, "Please let me finish. I'll allow time for a few questions when I've made my full statement."

"I just wondered," the male reporter continued, "if you'd seen the report released about an hour ago that Henry Knight and Reginald Holt were both apprehended by Border Force officials when they reentered the country this morning."

Kara's face reflected the same shock that slammed Daryl.

* * *

A shockwave hit Kara, knocking the breath from her. "I... What?" she asked, her voice a shadow of the command and assurance it had moments earlier.

"An arrest warrant had been sworn out for them in the United States and, in cooperation, British authorities had been on alert for them," the BBC reporter continued. "Do you have a response to this development?"

"I, uh..." When her knees wobbled and she swayed, Kara gripped the podium with her uninjured hand to steady herself. She didn't like this feeling of being caught off guard when she'd wanted to project nothing but placid assurance and courage. She shot a glance to Imogen, who was head down tapping and scrolling frantically on her iPad. When her assistant looked up and met her gaze, Imogen, wide-eyed, gave a small nod of confirmation.

"I hadn't heard," Kara said as calmly as she could. "But in light of the events of the past few weeks, it is welcome news." She took a breath, finding her composure again and continuing her planned statement. "Reginald Holt, at the behest of Mr. Knight, tracked me down in North Carolina earlier this month and waged a terror campaign against me that included death threats, breaking my fingers—"

Here she held up her injured hand for the reporters to see, and the room filled with the sound of cameras clicking and flashbulbs blinking.

She gave more detail about the other horrors inflicted on her and concluded the summary by saying, "Henry Knight has used his wealth and influence to manipulate public opinion against me in order to protect his investment in Ian Stafford, whose sole worth to him was as a moneymaker as the star of his football club. When warned that Ian had an addiction that needed intervention, Knight brushed aside my concerns and made me the villain. I regret that I gave into my fears, heartbreak and humiliation and chose avoidance and hiding rather than standing up to the bully that Henry Knight is. As a result of my regrettable timidity, Ian Stafford didn't get the help he needed in time."

She paused to gather herself. This next part would be the hardest, and she wanted to stay strong. She didn't want to break down in tears before this field of paparazzi cameras. In the brief silence as she tamped her jagged nerves, a voice from the back of the room shouted, "What happened to your arm? Did you try to kill yourself?"

She gritted her back teeth and squared her shoulders. "I haven't finished my statement, but thank you for this opportunity to address the rumors concerning my injury." She held up her arm again. "While I did, in fact, sustain a cut on my hand that required stitches in hospital, the cut was purely accidental. I am not, nor have I ever been, suicidal. In fact, despite the traumas and terror inflicted on me by Reginald Holt and Henry Knight, the past few weeks have been…blessed."

A murmur of intrigue rippled through the room.

"I say that because, quite by accident, I came to know a man and his loving family who surrounded me in kindness, generosity and unconditional support. I can honestly say that without him, I would not be here with you today. A chance meeting on a transatlantic flight has changed my life in all the best ways." She stopped, feeling her throat tighten, and swallowed hard.

"Is the man you speak of the one you were photographed with in Georgia last March and again several days ago outside the apartment building in North Carolina?" another journalist shouted.

She shoved down her irritation. She should have known the media couldn't resist interrupting and pelting her with questions before she opened the floor for follow-up. Pushy was the local paparazzi's permanent setting.

She sighed. Her goal had been to set the record straight, to put out the truth and to reclaim some manner of self-respect and courage with her choices. Raising her chin, she answered simply, "Yes. The same man."

The room erupted in a cacophony of shouted queries.
"Who is he?"
"What's his name?"
"Who was the woman with you when you went to the hospital?"
"What family do you mean?"
"Can you explain what you—"

She glanced at Imogen, who only rolled her eyes and shrugged.

Finally raising a hand to signal for quiet, Kara leaned closer to the microphone and said, "Please hold your questions for now."

She'd expected to be bombarded with questions about Daryl and the Camerons, especially once she mentioned their part in the events of the last few weeks. Initially, she'd wanted to shield them, but like the reporter mentioned, she had been photographed with Daryl. His name was already out there floating alongside the internet rumors. While it was too late to save him from the scrutiny associated with his connection to her and the debacle created by Henry Knight, she could help spin the attention in a positive light. She wanted the public to see him as the man she'd come to know and not just a titillating source of gossip and speculation.

When the clamor had subsided, she took another bolstering breath and began again. "I did not know the man I was photographed with before I went to the US last spring, seeking a refuge from the whirlwind of negativity and vitriol aimed at me thanks to the lies spread by Henry Knight and his minions. What's more, Daryl did not know who I was. But fate brought Daryl Cameron into my life, and I thank my lucky stars for this blessing. His kind and compassionate nature was immediately evident and never failed throughout the ordeals I have faced in recent days. He has been a loyal friend, a brave protector and a trusted companion as I navigated stormy seas. He has endured hardship and risked his own life to defend mine. He has buoyed my spirits with his warmth and optimism, his laughter and quiet strength. I'm so grateful that he is in my life. He is the truest sense of the word *hero*." Her voice cracked, and she cleared her throat before ending with a final thought. "Daryl Cameron, quite simply, means the world to me."

Chapter 24

Once Kara had taken a few questions and the presser ended, Daryl set his phone on the table and scrubbed both hands on his face. He couldn't say what he was feeling. Emotional stuff had never been his strength, and right now his head and heart were such a confusing cocktail that he would need some time, and probably one of his sisters' advice to sort through everything.

Isla. She was so hyper-connected to her emotions and everyone else's, she'd know exactly what he was thinking and what he should do. Assuming he wanted to do anything other than shut all this turmoil down and go back to California to pick up where his life had been put on hold a few weeks ago.

His father leaned back in his chair and laced his fingers as he rested his hands on his belly. Neil sighed contentedly. "Well, at least you have one answer you've been looking for."

Daryl roused from his own muddled thoughts and gave his father a querying look. "Do I?"

His father chuckled and nodded toward Daryl's phone. "She just said she loves you. Wasn't that what you were needing to know?"

Daryl scowled. "Dad, I think you need to get your

hearing checked. She said nothing about being in love with me."

His father grinned. "Maybe not in so many words. The actual words *I love you* are too intimate and private to be said explicitly to a crowd of journalists. But I'd bet my right arm that she'll say them to you the next time you talk privately."

Daryl's gut seesawed, and he grunted. "Yeah, except we aren't talking privately. We aren't talking at all, really. When she walked out of the hospital with barely a goodbye, I got the message loud and clear that she was done with me. I'd served my usefulness to her, and she couldn't get back to London fast enough. I saw no need to prolong the inevitable, so I haven't been in touch with her since she left." In a morose mumble, he added, "Not that she's contacted me, either."

His father sat forward, pressing his palms to the tabletop. "I'd say she just communicated with a bullhorn, son. You know how she feels about her privacy and the paparazzi, yet she laid her life out for scrutiny and told the world how much you mean to her. That's big."

Daryl groaned and pinched the bridge of his nose. "Doesn't matter, anyway. I have no expectation of a life with her. I'm not…" He sighed, not sure how he wanted to finish that sentence. "Well, never mind."

He pushed his chair back and stood, intending to carry his mushy cereal to the sink.

His father pushed his chair back, as well, and caught his shoulder. "No. Hang on, buddy. Finish that sentence. You're not what?"

He heard a slightly scolding tone in his father's voice. He shook his head. "Nothing. Forget it."

"I can't forget it, son. Because it echoes a feeling I've had about you for years."

Daryl angled a puzzled look at his father, his belly churning.

"You were going to say you weren't good enough for her, or that she was out of your league, weren't you?"

Daryl didn't answer but ground his back teeth and dropped his gaze to the table. His dad wasn't exactly right, but he was close enough.

His father loosed a bitter scoff. "Daryl, I've sensed this striving in you since you were old enough to recognize you were adopted. This restlessness in you that says you have to do more, push harder, reach higher to be part of this family." His dad gripped his shoulder harder, turning Daryl to face him.

Daryl's heart thrashed in his chest. He raised his head to meet the blazing look in his father's eyes. He wanted to deny that his father had tapped into his deepest longing and secret doubts, but his throat closed. He had to swallow several times to shove down the sudden sense that he might actually cry. In front of his father. Unacceptable.

He turned his head toward the far wall, struggling to blink the moisture from his eyes before his father saw it.

"Daryl, look at me," his father said in a tone he hadn't used since Daryl had talked back to his mother as a teenager. He waited for Daryl to meet his gaze before continuing, "Hear me, son."

A sparkle of something winked in his father's eyes, some reflection of the kitchen lights or—

Daryl's chest seized as he realized his father's eyes were tearing up.

"You are *more* than enough just by being who you are,"

Neil said, his voice thick with emotion, "and I am sorry if something I said or did as I raised you gave you even a hint that I felt otherwise." He paused and cleared his throat. "Daryl, I am immensely proud of you and your achievements, but more important, I am overjoyed with the man of character you are. I have always admired your work ethic, your talent and intelligence, but it's always been your heart, your loving soul and gentle nature that has impressed me most."

The breath he'd been holding stuttered out of Daryl, and he managed a thin, "Thanks."

"You don't have to prove anything to me or to *anyone*. You are exactly right for this family, just as you are, and anyone who doesn't see that, isn't worth your time."

Daryl sighed, wanting to dismiss his father's assurances as the kind of paternal bias and pep talk all parents give at some point. He gave a small nod and tried to pull away from his dad's grip. But his father wasn't through.

"Daryl." Again the firm, all-business tone that meant Daryl needed to heed or else.

"I hear you. Thanks."

"Daryl."

His insides swimming and trembling, he glanced up again and met his father's eyes.

"I love you, Daryl. *You*. You don't have anything to prove to me or anyone else."

As he stood there, holding his father's teary gaze, something buried inside him cracked. The scared little boy who'd come to live with a white family when he lost his mother to cancer stirred inside him. The boy who'd consistently tried to be more, tried to earn his adoptive parents' love, tried to prove he deserved the family who had taken him in and loved him so well, released the fist that had clung to his soul. A strangled sound wrenched from his throat as his father pulled him into an embrace so tight he could barely breathe. And he hugged his father back just as fiercely. "I love you, too, Dad. I love you, too."

Chapter 25

Kara made her way through the Charlotte, North Carolina airport, headed toward baggage claim. She smiled and met the gazes of her fellow passengers, many of whom did double takes and whispered to each other as she passed them in the concourse. When one young girl ran up to her with a notepad and asked for her autograph, Kara had a short conversation with the preteen and her mother as she signed the girl's notebook.

In the thirty-six hours since the presser ended, she'd rehearsed what she wanted to say to Daryl more diligently than she'd ever run lines for her film roles. She hadn't told him she was coming. She didn't want to give him a chance to refuse her or build a case for why they were wrong for each other before she could present her request in person. She needed to appeal to him in person, on his turf, to make up for fleeing so quickly earlier in the week.

She'd start with apologizing for that abruptness. She'd been so stunned about Ian, so overwhelmed with homesickness, so torn over leaving Daryl that she knew if she didn't go quickly and take care of the business in London, she might have talked herself out of going.

Walking through the American airport felt oddly familiar. In recent months, she'd grown accustomed to hearing American Southern accents on people's tongues. She welcomed the hints all around her that she was back in Daryl's home state—the Carolina Panthers and University of North Carolina jerseys for sale in airport shops, the abundance of fragrant coffee shops, the signage advertising vacation getaways in the Smoky Mountains. Her heart lifted. Vacation getaways like Cameron Glen.

She quickened her pace, all the more eager to reach his family's retreat and fall into his arms. As she passed the line of passengers queued for security clearance, she even imagined she saw Daryl—

Kara stopped so abruptly, the woman walking behind her crashed into her. She apologized to her absently as she stared at the handsome man across the lobby. She squinted as she moved closer to the security lines, trying to get a better look at the man's face.

And then he turned. Locked eyes with her.

Kara's heart leaped, and a glad cry squeaked from her. She ran to close the distance between them, laughing with pleasure at the sight of the man who hadn't left her thoughts in days.

He ducked under the stanchion ropes that organized the security queue and moved toward her with long strides and a steady gaze.

She flung herself against him, wrapping him in an enthusiastic hug. "Daryl! My God, Daryl! What luck. I almost missed you! Where are you going?"

She backed from the embrace and beamed up at him. But he wasn't smiling. Something cold landed in her core. "Daryl?"

He gave his head a small shake as if rousing himself

from a trance. "I… I was going to London. To find you and…settle things between us before going to California."

"California?"

"That's where I live, where my job is."

"Oh. Right."

Her smile faltered. What was wrong? He didn't look happy to see her. Was she too late? Had she hurt him too badly or misunderstood his resolve that they had no future together? Acid puddled inside her but she was determined to maintain hope and a cheerful countenance.

"Why are you here?" he asked.

She chuckled stiffly. "To see you, of course, you dope."

One black eyebrow sketched up. "I see."

She cocked her head to the side, studying him. "Do you? You don't seem happy to see me."

"I'm just…surprised. I mean, you left so fast, without explaining—"

She nodded and grabbed his elbow. "I know. I… I can explain. I want to explain. That's why I came, in fact. I knew a phone call or texts wouldn't do. I wanted—"

She paused and glanced around them. The middle of a crowded airport terminal was not where she wanted to have this discussion. "Can we go somewhere more private? I have so much I want to tell you."

He drew a deep breath and rubbed both palms on his blue jeans. He cast a glance toward a coffee shop then to a restaurant with a bar. "Sure. Where?"

She shifted her weight. "Ideally, Cameron Glen. But if not there—"

"I checked a bag," he interrupted, pivoting to face the airline departures desk. "I'll need to reclaim it, if I'm not going to England."

She aimed a thumb toward the escalators to the ground floor where baggage claim and public transportation were located. "And I have to claim mine."

For a few seconds, neither said anything as they stared at each other, their unresolved situation hanging heavily between them.

Finally he pointed to the nearest sign, an electronic screen advertising a downtown hotel, and said, "Meet me back here once we both have our luggage?"

She exhaled and gave him a hopeful smile. "Deal."

Daryl was able to call his father and have him return to the airport to retrieve him and Kara. An awkward silence filled the car as the three of them made their way back to Cameron Glen. Daryl's chest squeezed with anticipation, but he fought not to get his hopes up. Sure, she was here, but he refused to read too much into that fact.

After his father had convinced him to fly to London and find some closure with Kara one way or another, Daryl had fought the restless yearning inside him. Hadn't he been the one to tell her they were too different and had no future? He'd stopped them from making love. He'd given her every reason to believe the opposite of the truth. He was in love with her and needed her at his side for his future to be complete.

When they finally, *finally*, reached Cameron Glen, he led Kara down to the same bench by the fishing pond where they'd talked a few weeks earlier when she'd sought him out to be her protector.

Once they were settled, a light autumn breeze that smelled of fallen leaves wafting across the water, he turned to her.

"Kara," he said at the same time she said, "Daryl."

They chuckled, and she quickly said, "Please, let me say what I must first."

With a hand gesture toward her, he invited her to continue.

She took a deep breath, and he saw the moisture that sparkled in her eyes. "When I left the hospital last week, I told you that I was eager to get home because I was homesick. And I was. But once I was back in London, I still ached, and I realized I wasn't really home…because I wasn't with you."

Daryl held his breath. Was she saying…?

Kara reached for his hand and smiled. "You are my home, Daryl. The reason I feel so safe with you, so happy with you, so at peace with you is because I love you. I think my soul recognized you from the moment you took my hand during the turbulence on that flight from Amsterdam to Atlanta this spring. Something inside me knew I could trust you, that you were right for me, that I belonged with you. Maybe it wasn't an accident we sat next to each other on that plane. Maybe it was fate. I don't know, but I'm so glad I found you."

A sound like a bee buzzing by filled his head. He took a beat, rubbing his ear and realizing it was adrenaline and joy that filled him with this loud hum and pounding heart. He opened his mouth. Closed it.

"Daryl? What's wrong?"

She sounded scared, and he had to quiet her fears, his eternal instinct to protect her and make her safe rearing its head. He managed a soft chuckle. "I, um…need a second."

"I know you said we weren't in love and that you and I had too many differences," she hurried to say in the silence when he was gathering himself, "but that's not my truth. I cared for you from day one, and I think I started falling in love with you over that first Southern breakfast at the diner in Georgia. You are different from the other men I know, but in all the best ways. And I love that you—"

He caught her face between his hands and silenced her with a kiss. When he raised his head to meet her eyes, her cheeks and his were both damp. "I love you, too, Kara O'Quinn."

Now it was her turn to gawk wordlessly, clearly choked with emotion.

He swiped tears from her chin with the pad of his thumb. "If you'll let me, I want to be more than your bodyguard for the rest of your days. I want to be your family, your best friend…your lover…" She nodded enthusiastically, and so he risked taking his wishes further. "And your husband?"

Her emerald eyes widened, and a glowing smile lit her face. "The role I was born to play!" She laughed and wrapped her arms around his neck. "Yes, Daryl. Oh, yes! I want you to be my husband."

Capturing her lips again, he sealed the deal with another kiss.

* * * * *

Get up to 4 Free Books!

We'll send you 2 free books from each series you try PLUS a free Mystery Gift.

FREE Value Over **$25**

Both the **Harlequin Intrigue®** and **Harlequin® Romantic Suspense** series feature compelling novels filled with heart-racing action-packed romance that will keep you on the edge of your seat.

YES! Please send me 2 FREE novels from the Harlequin Intrigue or Harlequin Romantic Suspense series and my FREE gift (gift is worth about $10 retail). After receiving them, if I don't wish to receive any more books, I can return the shipping statement marked "cancel." If I don't cancel, I will receive 6 brand-new Harlequin Intrigue Larger-Print books every month and be billed just $7.19 each in the U.S. or $7.99 each in Canada, or 4 brand-new Harlequin Romantic Suspense books every month and be billed just $6.39 each in the U.S. or $7.19 each in Canada, a savings of 20% off the cover price. It's quite a bargain! Shipping and handling is just 50¢ per book in the U.S. and $1.25 per book in Canada.* I understand that accepting the 2 free books and gift places me under no obligation to buy anything. I can always return a shipment and cancel at any time by calling the number below. The free books and gift are mine to keep no matter what I decide.

Choose one: ☐ **Harlequin Intrigue Larger-Print** (199/399 BPA G36Y)   ☐ **Harlequin Romantic Suspense** (240/340 BPA G36Y)   ☐ **Or Try Both!** (199/399 & 240/340 BPA G36Z)

Name (please print)

Address   Apt. #

City   State/Province   Zip/Postal Code

Email: Please check this box ☐ if you would like to receive newsletters and promotional emails from Harlequin Enterprises ULC and its affiliates. You can unsubscribe anytime.

Mail to the Harlequin Reader Service:
IN U.S.A.: P.O. Box 1341, Buffalo, NY 14240-8531
IN CANADA: P.O. Box 603, Fort Erie, Ontario L2A 5X3

Want to explore our other series or interested in ebooks? Visit www.ReaderService.com or call 1-800-873-8635.

---

*Terms and prices subject to change without notice. Prices do not include sales taxes, which will be charged (if applicable) based on your state or country of residence. Canadian residents will be charged applicable taxes. Offer not valid in Quebec. This offer is limited to one order per household. Books received may not be as shown. Not valid for current subscribers to the Harlequin Intrigue or Harlequin Romantic Suspense series. All orders subject to approval. Credit or debit balances in a customer's account(s) may be offset by any other outstanding balance owed by or to the customer. Please allow 4 to 6 weeks for delivery. Offer available while quantities last.

Your Privacy—Your information is being collected by Harlequin Enterprises ULC, operating as Harlequin Reader Service. For a complete summary of the information we collect, how we use this information and to whom it is disclosed, please visit our privacy notice located at https://corporate.harlequin.com/privacy-notice. Notice to California Residents – Under California law, you have specific rights to control and access your data. For more information on these rights and how to exercise them, visit https://corporate.harlequin.com/california-privacy. For additional information for residents of other U.S. states that provide their residents with certain rights with respect to personal data, visit https://corporate.harlequin.com/other-state-residents-privacy-rights/.